A Pre-Med(itated) Murder

www.mascotbooks.com

A Pre-Med(itated) Murder

©2025 Niru Mohandas. All Rights Reserved. No part of this publication may be reproduced, stored in a retrieval system or transmitted in any form by any means electronic, mechanical, or photocopying, recording or otherwise without the permission of the author.

This is a work of fiction. Names, characters, businesses, places, events, and incidents are either the products of the author's imagination or used in a fictitious manner. Any resemblance to actual persons, living or dead, or actual events is purely coincidental.

For more information, please contact:
Subplot Publishing, an imprint of Amplify Publishing Group
620 Herndon Parkway, Suite 220
Herndon, VA 20170
info@amplifypublishing.com

Library of Congress Control Number: 2024919927
CPSIA Code: PRV1024A
ISBN-13: 979-8-89138-362-3

Printed in the United States

To the loves of my life,
Govindh, Deene, and Sonia.

A Pre-Med(itated) Murder

A Neena Sundar Mystery

Niru Mohandas, MD

Prologue

The golden rays of the setting Indian sun filtered through the slats of the wooden shutters. The odor of car exhaust and animal dung combined with the fresh scent of jasmine and the tantalizing aroma of samosas from a corner stall created a distinctive fragrance. The gentle breeze lifted a stray lock of the young woman's silky dark hair. She stood close to a tall, lean young man, his long fingers clasping her delicate hand. Against the paleness of his skin, her hand glowed like a polished sandalwood sculpture. The official standing behind the counter in front of them requested their paperwork, and after scrutinizing them, he presented a sheaf of papers for their signature. The young man released her hand so that they could both sign each of the forms. They left the office with their paperwork and one official document. As they stood outside on the steps of the government building, the young man brought his companion's fingers lightly to his lips and his soft hazel eyes gazed lovingly into her dark brown ones.

Thursday July 2, 1992

Chapter 1

"Tape, tape, tape!" screamed a voice in her ear. It had become a recurrent theme over the past twenty-four hours and occupied much of her waking moments. What a bizarre thing to be thinking about! What has tape got to do with anything? The year was 1992 and many types of tape came to mind . . . cellophane tape, duct tape, film tape, cassette tapes. However, it was the demand for surgical tape that preoccupied her mind these days. As a third-year medical student and one of only two women in the rotation, most of the menial tasks—like carrying the box of surgical tape—often fell to her lot. This was not quite what Neena had in mind when she envisioned herself as a physician who would tend to the injured and defy death.

Neena would be the first physician in her family. It had been a lifelong dream and was, possibly, a self-fulling prophecy. Being the precocious and enthusiastic person that she was, Neena presented herself to the world a full month ahead of time in the early hours of a Sunday morning twenty-four years prior. Even routine births in India had a high risk of complications at that time and a baby born over four weeks early did not stand a strong chance of survival. Neena's maternal grandfather, upon hearing that his first grandchild had been born prematurely, was so worried that he fled the hospital in dismay. His hurried steps took him to the door of his good friend Mr. Das, who was well-known for seeing the future. Neena's grandfather rapped sharply on his friend's door without concern for the late hour. Though he had been suddenly roused from sleep, Mr. Das appeared at the door in a short time and ushered Neena's grandfather inside. Mr. Das was a dark-skinned, unprepossessing man, whose monumental calm enveloped all those around him like the folds of a soft blanket. He listened patiently as her grandfather poured forth his worry over the precipitous arrival of his tiny granddaughter. Placing a comforting arm on his friend's shoulder, he proclaimed in his deep, calm voice, "Do not worry, my friend. This child will not only live, but one day she will become a doctor."

Neena must have heard the story of her birth countless times. She always believed that this prophetic statement had shaped her thoughts and goals from the very beginning. After her birth, the doctor had quickly wrapped Neena in a cotton blanket, placed the small bundle on an empty bed and continued to care for her mother. After a few minutes the staff in the delivery room heard an astonishing sound. The little four-pound bundle was determinedly and vigorously sucking her thumb!

Neena was only four years old when she categorically stated her intention of becoming a doctor. To Neena, becoming a doctor had seemed inevitable and Mr. Das's prophecy had often given her immense confidence and reassurance. She distinctly remembered one summer day when she was thirteen. She and her best friend were in a rickety car at the apex of a creaking wooden roller coaster in Point Pleasant, New Jersey. The thought of her imminent demise flitted briefly through her brain but Neena knew that she couldn't possibly die that day since she had not yet become a doctor!

On this morning, in the first week of July 1992, Neena sat up in bed with a start, realizing that her alarm clock was not actually screaming, "Tape!" but instead emitting its usual high-pitched whine to drag her from sleep to wakefulness as quickly as possible. She brought it within a few inches of her bleary, myopic eyes and her brain registered the ungodly hour of 4:30 a.m. With a heartfelt groan Neena pulled off the sheets and stumbled toward the bathroom. Within twenty minutes she had showered, inserted her contact lenses, and put the tea kettle on.

Neena always prided herself on her speed and efficiency, no matter what the task at hand. She once read a short story in *Reader's Digest* about the father of a family of twelve kids. He had discovered that the fastest way to get dressed was to put socks on before pants and to button his shirt from the bottom up. The methodology described by the harried father had deeply impressed twelve-year-old Neena at the time and these strategies had unconsciously found their way into her own system of dressing.

While she waited for the kettle to start whistling, Neena pulled on a pair of freshly ironed black slacks and slipped her arms into a light summery shirt. She buttoned her shirt from the bottom up, and quickly gathered up her black curls into a ponytail. Neena slipped on a pair of comfortable black flats and slung her old blue messenger bag over her shoulder. She took a last critical glance in the mirror. With a sigh at the sight of her already-frizzy head, Neena patted her bangs down and headed out the door.

Since Neena was juggling keys, a bulging bag of books, and a cup of hot tea, she didn't get a good look at her car until she was actually at the curb.

"Oh, fudge!" she said in exasperation.

Overnight, her small gray 1983 Toyota Tercel had been neatly boxed in by a station wagon in the front and a large shiny sedan in the back. Neena did not mind the manual transmission in her car since she enjoyed shifting gears. Unfortunately, her car also lacked air-conditioning, power windows, and most important to her current predicament, power steering! Exasperation was quickly followed by anxiety. Neena stowed her bag in the back seat, hung her white coat on the hook and settled herself in the driver's seat. She started the ignition and worked the clutch, brake, and accelerator. Inch by inch Neena carefully maneuvered backward and forward until at last she was free. By the end of this process, her arms were aching with the effort of turning the wheel. With an anxious look at her watch, Neena put the car in first gear and took off.

The drive to the large private community hospital where Neena was assigned to do the first month of her surgery rotation was located in the suburbs of a major inner city about twenty minutes from her apartment. She had become quite adept at shifting gears while eating, drinking, and tossing exact change into the toll booths of the Garden State Parkway. Neena was thankful for the relative coolness of the early morning air which blew in through the open car window and ruffled her curls. She directed her car off the highway and onto the exit ramp toward the small but affluent town of Littlefield, New Jersey. The charming downtown area was filled with small shops and boutiques as well as a variety of cafes and restaurants. The storefronts were beautifully maintained and colorful summer blossoms spilled from urns and baskets in front of many of the establishments. Traffic at that time of the morning was sparse and the aptly named little town was just waking up to a glorious morning. At a more leisurely time, Neena would have loved to sit at one of the outdoor tables, sipping a frothy cappuccino while reading one of her favorite mystery novels.

To Neena's delight, she had realized by the end of her first day in the hospital that each patient was actually a medical mystery waiting to be solved! A doctor was very much like a detective. He or she was presented with a patient's complaints or symptoms, which were like a series of clues. The doctor then examined the patient, looked for tangible evidence, formed a theory and then, hopefully, made a successful diagnosis for which a treatment plan could be implemented. This in turn would result in a cure, which would then close the case! Neena was excited to see what mysteries this day would reveal. She took another sip of her now-tepid tea and returned the cup to the holder just in time to downshift.

Within a few minutes she passed through the commercial area of Littlefield and was approaching the outskirts of the city. Every now and then Neena glimpsed a view of an elegant home surrounded by wide expanses of green, manicured lawns. A sign indicated the entrance for Littlefield Community Hospital. This tree-lined drive was a pleasant change from the drab security stations which punctuated the road leading to University Hospital, a large inner city medical center, where most of her education and training would take place.

Although it had been in existence for almost a hundred years, LCH had been renovated regularly and tastefully. The bright, airy lobby was topped by a ceiling full of skylights and beautifully furnished with plush chairs and sofas in soothing shades of oat, biscotti, and fawn, more commonly known as, beige, beige, and beige. However, the choice of color belied the quality and elegance of the hospital's decor. On the right was the gift shop, displaying an array of flowers, balloons, and thoughtful items for patients. On the left, in the corner was a small coffee shop, aptly named The Coffee Corner, from which wafted the rich fragrance of roasted coffee and freshly baked cookies.

Neena, deciding that she was in need of a bit more caffeine before facing the day, went into The Coffee Corner and ordered a cup of the fragrant brew. Just as she had finished adding generous amounts of cream and sugar, someone jostled her right elbow. Luckily, she had just pressed the plastic lid firmly in place so only a small amount of her coffee sloshed up and around the rim.

"Oh dear, I'm so sorry, Doc!" said a soft, cultured voice.

Neena turned around, looking for the doctor to whom the apology was addressed. However, there was no one else in the cafe and she found herself at eye level with one of the volunteers who worked at the welcome desk. Ms. Helen, as her name tag identified her, had in fact been her first point of contact in the hospital yesterday. Neena had been anxious, as well as excited, for the first day of her clinical rotation. When she had stopped to ask for directions to the surgical wing, Ms. Helen's warm smile and cheerful greeting had instantly put her at ease.

She returned the older woman's smile. "It's okay, no harm done. Please call me Neena. I'm not a doctor yet."

"You're a doctor in the making and that is good enough for me," was her generous response.

Neena took a sip of her coffee. "Good morning, by the way."

"Good morning to you as well!" said Helen, smiling. Neena smiled back and walked back through the lobby. She rounded the long, elegant mahogany reception desk which dominated the space. The desk was always staffed by a team of smiling, helpful volunteers. Misses Barbara, Lavinia, and Helen, the senior volunteers, had been fixtures of the hospital auxiliary committee. When she had first seen them yesterday, with their beautifully coiffed snow-white hair and crisp pastel-colored pinafores, Neena thought they had looked as sweet as a trio of teatime petit fours. She gave the two ladies at the desk a wave and hurried toward the elevators.

Neena went first to the fourth-floor residents' lounge where she dropped off her bag, picked up the box of surgical supplies, and took the stairs up to the surgical wing. The surgical team always started their preliminary rounds on Six East and worked their way down to the floor below, which was also dedicated to surgery patients. The floors were gleaming while the walls were artfully decorated with drawings, paintings, and photographs. There were calming shades of blue and green everywhere. Small discrete gold plaques commemorated generous donors of the wing or department that was named in their honor.

As Neena approached the nurses' station she veered slightly to one side so that she could unobtrusively join the small group of medical students who had already gathered. The head nurse, Nurse Marge, was glaring at the gaggle of students crowded around the nurses' station who, in their short, pristine white coats, resembled a flock of squawking ducklings. Marge was a large imposing woman with a head of grizzled, wiry red hair pulled into a fierce bun at the top of her head. Small tufts of hair escaped the bun in irregular intervals along the crown of her head like the spikes of a triceratops. The tight bun narrowed Marge's murky green eyes into thin suspicious slits and constricted her lips into an almost invisible thin line. Marge considered the area to be HER nurses' station and was displeased to see it covered with the messy sprawl of students' books, clipboards, and coffee cups. Neena had quickly made it a point to steer clear of Nurse Marge's reptilian gaze.

Despite the early hour, the third-year students were bright-eyed and energetic. Until two days ago all of their medical knowledge had come only from books. Sitting in the great lecture hall for eight hours a day had really not taught them anything about actually caring for patients. The students hadn't even touched a patient yet, other than their anatomy lab cadavers. Neena was worried that she may not be able to apply all the information she had memorized thus far in a practical situation. However, it was some small comfort to know that at least they looked the part.

The white lab coats that symbolized the students' status were reminiscent of the short pants that young boys wore in days gone by, until they were old enough to graduate to full trousers. Although this was only the second day of clinical rotations Neena already longed for the day when she would have the privilege of wearing a long white coat. The longer the coat the higher the aspiring doctor was on the training ladder. Neena only hoped that her knowledge would increase exponentially! But, here she was at last, about to see real patients and learn how to be a real doctor.

Another interesting characteristic of the doctor-in-training was the quantity of handbooks and supplies crammed into the pockets of their coats. They each carried a pocket diagnostic set which contained an ophthalmoscope and an otoscope, a handbook on frequently used antibiotics, and a condensed version of Shwartz's surgical textbook, which was CliffsNotes for the surgery student. In addition, there was a quantity of pens, a calculator, and a few pairs of latex gloves. The final item, a brand-new stethoscope, was also stuffed into one of their jacket pockets and extricated only with great difficulty.

As Neena bent down to place the bulky box of tape on the floor she found herself looking into a pair of light caramel brown eyes, set in an unfamiliar tanned face. The owner was in the process of tying the laces of his brown shoes. Under his bright white coat he was dressed head to toe in brown. As Neena straightened she saw a gleam of white teeth which were framed by a neatly trimmed black mustache. Neena, mentally dubbing him as The Brown

Guy, smiled briefly in return and continued organizing her box of supplies. He looked like a new medical student but she was too preoccupied with her box to give him a second glance or thought. Besides, men with mustaches did not interest Neena one whit.

One of the students, Calvin Cheng, turned to Neena with a smile and asked, "Hey, Neena, how far have you gotten in the syllabus so far?"

She and Calvin had become friends during their first two years of medical school. They sat next to each other in the lecture hall, exchanged notes, and often studied together. Calvin was quiet and very smart. He worked hard at school and in his free time played piano and chess. Although he was taller than the average Asian, all those hours spent in sedentary pursuits had taken their toll. He had the round, smooth-cheeked appearance of a little boy and had grown chubby around the middle.

She gave him a look of exasperation, tinged with worry.

"Calvin, it's only the second day of the rotation! I read the introduction and started on chapter one." She was worried that twelve weeks was not enough time to learn all that material. She was sure that Calvin had probably read and memorized the entire textbook by now and would be ready to take the unit test at any time. Interpreting her expression correctly he gave her a reassuring pat on the arm and said, "Don't worry, Neena. You know you always do great."

Medical school was a constant exercise in cramming as much knowledge into the brain as was humanly possible in the shortest amount of time. One of Neena's tried and true methods of memorization was to concentrate on certain facts or details in certain locations. For instance, when studying for her biochemistry final she stood in her living room as she listed the steps of the urea cycle, going around and around the room until she had committed the details to memory. Then she would move on to another room, say the kitchen, to memorize the Krebs cycle. Each time she finished memorizing a particular lesson she would then file it away in the capacious filing cabinet that was her brain. Then during the exam she would simply picture herself in the appropriate room and rifle through the folders of her mental filing cabinet until she was able to successfully pluck out the necessary information. Neena considered test-taking as one of her main talents in life thus far.

Neena exchanged brief greetings with Joe Mercurio and Neelesh Shah, who were fellow third-year students on the team. Within a few minutes they were joined by half a dozen others, all surgical residents in various levels of training. The leader of the group was Dr. Michael Windsor, the chief resident for the year. The position of chief resident in surgery was awarded to the strongest resident in the senior class. He was the one who was in charge of the entire team and reported directly to the Attending surgeon. There was a strict hierarchy in medical training, with each year responsible for reporting to the residents above them, and tasked with guiding the residents and students junior to them.

Dr. Mike Windsor looked like he had stepped off of the set of *General Hospital*. He was a tall, athletic-looking young man with closely cropped light brown hair, who walked through the halls with long, quick strides. His scrubs were never wrinkled and his white coat was pristine. When not in scrubs, his shirts were neatly pressed and it was obvious that he actually ironed the entire shirt and not just a strip down the middle as the third-year male medical students were wont to do. Neena's male classmates had not yet gotten over the shock of having to put on real clothes before they showed up in the morning, rather than rolling out of bed in their sweatpants. She had heard one of her classmates expound on his time-saving strategy, "Why bother ironing the rest of the shirt when the middle strip is the only part that's going to show?"

Mike walked up to the nurses' station and then, in what Neena thought was an act of bravery—verging on folly—actually greeted Marge.

"Good morning, Marge! You're looking well this morning!" he said. Unbelievably, instead of the irritated grunt she usually gave in response to any doctor-in-training, Marge's posture relaxed ever so slightly. This small amount of slack allowed her to infinitesimally incline her head and turn up one corner of her mouth, in what Neena thought was Marge's version of a smile.

"Marge the Barge has a sweet spot for Mike," Neena heard one of the residents whisper. "Shhh!" someone else hissed as Mike turned to face the group. The first-year surgical resident, Duncan, who was standing behind Mike, gave them a lazy wink of his eye. But Mike looked disapproving and ushered them away from the nurses' station.

When they had formed a semi-circle around Mike he said, "You will find that the nurses and support staff can either be your best allies or they can make your life more miserable than you can possibly imagine. There are so many things they can teach you about patient care if you take the time to listen and observe. Some of these nurses started their careers a decade or more before many of you were even born. I strongly suggest that you treat them with the respect they deserve."

Neena, who had been caught up in the newness of this first week, had not spared a moment to consider how the nurses would feel about the constant rotation of rookie doctors on their floors. She thought how frustrating it must be for them to have to constantly work with new trainees. And, to add insult to injury, Neena had often noticed the dismissive or even disdainful attitudes projected by some of the students and residents toward the nurses.

Mike then gave the group a quick, comprehensive survey. His eagle eye landed on the newcomer in the group. He glanced at the new guy's ID tag, seemed perplexed, and looked into his face for elucidation. In a quiet but assured manner, The Brown Guy held out his hand and finally spoke. In crisp British English, with just a hint of an Indian accent, he introduced himself.

"Hello, Dr. Windsor, my name is Raj. I've just transferred to your medical school and was told by the clinical coordinator to report to you. Sorry for missing the first day of the rotation but my visa was delayed."

Mike, who was on eye-level with the new student, gave Raj an appraising glance, appeared to be satisfied with what he saw and returned the handshake.

"Welcome, we can always use another pair of hands. And call me Mike. You'll need to get a pair of scrubs from the OR before the afternoon but you're fine for now. Get a copy of our census from Dunk," Mike said.

"Uh, Dunk?" said Raj in confusion.

"This guy, over here," said Mike as he hooked a thumb toward the tall, blond-haired, blue-eyed resident next to him.

Duncan Goodwin, aka Dunk, was the first-year surgical intern and therefore had the most contact with the medical students. Dunk was the one who shepherded them down the halls and through the intricate maze of stairwells. Surgical residents did not wait for elevators and therefore neither did the medical students assigned to them. It was good exercise and helped break up the monotony of constantly standing on rounds or in the OR.

Duncan's eyes opened slightly in surprise and then a slight frown marred the tanned surface of his forehead. *Maybe he is surprised to have a foreign medical student on the team*, thought Neena. But, in an instant his face smoothed out and the look was replaced with his usual faintly sardonic smile. Duncan quickly shook Raj's hand and passed over a few photocopied pages. The rest of the medical students gave Raj quick nods of acknowledgment and turned to await instructions.

Neena suppressed a giggle as she thought of the first time she had met Duncan. The decidedly unorthodox introduction had been performed by their fellow student, Victoria Cabot.

"Duncaaaan!" Victoria had screeched on their first day of the rotation. Then the team was witness to the even more astonishing spectacle of Victoria launching herself into his arms. For a split second it seemed as if Victoria's head-long rush would topple Duncan's tall, thin frame. However, he stood firm against the onslaught as Victoria jumped up to wrap her long skinny arms and thin fingers around his neck in a tight grip. Duncan was a lot stronger than he appeared since he had effortlessly grabbed both of her arms and set her down with a thump a few feet away.

"We met in boarding school!" Victoria gushed to her audience of startled medical students, and did not at all seem abashed at the unceremonious way in which she had been detached from him.

"That we did," acknowledged Dunk with a lazy smile. Dunk, a name which eminently suited him, looked as if he had just walked off of the beach and exchanged his surfboard for a clipboard. A shock of bleach-blond hair frequently fell over his tanned forehead and with a practiced gesture he flipped it back. When he was concentrating, he tended to narrow his sea-blue eyes and this, along with his open-legged stance and habit of slightly rocking back on his feet, completed the image of a surfer balancing on a wave. But he was no beach bum. He had attended a top Ivy League university and graduated from a prestigious medical school. There was an air of quiet wealth around him, from the worn but costly leather loafers he wore, to the handsome Swiss watch on his wrist, and the Mont Blanc pen that he carried—as did surprisingly many of the other surgical residents—in his breast pocket.

Mike clapped his hands together and in his clear, authoritative voice he called out, "All right people, let's get moving. We have a full house today."

Chapter 2

It was exactly 6:30 a.m., and this morning, like the one that had preceded it, they started their preliminary rounds. Dr. Windsor, as the leader, was always in front and the rest of the team usually arranged themselves according to hierarchy. Neena felt like one in a row of obedient ducklings following docilely behind the papa duck. Everyone knew their place in the pecking order. Everyone other than their fellow student Victoria Cabot that is. She was a tall young woman who was almost at height with Mike and somehow managed to position herself right next to him. As she walked briskly beside him, her long, dirty-blond ponytail swung back and forth on her head like a pendulum. Two years ago, on the first day of anatomy lab, Victoria had pranced up to the group and introduced herself, "Hello, I am Victoria Cabot, of the Boston Cabots." *What is a Boston Cabot?* Neena had wondered, and who cared anyway? Victoria wore her sense of entitlement like a royal mantle and looked down the length of her long, thin nose at the lesser beings around her. Neena had been extremely disappointed to learn that they were on the same team since Victoria had a habit of monopolizing the attention of any instructor.

One of the aspects of medicine that Neena loved was that there is no limit to the knowledge there was to acquire. Despite over a hundred years of modern medicine, the human body was still essentially a mystery. She looked in growing annoyance at Victoria as she peppered Mike with questions which were meant not as much for learning new information but to demonstrate how much she already knew. Since it was only the second day of their rotation it was unlikely that she knew much. Neena thought it was crucial to identify knowledge gaps so that they could be appropriately filled. This would then form a bridge to the next body of information. Dr. Windsor, as the most senior member of the team, had a great deal of knowledge to impart. By simply talking at Mike, rather than listening to him, Victoria was doing herself and the team a great disservice.

Trailing behind the senior residents was Dunk, the intern, followed by a fourth-year student, and then the most inexperienced members of the team, the third-year medical students. The other students assigned to this rotation were Neel, Calvin, Raj, Joe, and last but not least, Neena. At only a little above five feet tall, she was considerably shorter than all the others. Neena hadn't realized that surgeons, like presidential candidates, were typically six feet tall! Neena's eyes were approximately at the mid-thoracic level of the guy in front of her and although she glanced at the expanse of white coats in mild annoyance, she had no problem in keeping up with their pace. Neena was used to walking in long, fast strides, as she had learned to do in high school and college when she was trying to keep up with her many tall friends.

They had been walking at quite a clip and Neena didn't realize they had stopped until she almost ran into Joe. Mike was already in the room and was waking the patient, an elderly diabetic gentleman who had recently undergone a BKA, a below-the-knee amputation. Victoria, who had appointed herself the keeper of the gloves, stood right next to Mike holding the box. She proffered him a pair and Mike quickly pulled them on. Neena heard Mike say, "Good morning, Mr. Williams. How are you feeling today? Is it okay if we take a look at your dressings?"

The students had quickly learned that all patient encounters were viewed and documented within an established framework known as the SOAP Note. "Subjective, Objective, Assessment, and Plan," Neena repeated to herself. The subjective encompassed everything the patient was experiencing, such as pain, nausea, vomiting, fatigue, etc. The objective consisted of concrete information such as vital signs, diagnostic testing, and the physical exam. The sum of the subjective and objective, almost like a mathematical equation, usually resulted in the assessment, or the diagnosis. Finally, there was the plan, or the course of treatment for each patient. Neena loved how neatly the SOAP note helped to organize so many pieces of information. With each patient encounter, Neena had formed a mental grid using these four components and she imagined herself as a detective, trying to solve a case. She thought of the subjective as mysterious clues and the objective as the evidence. The assessment or diagnosis was similar to the denouement in mystery novels and the plan was how the symptoms or "bad actors" were treated.

Mike was politely but efficiently eliciting the details of Mr. Williams's overnight condition, while his immediate junior resident, Dr. Ron Roberts, had already unceremoniously whisked the sheet off of the patient's lower body. Whereas Mike was kind and polite, Ron exhibited the worst of the surgical specialty's stereotypical features. He was arrogant and brusque to the point of rudeness toward his patients. He demonstrated little empathy for their suffering and seemed to treat each patient as simply another nuisance to be checked off of his to-do list or, in the case of interesting diagnoses, as just another challenge to his superior intelligence. As one of the senior residents, teaching was also one of Ron's responsibilities, but he treated his junior residents as his lackeys and looked at the students with disdain.

The second-year resident expertly cut away at the bandages that swathed Mr. Williams's stump of a leg. He stepped aside so that Mike could examine the surgical wound. In the meantime, the third-year resident listened to the patient's lungs, while Dunk, the first-year resident, checked the vital signs clipped to the foot of the bed. Poor Mr. Williams looked groggily around the room, which was suddenly full of white coats. Neena had not yet managed to maneuver her way into the doorway when she heard the clarion call of, "Tape!" Of course it was Ron. She rushed forward and thrust a roll of surgical gauze and tape into his outstretched hand. Neena avoided looking into his dark, angry eyes, which were set beneath a wide, jutting forehead and bushy black brows. With his thick neck, loud voice, and forceful manner, Neena was at once reminded of a bison she had seen in Yellowstone National Park. She hoped that one day soon she would be able to hand him the tape before he could shout for it. She glanced interestedly at Mr. Williams's stump of a leg but in less time than it took to describe it, they were finished with Mr. Williams and on to their next patient. In this manner they managed to see all twenty-five of the patients on the surgical service in less than two hours.

Their rounds were only a dry run for actual rounds with the surgery Attending. Mike, the chief resident, was second-in-command to the even greater Attending on service for the month. To be an Attending was the ultimate goal, and Neena could only think of it with a capital "A." This was the culmination of an educational journey that, beginning with kindergarten, could span at least twenty-five years. The Attending had the final word in all matters and many in his team quaked under his critical glare. What did the Attending want them to do? How did the Attending want his patients' wounds wrapped? What antibiotics did the Attending want to use? What type of IV fluids did the Attending prefer? The capitals are quite necessary, for the Attending was a Great Being. He was the one who held their happiness—not to mention their grades—in his hands, at least for this month.

The surgical team gathered in the small conference room which was located near the elevators on each floor and waited for the Attending to join them. Neena helped herself to a cup of the strong, bitter coffee that the hospital provided for the residents and students. This coffee had obviously not come from The Coffee Corner. She added extra cream and sugar to her cup. Neena preferred tea, especially when it was fragrant with cardamom and cloves, but the frequent application of caffeine had become a necessity during the long days in the hospital which were followed by hours spent studying at home. There was also a selection of donuts and pastries on a platter. This being a hospital, Neena had expected fruits or something else healthy but it seemed that donuts were what they fed the trainees. She selected a pastry dripping with strawberry jam and walked over to the corner where her fellow students and Duncan were sitting.

Victoria, naturally, had already seated herself in the most comfortable chair and was trying hard to engage Dunk in a conversation. "Do you go to the Hamptons on your days off?" she asked, batting her sparse blond eyelashes at him. "I hear it's just a quick helicopter ride away. Can you believe I've never been to the Hamptons? It must be beautiful there," she gushed. "Daddy has a house on the Vineyard so I go there whenever I can." She looked up at the group. "That's Martha's Vineyard. In case you were wondering," she explained.

The boys were sitting on the folding chairs or leaning against the wall with cups of coffee in their hands. "I wasn't wondering. Were you wondering, Joe?" asked Neel in a serious voice, but his green eyes gleamed mischievously.

"No, not really, Neel," answered Joe with a grin. Joseph Mercurio was tall and thin, with short black hair that was liberally spiked with hair gel. He came from a working-class Italian family and Neena sensed that he too was proud to be the first doctor in his family.

Victoria's pale blue eyes glared in their direction. "Hmph!" she said, whipping her head and ponytail around to face Duncan.

Duncan looked at her with amusement, "Yeah, sure Vicky, you should come over sometime. My uncle usually lets me use his helicopter if it's free."

Neena knew from painful experience that the other girl hated being called 'Vicky' and waited for the usual blistering correction. But to her astonishment Victoria simply batted her eyelashes and simpered, "Oh, Duncan, that would be awesome!"

Neena turned away in disgust and heard Raj say, "I'm still a bit jet-lagged and it was so busy before I left India that I almost can't believe I'm actually here."

"I didn't think our school took international students," said Neel.

"The dean of my medical school back in India told me of a scholarship at an American medical school for clinical rotations and thought that I should apply. I didn't seriously think I'd get in, especially since competition is so fierce in India. I was stunned when the dean told me I had been accepted."

Duncan, flipping a shock of bleach-blond hair out of his eyes, reached out with one long arm and lifted Raj's ID tag, which read, M. Raja. "What's the 'M' stand for? Is it something hideous and that's why you go by your last name?"

Neena looked at Raj with some sympathy as he started to explain, "The 'M' is the first initial of my father's name, Markandaya. Where I'm from we don't use last names or family names."

"You mean like Madonna or Sting?" asked Duncan.

Now it was Raj's turn to look confused. "Uh, what?"

"Well, these singers are only known by their one stage name," Neena explained. "Most people don't even know what their real names are."

"Yes, I know, but this is my real name," Raj said. Duncan, who had lost interest in the subject, shrugged and turned away to talk to one of the residents.

"Don't worry about it," she said to Raj. "People will get used to it." Many immigrants to America ended up changing or altering their names to fit the conventions and the linguistic abilities of the people in their new country. Neena's father decided to split up his one long polysyllabic name. What had been T.R. Shanmugasundaram in India, became Shan Sundar in the USA. Thus, Sundar became her last name as well. During the many standardized tests she had taken in her life she was always exceedingly grateful for this convenient contraction. Otherwise, how would she ever have fit a sixteen-letter last name on a scantron test form!

There was suddenly a flurry of movement near the door and the sea of white coats parted to reveal the Attending, Dr. John Silverman, under whose auspices they were working this month. He was a tall, distinguished-looking man in his early fifties with dark hair that was graying at the temples. His face seemed especially tanned in contrast to the crisp white of his shirt and he was dressed elegantly in a well-cut, lightweight gray suit and dark leather shoes which were polished to a shining finish. Neena thought, with some amusement, that this is probably what Mike would look like in another twenty years.

Mike had a few words with Dr. Silverman and then they were off. As they walked, Dr. Silverman shot surgical questions at all and sundry. This was supposed to be part of their didactic lessons during the day, in addition to the lunchtime conferences and weekly Grand Rounds lectures. The residents nearest to him bore most of the brunt but Joe and Calvin got in a few answers, ahead of Victoria, on behalf of the medical students. Neena was bobbing up and down on her toes and tried to call out an answer or two but since she was bringing up the rear usually one of the people positioned closer to the Attending beat her to it. This was one of the many times that Neena found her lack of inches a distinct disadvantage.

They covered the same route as earlier only in reverse order, and stopped briefly at each patient's bedside again. Each time one of the residents gave a two-line synopsis, the Attending spoke briefly to the patient and then signed off on the chart which was held out to him by one of the students. As Dr. Silverman headed out of one of the patient rooms, his eyes finally fell on Neena, and he shot out, "What are the four main etiologies for fever in a post-surgical patient?" She was momentarily taken off guard since she hadn't expected to be questioned, but rallied instantly. She quickly remembered the mnemonic of the four W's. "The main causes of fever are trauma from the surgery itself, infection at the surgical site, pneumonia, and urinary tract infection." She got it all out in a rush and waited with bated breath. The four W's: wound, wound, wind, and water. It was only one of dozens of mnemonics she had learned or devised so far in her medical career. Dr. Silverman gave her a nod of approval and left the room. Neena let her breath out in a small whoosh and Calvin gave her a silent high five as they filed out of the room.

Their last patient was occupying the bed closest to the window in a double room and as the team filed in, Neena again found herself near the doorway. She strained to hear the discussion at the patient's bedside and, feeling frustrated, finally allowed her attention to wander. She glanced at the patient occupying the bed closest to the door and then did a double take. It was a thin, elderly woman, propped up on pillows, her white hair straggling out on the pillow behind her. Her faded blue polka-dotted hospital gown hung limply on her gaunt frame and she did not acknowledge the doctors' presence. This in itself was not unusual. Neena had seen many patients like this over the past two days. They were ill, tired, and often alone. It was not surprising that the elderly patients often registered little emotion at the dozens of people who walked in and out of their rooms each day. However, this patient was staring blankly at her and the thin chest under the hospital gown was ominously still.

After a few shocked seconds Neena tugged at the sleeve of the white-coated individual next to her, which happened to be Calvin. "Calvin!" she whispered. Gaining no response she tugged and whispered again, "Calvin!" He shushed her with mild annoyance and turned back to listen to the Attending. Neena pointed mutely to the patient in front of them. Calvin registered the same facts she had and immediately turned to the person next to him. Like some bizarre form of the childhood game of "Telephone," each member of the team commandeered the attention of the person next to him, until the message finally reached Mike who broke off in mid-sentence and flung open the dividing curtain. Mike ran from the room, and then several nurses ran back in with him. Within a minute they heard the overhead speaker go on and "Code Blue" was announced.

Suddenly the room was a beehive of activity. More white coats raced into the room, pushing a bright red code-cart in front of them. Dr. Silverman took charge of the code and called out orders in a rapid-fire staccato. Half a dozen residents jumped, as if shot, to do his bidding while the medical students squeezed into the back of the room and looked on in bewilderment at their first code. After almost thirty minutes of frenzied activity, Dr. Silverman called a halt to the resuscitation efforts. He proclaimed the time of death and they all filed soberly out of the room and stood in the hallway, somewhat at a loss. Other than the cadavers Neena had worked on during her first-year anatomy class, this was the first dead person she had ever seen in her life.

Ron glanced at his wrist. Neena was not surprised to see that he, too, had an expensive-looking gold watch.

"Okay, people, let's get a move on," he barked. "Here's the OR schedule for the day." He jabbed his finger at several residents and students. "You, you, you, and you," he said, "are with Mike in OR number one." Then Ron turned to the rest of them. "Duncan, Raj, Neel, and Neena, you're with me. Head to OR number two and get ready to scrub!" Neena and her classmates looked at each other in mild bewilderment. She had assumed that there would be some discussion or debriefing after the unsuccessful resuscitation attempt they had just witnessed. But there was clearly no time for that. Nor was there ever, as she was to find out over the course of her training. With a deep breath she hurried down the hall to deposit her tape box and ran to join her team in the OR.

Chapter 3

Narrowed eyes and a furrowed forehead were visible above the mask. There was something unusual about the new student. An idea, as slight and elusive as a moth, flitted around, but it would not alight on any solid memory or fact. The team was waiting so the thought was mentally swatted away for the time being.

Neena emerged from the women's locker room into a forest of tall, blue-clad people as both of the surgical teams milled about outside the doors to the OR. With their identical blue scrubs, booties, masks, and poofy hair caps it was almost impossible to tell most of them apart. The only visible parts were eyes, foreheads, and arms.

Neena and her classmates headed to the bank of gleaming stainless steel sinks and listened closely as Ron explained the proper scrub technique. They each reached for a small white packet that contained the scrub brush, which when wet, released an antibacterial soap.

"Take your time, scrub from the elbows down, pay close attention to your fingertips, the small plastic utensil is to clean under your fingernails. Rinse well from the fingers down, and do NOT touch anything else from that point on!"

Once they had finished they all carefully held up their wet hands, feeling quite professional indeed in the gesture they had seen demonstrated so many times by surgeons on TV. With water dripping down her arms, Neena followed the team into the operating room. She watched carefully as the OR nurse helped Dr. Ron Roberts suit up. When it was her turn the nurse assisted Neena into a sterile blue gown and deftly drew on a pair of sterile gloves. Neena then joined her classmates who were already waiting with their hands carefully folded and held against their chest, as the surgery residents had done.

The Attending was the last to arrive. He quickly suited up, walked briskly to the table and positioned himself on the patient's right side. The patient, who had been draped and prepped, was about to undergo hip surgery due to complications related to her obesity. Ron, as the first assistant, was positioned opposite Dr. Silverman. Then Dunk took his place next to Dr. Silverman, thereby completely obscuring the patient from the students' view. Raj, Neel, and Neena exchanged lifted eyebrows and waited for an opportunity to see something, anything. After a few minutes Ron beckoned to Raj and Neel to join him at the table. Not surprisingly, Neena's view was not thus improved and she was not asked to step forward. Disappointed and annoyed she gazed at the blue backs of the team and hoped for an opportunity to get closer to the operating table.

The OR was quiet, with only the soft murmurings of the surgeon, requesting various instruments, which were quickly and efficiently handed to him by the OR tech. Since Neena could not see or hear anything she fell into a sort of wakeful doze. Suddenly, she jumped as Ron called out her name in loud, strident tones. "Neena!" he said. "Come over here and stand to my left." Excited

A PRE-MED(ITATED) MURDER

to finally be called to the table she carefully made her way around to the left side of the patient where Ron stood. Raj moved slightly so that there was room for her. The OR assistant helpfully stepped forward with a small stool for Neena to stand on. With eager anticipation she stepped up and glanced interestedly at the surgical field. Ron, who was supporting the patient's left leg, shifted slightly so that Neena could get closer to the operating table. As she turned to thank him he looked at her with a strange glint in his narrowed eyes and said, "Put your arms out, palms up!" As soon as Neena had done so he lowered the patient's leg onto her outstretched arms and stepped away!

Neena was too startled at first to say anything, not that she would have protested anyway. At first, she was happy to finally have a spot at the table. However, within a few minutes, as she started to feel the weight of the patient's leg, she realized that this could quickly become a problem. Neena, a petite woman who did not weigh much over 100 pounds, was now holding a leg which alone must have weighed 100 pounds! As the minutes went by the leg became heavier and heavier and heavier. Neena was having trouble concentrating on anything but the task of keeping her arms steady and the leg elevated at the requested height. She could barely hear the surgeon's words. Her breathing became quicker and beads of perspiration sprang up on her forehead. Luckily her mask hid the grimaces of pain, but as she tried to channel all her strength into her forearms, the crinkling of her eyes was clearly visible. As Neena's arms started to burn and tremble she realized that she could rest her elbows on the bony prominences of her hips, thus supporting her arms and weight of the leg. After a few minutes she felt her burden lessen slightly as Raj's hand surreptitiously slipped under hers. Neena momentarily closed her eyes. When she opened them she found a pair of startlingly green eyes, soft and warm as moss, looking across the table at her. The eyebrows lifted concernedly and she could feel Neel's strength and sympathy being directed to her. Feeling grateful for the support of her classmates, Neena took a deep breath, shifted her arms slightly, and prepared to continue until she was requested to stop. She was determined not to let her team, and most importantly, the leg, down.

Chapter 4

At six o'clock that evening, Neena finally turned onto her quiet tree-lined street and gratefully pulled into a convenient parking spot. This part of town was filled with older two-story homes, each surrounded by a fairly large patch of green grass. Most of the homes were beautifully restored and maintained. A few, like the home she lived in, had added on a small apartment which could be used as a rental space. Neena's landlords, Dr. Christian Spencer and his wife Dr. Melanie Hart, a pediatrician and an Ob/gyn, respectively, were a fun, easy-going pair in their early forties. Chris and Melly, as they insisted she should call them, and their small brood of children had moved into the main house a few years ago. Neena had liked them immediately and counted herself as lucky when she moved into their small yet stylishly updated apartment.

Neena glanced up at the house as she stepped onto the flagstone path leading to her private entrance. She smiled and waved at the two small curly heads at the window, their faces pressed eagerly against the glass. From the patchwork of spots and smudges on the lower portion of the otherwise shining window it was clear that it came into frequent contact with little wet noses and tongues. The smaller of the two waved back at her and the other one let out a hopeful bark. Pinecone, the family's loving chocolate lab, almost never allowed Chris and Melly's youngest child, little Danny, out of his sight. With their brown curls and matching light blue eyes they comically resembled one another. Pinecone wagged and Danny waved until Neena was out of sight.

As she ducked under the flowering trellis that framed the side entrance and entered her apartment, Neena shed her shoes, bookbag, and white coat as she walked across the small living room. She sank gratefully onto the soft, shabby-chic sofa, which was upholstered in soothing pastel flowers and leaves, and put her aching feet up. After her twenty-minute drive home in the ninety-degree July heat in a car without air-conditioning, the cold air that blew from the window-mounted air conditioner was heavenly. Neena closed her eyes and sighed as the icy current blew her wet bangs off of her forehead. She reflected on her second day as a third-year medical student and wondered if the rest of her surgery rotation would be as eventful. It had been a fascinating day. The code this morning, the surgery at which she had "assisted," the lunchtime lecture on the management of the post-surgical patient and even the basic scut work, the menial tasks relegated to medical students and first-year interns, had all had a purpose. Today had only whetted her appetite and Neena was eager to learn more and do more.

But, one day at a time, she told herself. With a start Neena looked around and called out, "Idli? Idli, where are you?" She had startled many first-time visitors with this call. Her unusual summons was promptly answered, not by a magical plate of puffy steamed rice cakes, but by a little fluffy white cat. Neena's first sight of the little cat had been of a small, poofy mass curled into a perfect circle, her little head tucked under one paw. She was immediately reminded of the idlis her mother made every weekend for breakfast. Idli quickly jumped up on the sofa and snuggled in Neena's lap. Neena gently stroked her velvety hair. The feel of the warm, soft body quickly melted away the tensions of the day.

After some time Neena placed Idli on the floor and went to take another much-needed shower. Ten minutes later she padded into the tiny, yet well appointed, galley kitchen in a comfortable T-shirt and shorts, her damp hair wrapped in a thin cotton towel. She was feeling refreshed and energized. A quick dinner and a few hours of studying was the plan for the evening. Neena served Idli a small bowl of her favorite kibble and investigated the contents of her fridge. She noticed with regret that the container which had been filled with Mrs. Patel's aloo-gobi, a traditional potato and cauliflower curry, was empty.

Patel's Pantry was a convenience store a few blocks away which was well stocked with all of the typical items. However, the complex but delightful fragrance in the air hinted at the other treasures in store. The scent of the crisply fried spicy pakoras in the warming pan blended sensuously with that of sandalwood soaps, jasmine-scented candles, and musky incense. There were gleaming trays filled with small diamond-shaped sweets which were delicately dusted with silver. Next to them the bright monarch-orange-colored sweets which were intricately twisted and deep-fried glistened with butter and reposed on a bed of wax paper as gently as a butterfly nestled in a flower. In addition to these savories and sweets, Mrs. Patel also sold small containers of her home-cooked food. She offered curries made with a variety of vegetables and lentils, fragrant basmati rice, and pillow-soft rotis, which simply melted in one's mouth.

With a sigh Neena looked into her fridge and took stock. This did not take long since the only items it contained were a small bottle of milk, a carton of eggs, one small cucumber, and a few wrinkly carrots in the drawer. The fridge door held an assortment of condiments along with a varied collection of the spicy Indian pickles to which she was addicted. Neena added grocery shopping to her mental weekend to-do list. Luckily her cupboards contained a collection of staples like noodles, rice, beans, onions, and a colorful collection of spices.

Before leaving for med school Neena had learned a few simple Indian recipes from her mother and, when she had the time, she practiced her cooking. She found cooking to be challenging, yet satisfying, and she especially loved feeding her friends. Her dishes didn't quite taste as good as Mom's but her friends were always appreciative. Tonight, however, she opted for her most favorite and most speedy meal: ramen noodles with scrambled eggs, topped with slices of cucumber and a generous dollop of chili-paste. Happy in her belief that she had incorporated all of the major food groups, Nina quickly assembled her simple yet tasty dinner. She placed her bowl on a tray and carried it into the living room where she turned on the TV. Neena quickly flipped past the news channels. She was not interested in the nightly newscast which, filled with crimes and peoples' misfortunes, she found too depressing. Neena found the channel she was looking for and settled down for an entertaining half-hour with Alex Trebek on the popular game show *Jeopardy*.

The telephone rang as Neena finished rinsing her dinner dishes. Looking for a kitchen towel but not finding one, she reached up and wiped her hands on the now-dry towel on her head. She managed to answer on the fourth ring.

"Neena?" said a familiar voice.

"Hey Cecilia, how's it going?" she asked in return. "I was just about to sit down to study. Why don't you come over and we can study together?" Cecilia promptly agreed and said she would be right over. Cecilia was doing her internal medicine rotation this quarter and it was always nice to have company when studying. Neena and Cecilia studied well together since they were both quiet and still when they studied.

Cecilia Preston had been Neena's best friend ever since the first day of medical school. They had literally run into each other as they were racing to find a restroom during the minute or so in between lectures in the great circular first-year lecture hall. On the first day, being unfamiliar with the layout of the school, each girl had left the hall, turned in opposite directions, and ran around the back curve of the hall only to meet in the middle. They looked in vain and, hearing the doors of the lecture hall closing, ran back into class. Neena and Cecilia took their seats and hoped that the next break would be longer. Unfortunately for them they had to sit through a few more hours before being dismissed for lunch. They met again at the bank of sinks in the ladies' room, took one look at the relief on each other's face, and started to laugh. "I guess I shouldn't have had those two cups of tea this morning," Neena had said ruefully. Cecilia rolled her eyes and declared that she could not face the day without her large cup of strong coffee. "I suppose, with practice, we can last through until lunch," she said. In fact, it was a skill that was put to the test many times during medical school, as was going without food, drink, and sleep for large stretches of time.

Cecelia lived in a lovely house nearby. And, although a brisk ten-minute walk was all that separated them, Neena knew Cecilia had arrived when she heard the slam of a car door. Idli, who seemed to have almost a canine instinct for visitors, had already taken up a stance of hopeful anticipation near the door. Like most cats, she was quite selective when bestowing her feline attentions but Cecilia was one of her favorite humans. Looking out of the front window Neena spied the shiny silver hue of Cecilia's new Jaguar and a pair of long slim legs swinging onto the sidewalk.

Unlike Neena, who rented a small space in a larger home, Cecilia's parents had bought her an entire house in this quiet, upper-middle class neighborhood in which they both now lived. Cecilia's home had also been tastefully refurbished and had every comfort that money and good taste could supply. However, rather than spreading out her books on her large, elegant dining table, she often preferred to study in Neena's tiny eat-in kitchen.

Cecilia sniffed appreciatively as she entered and asked, "Is that something yummy from Mrs. Patel?"

Neena laughed and said no but offered to whip up a bowl of her famous five-minute noodle dish.

She shook her head. "I've eaten but I always have room for some of Mrs. Patel's cooking." Cecilia reached down to pet Idli, who was winding around her legs and quietly purring her pleasure at seeing a friend.

Cecilia had an experienced palate and was something of a foodie. She enjoyed all types of cuisines and really savored the complex flavors of Indian cooking. She loved the intricate combinations of garlic, ginger, turmeric, chili powder, and so many more that created such a panoply of savory curries. She even appreciated Neena's cooking!

Neena hurried to clear her small cafe-style kitchen table, which substituted for a desk, since the bedroom was too small for anything but a bed and a dresser. As she turned back toward the table she bumped into the edge and let out a sharp cry of pain. Cecelia jumped up and came around to Neena's side.

"What happened?" she asked.

Neena shook her head and tugged at the drawstring of her shorts. She pulled them down slightly and was surprised to find a large aubergine-colored stain on her right hip that was clearly visible even on her light brown skin. She checked her left hip and found a matching discoloration. Neena realized that she must have given herself those bruises when she had placed her rather pointy elbows on her hips to help support the weight of the 100-pound leg.

"Oh my god, that's terrible!" cried Cecelia when Neena told her of her first OR experience. "Why on earth didn't Ron ask one of the guys to do that?"

Neena shrugged. "I think he was just bullying me because he could and because I was the only woman there at the time. He's that kind of guy. But you will be pleased to know that I held on until the very end! I think I may have to start some weight training though if there's more of that to come."

Cecilia opened her large well-used leather tote bag and started extracting her books from it. From a slim quilted bag she also produced a bottle of red wine.

"This," she said, "is our reward for later." One of the many new experiences which Cecilia had introduced to Neena was the pleasures of fine food and wine. Before meeting Cecilia, Neena had not drank much alcohol since usually only beer, and cheap beer at that, was the main offering in college. And, try as she might, Neena had never developed a taste for the bitter brew. She found, however, that quality French and Italian wines went down quite smoothly.

Neena laughed. "It's a school night, Cecilia. You know wine makes me sleepy."

"Well, exactly," said Cecilia. "We will just have a few small sips at the end of the evening. I still have to drive home, don't I?"

Cecilia smiled as she watched Neena set up her supplies for their evening study session. Neena had placed a row of highlighters and pens, neatly lined up, along with a mini-stapler, and a stack of Post-its in a variety of colors. Neena approached her studies in a methodical, color-coded manner. Important text was highlighted in yellow, very important information was underlined in red, and topics requiring additional research were noted by the small green question marks in the margins. Her notebooks and study guides usually had a bouquet of Post-its peeping out at regular intervals, with each color denoting a certain concept that needed to be mastered. Neena knew exactly what had made Cecilia smile. With a sheepish grin and a slight shrug of her shoulders she continued her pre-studying organization. Neena did not in the least mind her friend's good-natured teasing.

Both girls finished arranging their materials on the table and settled down to study. Idli settled beside them onto her favorite bed, a circular brown velvet pillow. Neena thought she looked like a dollop of butter cream frosting atop a chocolate cupcake. They studied diligently for several hours, only pausing now and then to nibble on some cheese and crackers that Neena had put on the table between them. By eleven p.m. Neena found her attention wandering off the page. Sighing, she closed her textbook with a snap and started returning items to her book bag. Cecilia put her things away as well and poured each of them some of the rich, garnet-colored wine into the small glass tumblers Neena had produced. They moved to Neena's comfortable sofa and put their feet up on the small wooden bench that Neena used as a coffee table. Neena sipped her wine and felt her shoulders relax and the tension of the day finally eased.

Soon, the quiet of the room was periodically broken by yawns alternating between Neena and Cecilia. Cecilia turned the elegant slim bangle on her wrist and glanced at the delicate oval of her watch. Though it did not have any numbers, only a diamond at twelve o'clock, she proclaimed the time as eleven o'clock and stood up, swinging her bag onto her shoulder. As soon as Cecilia had sped away in her classy car, Neena restocked her school bag and hurried to get ready for bed. A quick phone call assured Neena that Cecilia was home safely. Although their neighborhood was safe they were always careful to remember that a large city, filled with crime, was not that far away.

Neena finally sank into her bed with relief, and as she pulled up the soft covers she was careful not to upset the small furry bundle at the foot of her bed. Idli was a restful companion and her soft purring always quickly lulled Neena to sleep. She reached up to touch her head and found to her astonishment that it was still wrapped in a towel. As she tossed it to the floor Neena caught a glimpse of herself in the mirror. Her last waking image was of her head, full of crazy ringlets springing out in all directions. She smiled ruefully and sank back against the pillow.

Friday July 3, 1992

Chapter 5

Although it was only the third day of Neena's surgery rotation there was already a rhythm to the busy days that were filled with new sights and experiences. Neena had mastered the art of the tape box and was able to deftly hand Ron the appropriate gauze and tape for each patient. Usually in the afternoons, if there were no surgeries to observe, Mike assigned various tasks to each member of the team. The medical students were responsible for checking on lab results, reviewing official readings of X-rays, following up with consultants, and numerous other tasks that fell under the vast umbrella of "scut work" before their afternoon sign-out rounds. This afternoon, however, Mike said he had a special errand in mind. There was a surgery patient in the VIP floor who needed staples removed and Mike wanted one of the medical students to do it.

Mike looked around at the group assembled around him. Victoria was fairly quivering with anticipation. With her thin face, gaunt frame, and light gray eyes rimmed with dark brown eyeliner, she reminded Neena of a greyhound. As if she was at the races, Victoria jumped ahead of her fellow classmates.

Before even being asked she burst out, "No problem, Mike, I would be happy to go up to see the VIP." She gave him a knowing glance as if it would be obvious to anyone of the meanest intelligence that she, as a fellow VIP, was the one student who was eminently qualified for this task. However, Mike's cool blue eyes moved past Victoria and landed on Neena.

"I know you've seen it done before Neena, so grab a staple-remover from the supply closet and head up to the VIP wing," said Mike. Neena, who had supposed that Victoria or one of the guys would be selected for this task, looked up in surprise.

"There's a VIP wing?" Neena asked, perplexed.

"Yup," replied Mike. "It's on the top floor and reserved for the big wigs. The patient's name is Rodrick MacMillan. There's a separate elevator on the second floor that will take you straight up." He quickly turned back to his to-do list. Victoria arched an astonished sparse eyebrow at Mike. Crossing her long thin arms across her bony frame, she directed a hostile glance at Neena, turned on her heel, and flounced down the hall with her ponytail wagging furiously. Mike, who had not missed the interaction between the two women, gave Neena an encouraging smile. He turned toward the opposite hall and indicated with a movement of his sharp blue eyes the direction in which he expected Neena to go. With his long strides he had already disappeared along one of the endless corridors and as Neena looked around there was not a white coat in sight. Everyone had simply vanished in their haste to complete their assigned tasks for the afternoon.

Neena realized with a sinking sensation in the pit of her stomach that Mike had not opened the supply closet for her. His breezy suggestion to "grab a staple-remover" belied the actual complexity of this task. Now she had no choice but to ask Marge.

Nurse Marge, with her imposing frame, heavy jowls, and slit-like eyes, sat like a malignant creature behind the curved nurses' station. Neena approached Marge with the trepidation of a wanderer on a quest to seize a closely guarded treasure. As Marge held a large Styrofoam cup to her lips the steam rising from it gave her the appearance of a dragon expelling small puffs of smoke from its nostrils. Neena told herself that she was up to the challenge. Although her diminutive size often led people to underestimate her, those who knew her well also knew that there was a will of iron running through her small frame.

"Hello Nurse Marge," said Neena brightly. "Could you please help me get a staple-remover from the supply closet?" It was several seconds before Marge even acknowledged Neena's presence. She stood up and glared down at Neena from her great height.

"Now, why would YOU be needing a staple-remover?" she asked with suspicion. Marge glanced at the stacks of papers which Neena had placed on the counter. "It is a sterile piece of equipment and is only for use on patients."

"Oh yes, yes I know that," Neena stammered. "But I don't know the combination for the supply closet lock."

"I repeat, it is only to be used on patients," Marge said again, looking pointedly at Neena's neat stacks of stapled papers.

"Yes, I know that," Neena repeated. In her nervousness she became increasingly confused. After a few moments it dawned on Neena that Nurse Marge had likely assumed that Neena had no idea of what a surgical staple-remover was used for. In all fairness to Marge, she was probably within her rights to assume complete ignorance on the part of medical students, especially third-year students in the first week of July! Neena had heard the residents joke that the first week of July was the worst possible time of the year for any sick patient entering a teaching hospital. The first of July has historically been the start of all clinical years and training programs so every person on the team was "new" in some sense of the word. But, the end of June was one of the best months of the year to be ill since all of the doctors in training would have had another year of experience under their belts—or white coats, as the case may be.

Neena pulled her wits together and tried again. "Actually it was Dr. Windsor who asked me to remove staples for a patient on the VIP floor. A surgical patient," Neena added for good measure.

39

At this, Nurse Marge raised a shaggy red eye brow at her. "What other type of patient would require staples removed if not a surgical patient?" she asked. But at the mention of Dr. Windsor, Marge's face lost a little of its rigidity. With a slight snort, Marge whirled away from the counter. Neena stifled the giggle that was bubbling up in her throat and dragged her eyes away from the lumbering progress of the "dragon." Neena's gaze settled on the face of a man working in the hallway about ten feet away. He was standing on a stepladder replacing a light bulb in one of the sconces along the wall. When he saw Neena looking at him he gave her a quick smile and a surreptitious thumbs-up. It seemed that she had a spectator for her daring feat!

Marge returned with a small white packet and thrust it at Neena. Trying not to laugh, Neena accepted the staple-remover and offered a quick word of thanks. She turned her back on Marge and gave the man a triumphant smile. She felt victorious and fled with her hands clasped tightly over her treasure.

Neena was wandering around on the second floor looking for the VIP elevator when she saw one of the friendly volunteers who usually manned the welcome desk coming toward her. At a distance she could not tell which one of the ladies she was. Her soft white hair was still beautifully coiffed and in her pale pink pinafore she looked as sweet as the treats that filled the cart she was pushing. As she came closer, Neena noticed that there were trays of mini-cupcakes merrily frosted with colorful icing and cookies bulging with either chocolate chips, macadamia nuts, or M&M's on her cart, along with a large gleaming silver carafe.

She greeted Neena in a cheerful tone, "Good afternoon, doctor!" she said with a smile. Her eyes twinkled at Neena's surprised expression at being addressed thus.

"How about a little treat or a cup of coffee?"

"That would be wonderful but I'm in a bit of a hurry. I think I'm lost, actually. I'm looking for the elevator to the VIP suites."

Miss Helen pointed a well-manicured finger behind her. "I just came from there. The elevator is beyond that large potted plant at the end of this hall. Here, take a little something with you." And before Neena could object she placed a mini-cupcake in her hand.

"Thank you so much, Miss Helen. If you're still making your rounds when I'm done I will take you up on a cup of coffee."

"Don't worry, Doc, I will save you a cup," she said with another of her sweet smiles. Neena thanked her again, popped the little cupcake into her mouth and started briskly down the hall.

As Neena passed the potted palm tree she saw the gleaming doors of the private elevator to the VIP suite. She checked her reflection to make sure she didn't have icing on her chin and went up to the topmost floor. As the elevator door opened onto the eighth floor with a soft chime Neena stepped out into an elegant, subdued foyer. A plush mauve carpet eliminated the sound of her footsteps. There was a nurses' station, as on other floors, but this one looked more like a concierge desk. A smiling unit clerk in a crisp pale gray uniform performed the duties of a hostess.

"Good afternoon, how may I help you?" she said.

Feeling a bit awed, Neena momentarily forgot the purpose of her errand and after a few seconds stammered, "I'm here to remove Mr. MacMillan's staples?"

It should have been a statement but in her nervousness it came out as a question. Neena brandished the staple-remover at her and Marianne, as her name tag proclaimed, informed Neena that her patient was in suite number two. Neena turned in the direction Marianne had indicated and stopped outside the door.

Neena was feeling quite nervous at her first solo doctoring activity but the little cupcake had given her a boost of energy and strength. She fluffed her bangs, straightened her white coat, and knocked softly on the door. As there was no response, she carefully opened the door and stepped in. The room resembled a beautiful high-end hotel rather than a hospital room. The floors were dark wood and glowed warmly in the afternoon sun which streamed through a large window. The spacious hospital bed was neatly made and several plump pillows were propped up behind Mr. MacMillan, who was lying back with his eyes closed. For one startled second Neena had a horrible feeling of déjà vu but then breathed a sigh of relief as she saw his chest gently rise and fall. His light brown hair was in a neat crew cut, with just a few streaks of gray around the temples. The light stubble along his cheek and jaws made him look younger, like many of her fellow students when they came to class having just rolled out of bed. She knew from the summary on her to-do list that he was fifty-two years old and she was surprised at how young he looked. Until then she had always thought of anyone over fifty as OLD.

Neena called softly, "Hello, Mr. MacMillan? So sorry to wake you." She approached the bed and gently touched the hand that lay loosely on top of the covers. Suddenly Mr. MacMillan's eyes popped open, startling them both. He then gave Neena a slow, sleepy smile that started at the corners of his mouth and spread quickly to his warm brown eyes, flecked with green. Recovering, she smiled back.

"I am a student-doctor, Mr. MacMillan. My name is Neena." She extended her hand in greeting. Shaking his hand she explained, somewhat hesitantly, that she was there to remove his staples.

"Hello, Neena," he said. "Nice to meet you. Thank goodness you're here. These staples are driving me crazy!"

A common dictum during the course of medical training, regardless of the stage of one's learning, was: "See one, Do one, Teach one." As Mike had mentioned, Neena had indeed seen staples being removed. Now came the "do one" portion of the plan, which was actually quite daunting. After carefully washing her hands and pulling on a pair of gloves, Neena opened the sterile package which contained the staple remover. This did not look like the staple remover found in desk drawers, but had handles like a small pair of scissors with blunted tips. As the handles were squeezed together the outer edges of the staple were lifted up and out of the skin. Neena looked inquiringly at Mr. MacMillan since she had belatedly realized that she did not know where his staples were! She had been so nervous when she reached the floor that she had neglected to study his chart first. She was mentally kicking herself when Mr. MacMillan helpfully pulled his sheet aside, revealing his left lower leg. With mounting dismay Neena looked at the dozens of metal staples that looked like small railroad ties, tracking from his ankle to his mid-thigh! His incision looked very long and very pink against the paleness of his skin. Then, to her even greater dismay, he opened the top of his hospital gown and revealed more staples running down the center of his chest.

"I just had a CABG," he explained.

"Oh, hmm, yes, yes, I see," Neena said out loud, trying to sound as if she knew what that meant. *What on earth is a cabbage* she wondered? She decided it would be unprofessional to ask the patient and resolved to figure it out later.

Another dictum of any stage of training was to "fake it until you make it." Eyeing the staples as she would have eyed an obstacle course, Neena squared her small shoulders and planned her strategy. She would start at the bottom, she decided, and work her way up, since she felt more comfortable beginning as far away from the patient as possible. Suddenly Neena found herself alone and in close, fairly intimate contact with a patient, who was a man and a stranger. A stranger who was expecting her to take care of him, no less. Neena hoped that by the time she got up to the level of his chest that she would have gotten the hang of it. This was not a "case" or a bed number, but an actual human being and she was determined to do her best. Neena tucked one of her stray curls behind her ear, took a deep breath, and gently placed the instrument under the first staple. As it came quickly and smoothly out of his skin she could have shouted with relief!

As she slowly and carefully removed the second staple, Mr. MacMillan made small talk. Probably to distract himself—and Neena—from what she was doing.

"So, what year of medical school are you in?" he asked interestedly.

Oh my god, what would he say if he knew this was only my third day on the job? she thought. *He may refuse to let me take out his staples.* That's exactly what she would have done if the roles had been reversed. But, she forged ahead, in what she hoped was the tone of a confident and competent medical provider.

"I am in my third year and I'm currently doing my surgical rotation." Luckily, he did not press Neena for more details and she, in turn, did not have to burden him with the fact that this was one of the few times she had actually touched a live patient.

"I know a few of the surgery residents," he said.

Distracted by what she was doing, it took Neena a few seconds to reply.

"Hmm, that's nice," she said absently, removing the third staple successfully. Only a few dozen more to go!

"So, where are you from, Neena?" he asked.

"Oh, I'm a local girl, from central Jersey," she informed him.

He gave a small laugh and clarified, "No, I meant what country are your parents or family originally from?"

Neena laughed as well. "My parents are from India. I was born there but immigrated to the US when I was about two years old."

"Yes, I thought so," he said. "That explains your American accent," Mr. MacMillan remarked. "Do you speak any Hindi or Tamil?"

Neena's eyes widened in surprise. "Why, yes, I speak Tamil since my family is from Madras. I'm impressed that you even know the name of the language! Most Americans usually associate only Hindi with India. Unfortunately I didn't have the chance to learn Hindi since my parents never learned to speak it. I would like to learn someday, though."

"I learned to speak a few words of Hindi and Tamil," he said.

"Really, that's so cool!" said Neena. "How did you learn to speak either language?"

"Oh, there was a very friendly Indian doorman, named Dash, in my office building who spoke Hindi. If ever he saw me there at teatime on a Saturday afternoon he would always pour me a cup of the most delicious chai from his thermos. And then there was an engineer in my company from Madras. I've always been interested in languages and they would both teach me a little now and then, especially when they found out I was going to visit India."

"When did you visit India?" Neena asked curiously since she had not met many Americans so far who had been to India.

"It's been quite a few years but I used to travel fairly regularly. My work took me to both north and south India so I thought it would be helpful to learn a few phrases in both languages. It certainly came in handy as an ice-breaker. I gather my accent is atrocious and many chuckles followed my clumsy attempts to speak," he said with a smile. "How about you? Does your family go back often?"

"We go almost every year to visit my grandparents. When I was in grade school my sister and I would spend the entire summer there. It was a lot of fun. What's your favorite city there?" she asked.

Neena was bent over his leg in deep concentration. One of the staples was slightly embedded and surrounded by dark bits of scab. She reached for the sterile blunt tipped tweezers that were included with the staple remover. Finally, she gently lifted out the recalcitrant staple with a sigh of relief. Realizing that she was already at the level of his knee and feeling encouraged by her progress, Neena finally looked up at Mr. MacMillan. She found him with his face averted, eyes closed, and lips lightly compressed.

"Are you okay, Mr. MacMillan? I am so sorry if I hurt you!" she cried. Neena's eyes started to prick with quick tears of remorse and she fervently hoped that she wouldn't actually cry. Dripping tears onto her patient did not seem very professional. Luckily, she was able to hold her tears back. Mr. MacMillan quickly opened his eyes and when he looked at her, it was with a smile.

"No, no, I am fine," he reassured her. "You have been so gentle I barely felt a thing."

She appreciated his kind words and tact since Neena was sure that a few of the pauses in his speech and the quiet intakes of breath had probably been occasioned by her initial clumsy efforts.

Mr. MacMillan continued to keep up a steady stream of idle chatter. He had a kind voice and an easy way of speaking. He chatted about a variety of subjects and appeared to be a very intelligent man who took an interest in many things. He talked of a music machine that was in his grandmother's parlor which played music on its own. He was fascinated by the punched card system used in such music machines and said it had sparked his early interest in computers and hardware. He told her that he had been fortunate enough to invent a minute piece of hardware that has since come to be a part of almost every computer assembled! He had started his own company at the age of twenty-five and despite the challenges he has never regretted that decision. Neena looked at him in surprise as his words registered. He had spoken so simply and humbly about his success. The fact that he must be a very wealthy man finally dawned on her. Well, of course he would be since he was in the VIP suite! Suddenly she felt a little awkward. Neena was sure he would have probably preferred that a "real" doctor had been sent to take out his staples.

Mr. MacMillan did not appear to notice her hesitation. "Are you planning on opening up your own practice in the future?" he wanted to know.

Neena told him that she had not gotten that far in her planning, even though she liked to plan almost everything. He asked her about her goals and path to medical school. Neena told him about her childhood dream of being a doctor and how proud her parents were that she was the first doctor in her family. He then asked Neena about what she liked to do in her spare time. With a rueful smile she remarked that spare time had been in short supply the past few years. Neena mentioned that she often worked part time as a home health aide whenever she could to help pay for expenses.

"But, when I do have the time, I love to read mystery novels." She went on, "My favorite mysteries are those known as 'cozy's.'"

"What on earth is a cozy?" he asked. Mr. MacMillan chuckled when Neena explained.

"A cozy is a mystery in which a crime or murder has occurred but it is all very genteel. The dastardly deeds are presented in a softer, gentler way, hence the name 'cozy.'" She went on to explain that this was in contrast to "hard-boiled" mysteries which are very gritty with graphic descriptions of blood and gore.

Unthinkingly, she told him that she really didn't like blood and gore. At this Mr. MacMillan laughed out loud and then winced slightly as Neena's instrument extracted one of the staples rather more quickly than she had intended.

"You do know you are training to be a doctor?" he asked. "I think you may come across some blood and gore." His voice seemed very serious but when she glanced up at him she realized his eyes were twinkling and he was only teasing.

Neena smiled back. "Yes, I do know," she reassured him. "I don't mind actual blood and the surgeries that I've attended so far have been so interesting. I think with a controlled situation, such as surgeries usually are, that I am fine. I am not sure how I will react to trauma patients, though. I really don't like to see patients disfigured or suffering."

As she dropped another staple onto the little metal tray by her side Neena continued to tell him that she really hoped to become a pediatrician. She had always loved babies and had decided early on that the field of pediatrics seemed to best match her temperament and talents.

Neena moved slowly proximally (proudly remembering medical-speak for moving toward the head). As each staple dropped onto the small metal tray, it brought her a millimeter closer to the end. When she had completed removing all the staples in Mr. MacMillan's leg she straightened and stopped to catch her breath. While Mr. MacMillan was busy untying the top of his gown, Neena surreptitiously wiped beads of perspiration from her forehead with the back of her coat sleeve. As she pushed the damp locks back she correctly surmised that her bangs were no longer fluffy.

Mr. MacMillan looked up and asked, "Are you okay? You're doing great and it looks like we're almost done." Neena could feel her cheeks growing warm with embarrassment at being comforted and encouraged by her patient. Wasn't it supposed to be the other way around?

"Thank you, Mr. MacMillan, but you're the one who's doing great. I will be done soon," she said, and picked up the staple-remover again. Neena gently pulled back the folds of his gown and took a survey of the staples running neatly down the center of his chest. The image of a large silver zipper popped into her head. Neena imagined that if she pulled the zipper open she would be able to see his ribcage with his heart imprisoned within, like a cardinal trapped in its birdcage. The fragile, intricate, and amazing mass that was his heart would be beating softly and steadily, like the wings of that bird. A bird whose beating wings would never allow it to escape its bony confines. Pushing these fanciful thoughts aside, Neena bent over again to remove the final set of staples. She started at the distal end—the end furthest from the patient's head—and again felt inordinately pleased at having remembered this bit of medical terminology. She continued to carefully work her way up his chest. A little burst of happiness ran through her since she now had the hang of it and there was a natural rhythm to the process. Insert, click, lift, ping. Insert, click, lift, ping. Neena felt a tiny surge of confidence each time a staple dropped with a tinkle onto the metal instrument tray.

After removing approximately six staples she stopped briefly to take a breath. She hadn't realized that while intently concentrating she had been holding her breath. At the same time, she realized that the tip of her tongue was peeking out of her mouth. Conscious of the fact that this was not a professional look, she promptly closed her mouth and put an encouraging smile on her lips. As Neena was about to resume she noticed a mark on Mr. MacMillan's upper right chest that seemed to be etched with the clarity of a tattoo. It was about the size of a nickel and a light pink color against the white of his skin. What made it notable was that it was shaped like a perfect teardrop which curved slightly at its pointy end.

"That's a very interesting mark you have, Mr. MacMillan," she commented as she resumed her task. "The shape reminds me of a mango pattern that is commonly found on Indian textiles. Is it a scar or a tattoo?"

"It's a birthmark that many of the males in my family share," he replied.

"Rather strange, when you think about it."

As Neena removed the final staple she put it on the tray with a sense of relief and accomplishment. What had seemed like hours had actually been about twenty minutes.

"Well, I'm finally done, Mr. MacMillan. I hope it wasn't too uncomfortable. Thank you for being so patient with me."

He looked up at her with a kindly smile that crinkled the corners of his eyes.

"You have a very steady and gentle touch. Thank you, Neena, or should I say, Nandri?" he said, using the formal Tamil word for thank you. He extended his hand. "And, good luck with the rest of medical school."

Neena laughed in surprise and shook his hand. "I was happy to do it, Mr. MacMillan. Unfortunately I don't know the Tamil words for you're welcome." She placed all the used supplies in the red biohazard bin and washed her hands at the sink. Turning back to Mr. MacMillan she added, "I will stop by to check on you tomorrow." But his eyes were already closed and he had settled back onto his pillows so she let herself out of the room and quietly closed the door.

Nina retraced her steps back to the elevator. As she passed the "concierge desk" the clerk called out to her.

"Are you Dr. Neena?" she asked. "One of the volunteers left this for you."

She pointed to a cup with "Dr. Neena" written on it in a lovely cursive hand. It was filled with hot coffee, light and sweet, just as she liked it. How did Miss Helen know? Feeling as if she had finally done something useful for a patient, she happily took a sip of the delicious coffee. As Neena rode the elevator down to the second floor she quickly thumbed through her pocket surgical handbook. She giggled as her eyes alighted on CABG, aka "Coronary Artery Bypass Graft!"

At the end of the day the surgical team was sprawled across various articles of furniture in the surgical residents' lounge. This was the first area of the hospital Neena had encountered that did not appear to have been recently renovated. The walls were stark white, only relieved at intervals with cork boards filled with colorful notices and advertisements for roommates or sublets or used furniture. Little tabs had been cut into the ends of the flyers so that an interested party could tear off a piece containing a phone number. Many of them flapped briskly in the breeze of the air-conditioner like confetti at a parade.

There certainly was a celebratory feeling in the air. It was the end of their first, albeit short, week of their first clinical rotations! Neena had been on her feet since five a.m. that morning and until she sat down, she hadn't realized how tired she was. Joe was lying across the full length of a lumpy gray sofa, while Neel and Raj were reclining in two faded blue armchairs, their long legs extended in front of them. As Neena sank gratefully into the smaller sofa opposite them, Calvin plopped heavily onto the gray carpeted floor. In contrast to the exhausted neophytes, the surgical residents were standing near a row of metal lockers talking animatedly about their weekend plans.

As Duncan packed up his bag he turned to Ron and Mike and said, "See you tomorrow, same time, same place?"

"That works for me," replied Mike. "Four o' clock, Maple Tree Park?"

Dunk nodded. "The weather is supposed to be hot and humid but it should be a bit cooler by that time."

Mike zipped his duffel bag closed and turned to the group as he slung it over one shoulder. "If you guys are interested, you're welcome to join us. Do any of you play soccer? We usually play a pickup game in the park on Saturdays in the summer. A bunch of residents and students usually show up. Whoever is not on call, that is."

Neel straightened up in his chair. "That sounds like fun," he said. "What do you think, Raj?"

Raj, also sitting up, answered with a smile and a little bob of his head, which was neither a nod of acquiescence nor a shake of denial.

Duncan, who had paused nearby, looked confused. "Uh, is that a yes or a no?" he asked.

"He means yes," Neena said with a laugh. Of course, she and Neel were well accustomed to the distinctive and characteristic Indian head bob.

"Yes! I'd love to come," Raj clarified. "As a kid I spent most of my time playing soccer, but we call it football."

"Women are welcome as well, Neena," said Dunk.

"Believe me when I say that that is not a good idea. I have two left feet. I may have to work that day, so I'm not sure."

"Work? Come on, Neena, loosen up a little! All work and no play makes Neena a dull girl. At least come to watch. And bring a few friends, why don't you?" he added with a grin. She knew whom he meant in particular. Neena nodded and smiled noncommittally since she did not know Cecilia's plans for the weekend.

As Neena fumbled for her car keys she realized that Neel was patiently holding the door for her. With a grateful nod she slipped past him and joined the others in the stairwell. They clattered down the stairs and burst into the lobby. The late afternoon light held the promise of several more hours of sunshine and it was with a sense of satisfaction and relief that Neena looked forward to the weekend.

Saturday July 4, 1994

Chapter 6

Neena made her way to the park on Saturday afternoon. She carried a small blanket and her blue messenger bag, now filled with snacks and a favorite novel, rather than the usual pile of books and notes. She had woken early that morning and spent a few hours working at a nearby rehabilitation center as a nursing aid. She had worked there whenever her schedule permitted for the past two years. Not only did the extra money come in handy but she truly enjoyed interacting with the patients there. The patients were friendly and appreciative of any help they received. They were also mostly elderly, often alone, and they craved the company.

Although she had the title of nursing aid there were many days during which Neena had spent hours playing checkers with competitive grandpas or chasing after skeins of wool that escaped from the fragile grasp of grandmas. She really didn't mind though since she had always missed having her grandparents nearby. As a child, one of her favorite songs had been the one about Thanksgiving. "Over the river and through the woods." Each time she sang ". . . to grandfather's house we go," she felt a thrill of excitement. Neena marveled at the thought that some children had grandparents to visit. A small pang of loss usually followed but this nursery rhyme remained one of her favorites. When she was warmly greeted by the friendly denizens of the center, Neena experienced a mild jab of compunction at not being able to spend as much time with them as she had used to. But, even though her clinical rotations were keeping her quite busy she did her best to squeeze in a short shift whenever possible.

After a quick lunch at home Neena studied diligently for several hours. But, by four o'clock she decided she had done enough work for the day and needed a change of scenery. Neena changed out of her studying outfit of old running shorts and a T-shirt, into a pair of loose khaki pants and a pale pink scoop-neck cotton top. Slipping into a pair of worn yet comfortable leather sandals, she headed to her car.

As Neena came out of the gate on the side of the house she was greeted by Pinecone's enthusiastic barks. He scampered around her legs and leaned up against her, waiting to be petted. Neena bent over to caress the top of his head and scratch behind his ears. Where Pinecone was, Danny was usually soon to follow. And sure enough a little person came running down the flagstone pathway as fast as his chubby legs could manage.

"Neena, Neena, Neena!" he cried.

With a laugh she replied in kind, "Danny, Danny, Danny!"

He came careening toward her and she caught him up in her arms.

"How are you, Danny honey?" Neena asked. He responded by thrusting a brightly colored toy in her face.

"Look what I got!" The toy was a plastic car fashioned out of large multi-colored Legos.

"Wow, that's pretty cool! I used to love playing with Legos. Did you make this yourself?"

"All by myself!" he proudly asserted. "Didn't I mommy?" he asked, turning back toward the house. Feeling that Neena had expressed sufficient admiration for his toy, Danny started wriggling to indicate he now wished to be put down.

Melly appeared on the steps of the house and proceeded toward them, stopping intermittently to pick up the plastic blocks which littered the path.

Melly smiled at her little son and agreed, "Yes, you did, sweetie but maybe daddy helped you a little bit?"

Danny coolly ignored his mother's question since he was not keen on sharing his accomplishment. He promptly sat down and started to make vrooming noises as he pushed his car along the path.

Melly smiled down at her son's curly brown head. She turned back to Neena. "He's in love with his new Legos. He's always trying to get the older kids' Lego sets but since theirs have hundreds of tiny pieces we've told him he's not allowed to play with them," said Melly. "It can be hard being the baby of the family."

Neena wasn't so sure about that. Her younger sister, Nalini, had always enjoyed privileges and luxuries much earlier than Neena ever had. She supposed that she, as the firstborn, had had to initiate her parents in their role and that by the time her sister had come along, four years later, her parents had ironed out many of the initial wrinkles of parenting. Her mother and father have continued to evolve but Neena suspected that she would always be smoothing the way for her younger sister.

"So how are you? How did your first week of clinicals go?" Melly asked.

"It was great!" Neena said. "But one of the main things I've learned this week is how much I need to learn."

"Yes, well, you will never really stop being a student," Melly said. Seeing the look of disappointment which had started to replace Neena's bright countenance, Melly quickly explained, "Of course, you will learn all that you need to graduate. And it is in residency that you will really learn to be a physician. That being said, most of us are lifelong students and you will continue to learn about your field for as long as you are in practice."

Neena's face brightened again. "Yes, I see what you mean," she said. She did like to study and she enjoyed the challenge of a test. She loved the sound of opening a brand-new textbook and the smell of freshly sharpened pencils always reminded her of bright, new beginnings.

"Now, I look forward to going to conferences where I can listen to an authority in my field and be a student again," said Melly. "And, it gives me the opportunity for a little getaway with all expenses paid," she added with a smile. "But, I'm glad to see you going out on a beautiful day like this. I hope you're taking some time to relax and have a little fun?" she said, pointedly eyeing Neena's messenger bag.

Neena laughed and patted her bag. "For once my bag is filled only with snacks. I'm headed to the park to watch some classmates and residents play soccer." Giving Melly, Danny, and Pinecone a cheery goodbye, Neena walked to her car.

A short drive brought Neena to the park. As she entered the wrought iron gates of the park it was with pleasure that she took in the large leafy trees and expanses of grass. Although she found the city landscapes of concrete, glass, and steel structures very exciting, she did miss the open spaces and greenery of her childhood. Neena walked slowly along the tree-lined pathway, looking for one of the playing fields. As the path opened up to a large open area, she heard someone calling her name.

"Neena, over here!" She turned to see Cecilia waving at her from under the shade of a large oak tree.

Cecilia was lounging lazily against a large brightly patterned pillow. She was wearing a simple white cotton dress with thin spaghetti straps that contrasted beautifully with her even tan. With an elegant sweep of her hand she invited Neena to join her on the quilt she had laid under the lovely old tree.

As Neena dropped her things on the ground and sank onto the blanket next to Cecilia she found herself in receipt of a critical look.

"What have you been doing all day?" Cecilia demanded. "You look tired."

She added with an approving nod, "But, you look very pretty. That shade of light rose really sets off your lovely skin tone." She lightly touched Neena's sleeve where it met her skin. "Like a slice of strawberry cake next to a cup of sweet chai."

"You must be hungry," Neena said with a grin. "I'm just hot and thirsty. I felt like I was riding in a heated aluminum can," she complained and started rummaging in her bag for the water bottle. When she came up empty-handed Cecilia opened the small cooler next to her and poured lemonade into a paper cup.

"Here, drink this."

Neena drank thirstily and wiped her mouth with the back of her hand. "That hits the spot!" she said with a sigh. "I spent the morning at the rehab center and then did a few hours of studying," Neena explained to Cecilia. "How about you?"

Cecilia was investigating the contents of Neena's bag and took out the packet of sandwiches.

"Mmm, peanut butter and grape jelly, my favorite," she said as she bit into the soft white bread. The wonderful thing about Cecilia was that she enjoyed simple foods as much as she enjoyed haute cuisine. Neena smiled at her friend's contented munching.

Through a mouthful of food Ceclia mumbled, "I studied for a bit too but then was so tired I took a little nap. It was too beautiful a day to spend another minute indoors so I came here. I brought my book along though," she added virtuously. The large internal medicine textbook lay on the blanket near her and a bright yellow highlighter was sticking out of it to mark her last page.

"It looks like you're on page five!" Neena teased.

Cecilia, who was sipping her own lemonade, looked indignant. "I'll have you know that the print is quite small and dense. Don't worry, I plan on spending the rest of the weekend studying."

Neena actually wasn't too worried. Cecilia was a strong student and could get through masses of material in an efficient manner when she concentrated.

"But, right now I want to enjoy this lovely afternoon and the wonderful view." She gave her friend a mischievous look. Cecilia pointed a delicate, French-manicured finger toward the open space in front of them and adjusted her gold bangle watch, which now sported a white bezel to match her dress.

She delicately wiped a dab of jelly off her lower lip and got to her feet.

It was a lovely view. The grass was thick and velvety green. Large leafy trees bordered the open space and groups of bushes with bright pink and blue flowers were dotted throughout, adding splashes of color. However, Cecilia's finger was pointed not at the horticultural beauty in front of them, but at the group of shirtless young men scattered on the emerald field.

With a laugh Neena opened up the bag of corn chips that she had also brought along. Alternating bites of the sweet PB&J sandwich with the crisp salty chips, she chewed with a feeling of nostalgia. This had been one of her most favorite school lunches as a little girl.

She had to admit Cecilia was correct. The view was very nice. Duncan, Joe, Neel, and Raj were a few of the "skins." The diversity of their class, which was unexpected but so very important in the field of medicine, was demonstrated by the range of skin tones currently visible on the field. The complexions of the players ranged from pale white to dark bronze. Unfortunately, many of the fairer-skinned men sported patches of pink that would, most likely, soon develop into painful sunburn. Neena surveyed their anatomies with professional interest and came to the conclusion that their musculature was indeed well-developed and pleasing to the eye. She was, after all, a medical student.

A lively game of soccer was in progress. The players dashed up and down the field, occasionally colliding with one another. Many of them were very good and expertly headed the ball and tossed it around on their ankles.

Victoria was front and center, cheering loudly, mostly for Dunk. She was jumping up and down, clapping her hands.

"Awesome, Duncan! Way to go! Woo-hoo!" Dunk, who was simply standing still on the field at that moment, acknowledged his one-woman pep squad with a slight salute and a mocking bow.

Neena nudged Cecilia with her elbow. "Do you think she's abandoned Mike and moved on to Duncan?" she said softly.

"It looks like it. She's definitely his type." Then, they both turned to each other and said in unison, "Not!"

But Cecilia seriously pondered the idea. "Well, maybe she is his type. She is part of the New England aristocracy, is she not?" The slight curl of her pretty lip indicated her disgust for such shallowness.

"Dunk does look like a man who enjoys his luxuries. Anyway," Neena laughed, "if it gives Victoria something else to do other than monopolizing Mike every chance she gets then I'm all for it. These past three days she has been glued to his side and talks constantly. I wish he would tell her to shut up but he's too polite."

"A polite surgeon? Isn't that an oxymoron?" said Cecilia, referencing the familiar stereotyping of the surgical specialty.

Cecilia and Neena joined their classmates on the perimeter of the field behind a row of wildly cheering males, who ranged from medical students to senior residents. The crowd parted slightly for Cecilia, as it usually did, and they found themselves in the choicest position, thereby gently displacing Victoria. Neena noted two bright red spots on Victoria's pasty white face.

Neena was always surprised, and just a little bit envious, of the confidence and ease with which Cecilia approached life. She never seemed to be the least bit intimidated to approach anyone. Once, Neena had even noticed her chatting easily with the president of their medical school. Neena was always in too much awe of authority to feel comfortable in doing such a thing. However, in her time spent with Cecilia she had come to the realization that her own reticence, though appropriate in certain situations, may have precluded her from opportunities in the past. When Neena had spoken admiringly of Cecilia's courage in approaching even the most senior member of their medical school, Cecilia had said something that had struck Neena as profound. "Figures of Authority," said Cecilia, "should not be seen as barriers to success, but as ladders."

Neena's parents had always inculcated in her an immense and unconditional respect for her teachers, who had been the most common figures of authority in her life, other than her parents. Someone with the ability and inclination to impart knowledge was to be almost revered. Education and learning were so important that the Hindu pantheon even contained a goddess of learning, Saraswati. She championed and protected all types of learning, including the arts and music. Saraswati is often represented holding a book and a veena and seated on a rock, indicating that the pursuit of knowledge can be hard, like the surface of a stone.

While Cecilia's confident and outgoing nature opened many doors for her, Neena did not doubt that her friend's appearance played no small part in her success. Cecilia was supremely indifferent to the attention her lovely face and figure garnered. If asked, she would not have used adjectives such as beautiful or gorgeous to describe herself. She preferred her temporarily tanned summer skin to the milky white shade it promptly assumed as soon as the summer sun faded. And, she had often expressed the wish that her baby soft hair, to which no clip or tie could be attached, was richer and had more texture. In short, she believed herself to be simply average-looking and had always professed a preference for Neena's more exotic looks. It was this modesty, among her other qualities, which endeared her to her friends.

Neena, on the other hand, would have instantly exchanged her unruly mop of dark, frizzy hair for Cecilia's silky golden locks. And her skin tone, which Cecilia flatteringly compared to a cup of chai, but more closely resembled the color of milk chocolate in the summer, was not an attribute which she was used to hearing praised. Neena's mother had always tut-tutted at her darkened complexion following a summer's afternoon spent at the local swimming pool. Milk chocolate, sadly, was not a shade of skin color that was much admired by Neena's mother. Neena had always been hurt by this common attitude which she felt reflected very poorly on the Indian community.

However, at this moment a trite adage about the color of grass came to her mind. Once, Neena was at her favorite hair salon and had been bemoaning the effort it took to tame her wayward tresses. Her hair dresser sagely remarked, "The grass is always greener on the other side, but it still has to be mowed." Neena smiled to herself and, basking in Cecilia's reflected glory, moved to the front next to her friend.

They cheered and yelled encouragement to the players indiscriminately. Neena was not sure who won but the players ended their game with a great deal of high-fiving and chest-bumping. As they walked off of the field the "skins" were pulling on their shirts and the "shirts" were using the ends of their garments to wipe the perspiration from their faces. The medical students in their class headed toward Neena and Cecilia. They collapsed onto the grass in various stages of exhaustion and reached for their water bottles. The residents had formed their own group and gathered their belongings. Victoria rushed over to Dunk, proffering him a water bottle and trying to dab the sweat off his forehead with a towel.

"Look at her," said Neena, nudging Cecilia and arching an eyebrow at Victoria. "You'd think he's just finished a marathon surgery and she's the nurse assigned to wipe the surgeon-god's forehead."

Dunk, lost in thought, absentmindedly accepted Victoria's ministrations. Neena and Cecilia grinned at each other. The students walked past their classmates and they exchanged good-natured comments, but Dunk hurried by without a glance. Raj raised an inquiring eyebrow at Neena. She shrugged and they gathered up their belongings.

"Is anyone staying to watch the fireworks?" Neena asked.

"That's right, today is your Independence Day," said Raj. "I would like to but I am so tired after all that running around and I'm still not quite adjusted to East Coast time. Maybe I can catch them from the balcony of my apartment."

They all expressed a disinclination to watch the Fourth of July fireworks. Although Neena loved fireworks, she, too, was very tired after a few very eventful days.

As Neena, Cecilia, Raj, and Neel walked toward the parking lot Cecilia turned toward her classmates. "Would you two boys like to join Neena and me for brunch tomorrow at my place?" she asked. Cecilia and Neena had a standing brunch date on Sundays. It was the one morning of the week when they could sleep in a little and start the day with a leisurely meal. Since Cecilia spent many weeknights at Neena's home she always insisted on hosting Sunday brunch either at her place or at one of the many cafes and restaurants in Littlefield.

"Sure!" said Neel, and turned with an inquiring look at Raj.

"That would be great," said Raj with a look of pleasure.

"Wonderful, see you all at eleven then," she said with a smile.

As they approached the parking lot Neena looked around and asked, "Where's your car, Neel?"

"I left it at home and ran here this afternoon," he said.

Neel was an avid runner and tried to run at least ten to fifteen miles each week. He had the lean look of a runner but was well-muscled, as Neena had noted earlier in a most clinical fashion, of course. He had medium brown hair and a "wheatish" complexion, as her mother would have said. This adjective was one with which she had heard her mother and other Aunties use to describe a fair-skinned girl. It was one of the many English words which had morphed into a meaning and usage unique to the Indians who used them. Along with his "wheatish" complexion, another one of Neel's attractive features was his surprisingly light green eyes.

Cecilia asked, "Neel, are you planning on running back home or would you like a lift? I think your place is on my way." Her friendly glance included Raj in the invitation as well.

Raj declined saying that his apartment was only a few blocks away. Neel, however, quickly accepted. "I think I've done enough running for today. And, I've always wanted to ride in a Jag," he said with boyish enthusiasm.

"Would you like to drive then?" Cecilia offered. Neel, who was a car enthusiast, was momentarily speechless.

"Hell, yeah!" he said with a big grin. Neel deftly caught the keys Cecilia tossed in the air and the pair headed to the gleaming silver car. Neena watched them as they walked away and marveled at the ease with which Cecilia conversed with attractive young men. Cecilia not only had excellent communication skills but her success, Neena thought, was in large part because she also took the time to listen.

Neena, for all her admirable qualities, had not had the same success in the attracting-men department. She had had girlish crushes on classmates in high school and college but most of the males she had encountered seemed to consider her as more of a study buddy than a romantic interest. She believed that she enjoyed her mysteries so much since the heroines not only solved the mystery but always walked into the sunset with the man of their choice. "If only my life could be so easily scripted," she thought with a sigh.

Neena knew that Cecilia enjoyed gathering all the kindred spirits she could find. She was an only child and Neena suspected that Cecilia's childhood had at times been a little lonely. Watching the attractive couple walk away, Neena thought that Cecilia was like a force of nature. Like the soft currents of a babbling brook, she gently yet inexorably bore others along. Her kindness and generosity rippled impartially over all those in her vicinity. Neena disliked being the center of attention and was more than content to bob gently in her friend's wake. Neena waved goodbye to Raj and got into her own small, steaming car.

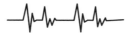

Raj waited impatiently for the light to change at the corner a few blocks from his apartment. A cool shower was the only thing on his mind at the moment after the energetic game at the park. It was a warm summer evening and the streets were filled with people. He was used to living in a big city and did not mind the crowds. Raj considered himself to be a savvy urbanite and had a system of distributing his money between various pockets. He had never yet been pickpocketed. Just as this thought passed through his mind, he felt a person standing a bit too close behind him. Raj quickly put his hands in his pockets and closed them over his money and keys. *Just in case*, he thought to himself. Suddenly he felt a hard shove in the middle of his back and found himself flying forward onto the crosswalk and into the path of oncoming traffic.

Sunday July 5, 1992

Chapter 7

On Sunday morning Neena allowed herself the luxury of sleeping in. She had been so tired the previous night that she did not even hear the Fourth of July fireworks. She was a firm believer in banking a few hours of sleep at least on Sundays, for withdrawal during the following week. Admittedly, these days there were more withdrawals from the repository of sleep than deposits. But, it felt marvelous to be awakened by the sunlight filtering through her lace curtains after having had her fill of sleep. She and Idli slowly and luxuriously stretched their limbs before finally opening their eyes. Idli morphed into a feline contortionist as she started her morning ablutions and Neena headed toward the bathroom for hers. Feeling invigorated and energized she emerged from the shower swathed in a fluffy bath towel. Neena pushed open her closet doors and inspected the contents.

Neena's closet was neatly organized by color. Rather than primary colors, which Neena thought were too bold for her to wear, she had filled it with clothing in the subtle shades of rose, melon, sage, and sky blue which she loved. Neena selected a light blue cotton top and her trusty khaki pants. She put in the small gold stud earrings she always wore and added a few thin gold bangles to her ensemble. This was her usual extent of "dressing up." Although she appreciated seeing other women wearing dresses or skirts, she had never thought these articles of clothes suited her. Having inherited what she termed "chicken legs" she was not eager to display her nether limbs. Her closet contained one black skirt which she reluctantly donned for interviews and funerals. Her lone dress, a loose-fitting, light gray A-line which reached to her mid-calf, made its appearance regularly at various school ceremonies, parties, and weddings. She next surveyed the floor of her closet to select from her extensive footwear. Neena had a weakness for shoes.

Neena was just pulling her front door shut behind her when she heard the insistent double twang of her telephone. She ran back inside and picked up the receiver. "Hello?" she said. She expected it to be Cecilia calling to request a last-minute ingredient for their brunch.

"Hello, Neena?" said a faintly familiar-sounding male voice.

"Yes?" she acknowledged, wondering who on earth this could be.

The voice sounded older. He went on, "Please forgive me for calling you at home but your chief resident gave me your home number. This is Mr. MacMillan. I am not sure if you remember me?"

"Of course I remember you, sir. Umm, how are you?" she asked in some confusion and with more than a little dismay. Had she left in a staple or caused some injury to him and he was calling to complain in person?

He must have heard the concern in her voice for he went on quickly in a reassuring tone of voice. "I am sure you must be surprised to hear from me but I wanted to ask you a favor."

Now Neena was truly astonished. Her? What more could she possibly do for a wealthy man like Mr. MacMillan?

He continued, "When we last met you had mentioned that you occasionally worked as a nursing aid. I was wondering if you would consider working for me? I will need some assistance when I am discharged with changing my bandages, organizing my medications, and the like. You had such a gentle touch when you removed my staples that I immediately thought of you. It would not be a lot of work and I promise to be a good patient." She could hear the teasing smile in his voice. "What do you say? Will you consider the position?"

Mr. MacMillan went on to present the details of the job and she had to admit that the timing and hours were convenient and the pay was generous. Neena already knew that Mr. MacMillan was well-liked and respected by the doctors and nurses at LCH. Even Mike, their chief resident, had discussed Mr. MacMillan with unusual warmth when they reviewed Neena's staple-removing activity. Neena realized she really liked Mr. MacMillan and felt a natural rapport with him. She accepted the position with pleasure and with the grateful thought that she would forever remember him as her first "real" patient.

Neena decided to walk the few blocks to Cecilia's house rather than spend any unnecessary time in her tin-box of a car. She planned on stopping at Patel's Pantry to pick up half a dozen of the crisp spicy samosas she knew Cecilia enjoyed so much. Neena had by now committed Mrs. Patel's schedule to memory and knew when the various delicacies were likely to come out of the kitchen and repose, for ever so short a time, on their gleaming warming trays. Adjusting the strap of her small cross-body bag more comfortably over her shoulder she reached for the door handle. She yanked the door open and as she quickly stepped inside, she ran directly into a white-shirted form. She rocked back onto her heels and gasped when she looked at the equally surprised face above her. Raj stood in front of her balancing two small white paper boxes. His usually symmetric features were disfigured by a large purpling mass the size of a goose egg on his upper-right forehead. The right side of his face was a cross-work pattern of abrasions and his knuckles were scraped raw. Neena took one of the boxes from him and stepped back onto the sidewalk.

"What in the world happened to you?" she asked, her face lined with concern.

Raj looked down at her and shrugged dismissively.

"Just a little accident," he said. "The pavement was crowded last night and as I was waiting for the light on my corner to turn someone ran into me from behind. I would have fallen into oncoming traffic if a big man next to me hadn't grabbed my arm. I'm fine, really," he said.

"Did you put some ice on your face?" Neena asked.

"Ice?" Raj said, skeptically. "I put a warm cloth on it. That's what my grandmother always did back home if anything was swollen."

Neena shook her head. "No, no, no, warmth will make the swelling larger! A cool compress will help the swelling come down by constricting the blood vessels!" This was one of the first tenets of first aid she had learned as a Girl Scout. Cold compresses for injuries and bruises, pressure on bleeding cuts, and immobilization of an injured finger with a popsicle stick! Although this knowledge had served her well thus far, she knew how woefully inadequate her skills actually were. But not for long! With this cheering thought, Neena—forgetting all about the samosas—fell in step next to Raj and they walked the last few blocks to Cecilia's house together.

Neena was not surprised to hear that Raj had never considered applying ice to his injury. In her experience, her parents and others of their generation and cultural background were highly suspicious of anything cold. In the winter she had not been allowed to drink cold orange juice, or eat ice cream, or even cucumbers for that matter. Cold food and drink would make you sick and everyone knew that eating cucumbers in the winter would result in the worst of throat infections. Although her mother had tried her best to ingrain these basic principles of infectious disease into her head, Neena had always been a bit skeptical. Was it not possible, she had once challenged her mother, to develop a fever and a "cold" in the middle of summer in Madras when it was a hundred degrees in the shade? Neena did not recall ever receiving an answer to this imminently logical question. She had, however, consistently refused to drink the warmed-up OJ she was offered whenever the temperature dipped below a frosty fifty degrees.

As soon as they arrived at Cecilia's house Neena was determined to get some ice on that goose egg to prove her point and, of course, to make Raj's head feel better.

Cecilia ushered Neena and Raj into the airy foyer of her elegant home. She and Neel, who had been lounging on the sofa, exclaimed at the sight of Raj's face. Clucking sympathetically, she pushed him down next to Neel and bustled off to the kitchen.

Neel raised his eyebrows in surprise as he caught sight of Raj's face. "What did you do? Walk into a pole or something?"

"That's exactly what I did," said Raj, and went on to explain how a passerby had probably saved his life in the process. "I hit my face against a nearby pole as I was swung around by my rescuer and then scraped my hands against the metal dustbin as I tried to break my fall."

Cecilia quickly returned with a small plastic bag filled with frozen green peas.

"Here you go," she said and pressed it into his hand. Raj stared bemusedly. Thankfully, before he could open it and politely partake of the offering, Cecilia gave him additional instructions.

"Put the bag on that bruise," she said. "The peas will fit the contours of your forehead better than a hard ice pack." Raj smiled at Neena's I-told-you-so look and did as he was told. After a few minutes he reported in tones of mild surprise that his head did indeed throb a little less than it had before.

Cecilia next returned from the kitchen carrying a small silver tray containing four tall, slim glasses filled with a pale orange, frothy liquid. "This," she said as she handed Raj the first glass, "will also help speed up your recovery."

Raj politely took a glass but did not take a sip. Neel, who did not seem to have any qualms about offending his hostess, asked bluntly, "What is it?" Cecilia laughed at his skeptical look as he considered the bubbly beverage.

"It's a peach Bellini," she explained. "Which is Prosecco mixed with fruit puree. Would you like me to add some beer to yours?" she inquired seriously. Neel grinned as he accepted a glass.

"Cheers," said Cecilia, and they all clinked glasses.

Neena took a long sip of her cool, sweet peach Bellini. She sank into one of the comfortable wingback chairs flanking the brick fireplace and crossed one khaki-clad leg over the other. She felt happy in this moment and although there was always so much studying to do she was determined to enjoy this brief reprieve. Even Raj seemed to have relaxed and put his empty glass down on the low table in front of him. Neena did not think the Prosecco in their drinks was very potent but a little alcohol went a long way to easing the tension of mind and limb. Raj leaned back against the comfortable cushions and stretched his long legs out in front of him. Neena thought he looked very nice in his crisp white shirt and well-fitting dark blue jeans. Neel, on the other hand, was dressed in a pair of wrinkled chinos and a slightly faded, and very wrinkled blue polo shirt. He did not appear to be a man who spent much time on his clothes and Neena suspected that he probably subscribed to the only-iron-the-middle-of-the-shirt philosophy. However, with his tall slender frame and boyish good looks he seemed to fit in wherever he was. His carefree air was a refreshing change from the stressed and uptight pre-med students Neena had known in college.

Neena was looking forward to the meal that was in store for them. Just as she had introduced Cecilia to a kaleidoscope of Indian dishes, Cecilia had, in turn, introduced Neena to many new and delectable foods and drinks. She had never heard of a Bellini, or a Caesar salad, or a steak *au Poivre*, until she had met Cecilia. Cecilia had a knack for combining delicacies from local cafes with other ingredients from her favorite specialty stores to create meals that were beautifully balanced to the eye as well as the palate. Neena always felt that one started eating with one's eyes and she loved to see a variety of colors on her plate, whatever cuisine she was eating.

Cecilia had set the rough oak table with honey-colored woven placemats and bright white ceramic plates. The centerpiece was a round glass vase filled with white roses and baby's breath. The silverware sparkled and cut glass tumblers were filled with bottled water, which had recently become all the rage. Neena could not believe it. People were actually buying bottles of water, which was absolutely free of charge from the faucet! But like many new fads, Neena knew that bottled water was a current-day status symbol. She, herself, preferred tap water but had no objection to drinking the pricey water which came in a tall bottle with the now-distinctive pink label.

As Cecilia moved back and forth between the kitchen and the dining room, Neena could not help but notice that the gaze of both of the young men kept wandering to her friend's tall, slim figure. Cecilia had a dancer's graceful gait and she looked as effortlessly elegant as ever wearing a loose-fitting black linen dress. She wore no makeup and her only adornment was a pair of small silver hoop earrings. The glow from her golden hair and sun-kissed skin was all that she needed. Neena, who always appreciated beauty in all its forms, also gazed admiringly at her friend.

When Neel tapped her on the arm, she belatedly realized he had been holding out the large wooden salad bowl for her to take. Neena helped herself to the crisp green salad dressed with a delicate concoction of olive oil, lemon, and fresh herbs. Neena hadn't known that a salad could be so classy. As a kid the only salad she'd ever had was iceberg lettuce drenched in Thousand Island dressing. Cecilia served everyone a generous slice of the warm ham and brie quiche. They all tucked in with good appetite as young people their age are wont to do.

Neel closed his eyes as he savored his first bite of quiche.

"This is delicious, Cecilia! Sure beats my usual morning meal of cold milk and cereal." Neel, as they learned, was not much of a cook and when he was home he relied heavily on cans of soup, boxes of mac 'n' cheese, and tins of tuna.

"At least the food at LCH's cafeteria is good. When we get the chance to eat, that is," he said, applying himself to his plate.

Although this was the first time the four had met socially, Neena found the conversation to be light and easy. She had worried that Raj may have felt out of place being so new to the country but she noted that he had a cosmopolitan air about him and she was glad to see that he spoke easily on numerous subjects. He also listened attentively and seemed genuinely interested in what the others had to say. Of course, much of the conversation consisted of apprising one another of their experiences during their first week in the hospital.

Cecilia told them about her first week of her internal medicine rotation at University Hospital. She had seen many diabetic patients who had been admitted in DKA, diabetic ketoacidosis. *Not to be confused with BKA*, thought Neena. Cecilia had been assigned three patients to follow. In addition to the woman with DKA, her other patients were a man with alcoholic fatty liver disease and a woman with cholecystitis. Cecilia asked them if they all knew the mnemonic for the latter condition. The others shook their heads.

"It's rather unfortunate," said Cecilia. "But it's the 3 F's. Fat, Forty, and Female. Apparently, that's the common demographic for cholecystitis."

"Did Neena tell you what happened during our first day in the OR?" Neel asked Cecilia.

"I can't believe Ron made you hold that patient's leg!" said Cecilia disgustedly. "That was so uncalled for. What a jerk! You should see the plate-sized bruises she has on her hips!" She gestured at Neena with a forkful of lettuce.

"Yeah, that was not right," Neena said. "I really thought I was going to drop the leg onto the table at some point. I would have too, without Raj helping me out. I never thanked you for that," she said, turning to Raj with a smile.

"I didn't realize at first how heavy that must have been for you. It must have weighed more than you! But you held up admirably, pun intended," Raj said, smiling in return.

Neel, helping himself to what Neena thought was his third slice of quiche, regaled them with a tale about an appendectomy he witnessed. Raj, who had finished his second slice, pushed his plate away and patted his mouth with his napkin. Neena had watched him eat with a slight fascination, expecting at any time to see bits of food get stuck in his mustache. Thankfully, he ate neatly. Seeing flecks of food in her dining companion's facial hair would certainly have put her off her own food. *Yuk*, she thought, and dragging her gaze away from Raj's mustache brought her attention back to what he was saying. Raj was animatedly describing a bowel resection he had attended yesterday. The surgeon had left the OR once the main procedure was completed, leaving Mike to close up, who then allowed Raj to do a few of the sutures. Raj looked quite excited.

"Was it similar to sewing up the pig?" Neena asked.

"I'm not sure," said Raj. "We didn't practice on fetal pigs in India. We practiced on actual patients."

"Really? Wow, that's awesome."

Neena was looking forward to doing some suturing of her own. She liked the precision of the surgical wound created by the surgeon's scalpel and the neat, exacting stitches that were so cleverly placed, bringing the edges of the wound into perfect approximation. She had some experience with a needle and thread since she had worked on many cross-stitch patterns over the past few years. She found it a soothing pastime and always felt pleased at seeing the small, neat rows of perfectly formed X's on her patterned cloth. Neena also thought that she had a steady hand, honed by many years of practice on her favorite game of "Operation." She usually managed to extract the little plastic heart, the funny bone, and the very tricky wishbone without triggering the honking alarm that sounded if the "surgeon" made a mistake.

Cecilia whisked away their plates and replaced them with smaller dessert plates. She brought in a colorful summer berry tart. Fresh strawberries and blueberries glistened like rubies and sapphires in the creamy custard of the tart. She served each of them a generous slice.

"Thank you for the sweets," she said to Raj as she opened the small white boxes, indicating everyone to help themselves. "I love the silvery diamond-shaped ones."

"You are most welcome," said Raj.

As Cecilia passed around frothy cups of her expertly prepared cappuccino, Neena said, "You are not going to believe who called me before I left home this morning."

"Well," said Cecilia, "since you look excited and pleased then it must be someone you like. Not your parents then," she surmised. Seeing Neena's look of surprise she laughed and went on hurriedly. "Not that you don't like your parents, of course, but I don't think you would look so excited. Hmm, let me see," she said, tapping her finger against her water glass. "Did Melly ask you to babysit? Or did someone offer you a kitten?" she teased. "Or maybe it was an old sweetheart?" she said with a twinkle in her eye. At this, both Neel and Raj looked more interestedly at her. Neena had great difficulty in disabusing her friend of the notion that she had not left any number of heartbroken boyfriends in her past. She could not believe Neena's assertion that thus far she had never been in a romantic relationship. Cecilia was convinced that there had been at least one tragic romance in Neena's past and it was this fact that accounted for Neena's otherwise inexplicable single status.

Neena rolled her big black eyes at her friend and shook her head. "Well, it was more of a rhetorical question since you'll never guess. It was a patient from the VIP floor in the hospital, Mr. MacMillan. I took out his staples a few days ago. It was my first time doing it and I was so nervous. I was sure the poor man must have been in agony but he was very nice. He actually started comforting me which was very embarrassing but I did get the job done. Anyway, he said Mike had given him my number and he called to offer me a job as his nursing aid."

Neena looked expectantly at the others but was confronted by various expressions which ranged from skepticism to concern.

"What?" she asked. "Why are you all looking at me like that?"

"Well, don't you think it's a bit odd? Someone in the VIP suite should be able to hire the best nursing care there is to be had, don't you think?" said Neel, who had already polished off his first slice of berry tart and was holding his plate up to Cecilia for another.

"Yes," added Raj, "that's what I was thinking as well. What made you accept him so quickly?"

"I really liked him. He was very kind and funny. He seemed genuinely pleased with me." Neena had found herself to be quite at ease with Mr. MacMillan by the end of the harrowing staple-removing session. His manner toward her was avuncular and she always tried to trust her instincts when meeting and assessing new people. "Besides, Mike seemed to know him and only had good things to say."

"I'm not so sure you should go alone to his house," Cecilia said, putting down her fork. "What would your mother say if she knew?"

"Cecilia, I'm not going to some house of ill repute or illicit den of iniquity," said Neena in a slightly exasperated tone.

"You sound like a Georgette Heyer novel," Cecilia said crossly, temporarily diverted from her main complaint.

"And you sound like an eighteenth century governess," Neena retorted. "It will be fine. Look, I'll talk it over with Mike, just to make sure. Will that make you happy?"

Cecilia did not look quite convinced. Neena looked at Neel and Raj for support.

"Neena, I would be happy to accompany you," Raj offered. "You can say that I am also interested in such a position and I simply wanted to see what you do."

At this the faint furrows between Cecilia's perfectly arched eyebrows faded a bit. "That's a great idea! Good thinking, Raj." She gave him an approving nod. Neel was also nodding his head in agreement.

"Okay, sure," said Neena. "I will still talk to Mike about Mr. MacMillan though."

She turned toward Raj. "That's really very nice of you, Raj. I'm supposed to go over there on Thursday evening at seven o'clock. Should I come pick you up on my way there? He lives on the western end of Littlefield, on Bougainvillea Boulevard."

Neel let out a soft whistle. "They may as well call it Billionaire's Boulevard," he said.

"I can come to your home," Raj said. "And then we can drive together."

Neena, who had just taken a generous sip of her cappuccino, nodded in agreement as she emerged from behind the large ceramic cup. Laughing, Neel leaned over and wiped a bit of froth from her upper lip with his napkin.

Tuesday July 7, 1992

Chapter 8

Neena joined her team on Tuesday morning in one of the small dark rooms on the lower level of the hospital. Today their Attending wanted to start rounds in the radiology department to review all of their patients' X-rays. One of the important skills that the students and residents were taught was to independently review and interpret their patient's X-rays. Although the radiologists were the experts in this field, a physician who could not interpret an X-ray was at a distinct disadvantage, particularly at night, when the radiologists had left for the evening. Therefore, if patient care was to proceed between those critical hours the doctors had to become proficient in this skill. A sudden shaft of light appeared and they all looked expectantly at the door. However, it was only Raj. He quickly slipped into the room, murmured his apologies and positioned himself at the back of the room. With the next shaft of light, the Attending strode briskly into the room.

Dr. Silverman stood near the light box and was handed a large X-ray jacket which contained all the tests for a particular patient. He took the first X-ray out of its jacket and slid it up into the light box with a swift swoosh and a snap. It was a chest X-ray and Neena peered intently at the black and white images. Dr. Silverman described a methodical and stepwise strategy of reading the X-ray so that nothing would be missed. Bones, air, and soft tissue were discernible. He started at the perimeters of the X-ray and worked his way inward. He directed the team's attention to the outer edges of the X-ray where the bones of the upper arms were visible, then he noted the clavicles and ribcage, diaphragm, and finally the heart. Having reviewed all that should be white on the X-ray, he moved on to that which should be black, namely air. He traced the air in the trachea for them with the tip of his Montblanc pen and followed it down the left and right bronchi. Then he looked at the air in the lungs, explaining how to assess the volume and condition of the lungs. There were two views of the chest, one was called the PA—the posterior-anterior—which was like a photo of the front of the patient. The other view, the lateral, was taken through the right side. It was very important, said Dr. Silverman, to carefully compare the two views, taking note of landmarks and discovering any inconsistencies.

He quickly took this X-ray down and replaced it with another one. This one was also a chest X-ray but seemed to be of a much smaller sized person. Then, he turned with a slight smile, the likes of which made Neena slightly apprehensive, and started calling on members of the team.

Dr. Silverman used his pen to point at them in turn. Each person had to interpret one aspect of the X-ray as Dr. Silverman had just demonstrated. Dunk was called on first to review the bones. As the first-year intern, he had two more years of experience than the third-year students. He flipped the hair out of eyes with a practiced gesture, squinted at the film as if he was scanning the horizon, and easily rattled off the findings in his casual drawl. Next, the pen, whose distinctive head gleamed in the semi-darkness, pointed to Bill, the fourth-year medical student, who was doing his acting-internship. He spoke very fast but Neena assumed he covered the required items since Dr. Silverman merely nodded at him. Finally, Dr. Silverman's pen cast about like an expert fisherman and landed directly on Neena. She took a deep breath and launched into the description, trying to remember the exact words he had used.

"There is no focal infiltrate or consolidation. There is no pleural effusion or pneumothorax. The stomach bubble is left-sided," she recited, hoping she didn't sound like a school girl practicing her lines for the second-grade play. Neena's interpretation of the X-ray hung in the air, alone and twitching in the silence like a hooked fish. Finally, he nodded at her as well and Neena let her breath out in a soft whoosh.

Dr. Silverman now turned to face the group. "So, what is your final impression of this X-ray? Is this a normal study?" he asked. He shook his head slightly at the residents, indicating that they were not to answer.

The students glanced around at each other and answered, almost in unison, "Yes!"

Neena saw Mike trying to hide a smile and Ron, standing next to him, made no attempt to hide his smirk. She now knew that this was a trick question. Neena scanned the black and white spots and lines but could not find anything out of the ordinary.

Dr. Silverman shook his head and clicked his tongue at them, apparently disappointed at the caliber of student-doctor he was tasked with training this month. He then decided to give them one final opportunity to redeem themselves. *More like re-doom themselves,* thought Neena, as Mr. Cook, her high school math teacher liked to say when he was presenting the class with a particularly sneaky problem.

"Does anyone see anything that shouldn't be there? This looks like a completely normal X-ray to you all, does it? Well then, tell me, what is that?" He jabbed at a spot near the top of the X-ray, just beneath the patient's chin. They all craned their necks forward to get a better look.

Finally, Neena heard a familiar voice and her fellow third-year, Calvin, came forward a little and offered, "It looks like a circular tag or disc was placed on top of the patient before the X-ray was taken. Is that it?"

"You're getting closer," said Dr. Silverman in a sing-song manner. He looked at them expectantly as if there was hope yet for these students.

Then to everyone's surprise, Raj spoke up, "I believe, sir, that this is an X-ray of a young child who has swallowed a coin."

The students let out a gasp of surprise. Of course it was! Neena now saw that the diminutive size of the chest was more compatible with a child than an adult. And the white disc was inside the patient not on the outside! *That wasn't fair*, Neena thought in annoyance. The team did not have any children on their service and so they would not have expected such an X-ray. But she appreciated his teaching strategy. Obviously simply looking at something was not the same as actually seeing it.

Dr. Silverman's studiously neutral countenance relaxed into an approving smile. "Yes, indeed. Nicely done, Raj," he said.

The team emerged from the radiology reading room squinting as their eyes adjusted to the bright lights in the corridor. Raj was the last one to leave the room and it was the first time that morning that his face had been clearly visible.

"Whoa, look at the size of that goose egg!" said Dunk, sounding impressed.

Mike looked up quickly from the sheaf of papers on his clipboard. "When did that happen? I didn't know you were injured when you left the soccer field on Saturday. Why didn't you say something?" He moved closer to examine Raj's head.

Raj shook his head. "It's nothing," he said. "No, I didn't get injured during the game." He went on to describe the accident that had befallen him. "If my hands hadn't been stuffed into my pockets then my face wouldn't have taken the brunt of the impact."

"Are you sure you're okay? Maybe you should go down to the ER and get checked out just in case," Victoria suggested, edging closer to Raj, her thin nostrils quivering. Neena looked sharply at Victoria. The other girl had initially tried to attach herself to Mike Windsor, then she had moved onto Ron, and most recently had transferred her interests to Dunk. Although Ron was a senior resident, he was, admittedly, rather hard on the eyes so she was not surprised that Victoria was looking toward more attractive vistas. However, until this moment Victoria hadn't even acknowledged Raj's presence and her sudden solicitousness made Neena suspicious. Although Raj was handsome, he was new to the country, without connections, and on a scholarship. He was certainly not the type of man to whom Victoria usually attached herself.

Raj shook his head again, winced slightly and insisted that he felt much better today. He had to endure several more exclamations of concerns from his fellow classmates who were regarding him as a patient requiring their diagnosis and care. Although he was in a hospital surrounded by doctors, some real (the residents) and most not (all of his classmates), he politely but firmly declined all of the varied treatment plans that were proposed. The team quickly headed toward the nearest stairwell. Raj and Neel were waiting for her but she waved them on.

"Go ahead, I'll catch up with you," she said and pointed toward the ladies' room at the end of the hallway. Soon, Neena emerged back into the hallway and stopped in surprise. At the end of the corridor she spotted Ron, who was staring intently at a paper in his hands. Neena thought Ron had been leading the team. *Why was he still here?*

She saw him in profile but he was too intent on whatever it was he was reading to register her presence. Suddenly, brows furrowed, he shoved the paper into his pocket. Neena hurried toward him and was about to call out but he had already turned away from her and disappeared into the stairwell nearest them. As Neena entered the same stairwell seconds later she noticed that the door nearby had a sign labeled "Billing." Her curiosity was instantly piqued and Neena wondered what Ron could be doing in the billing department. But, just as quickly, as she hurried up the stairs to rejoin the team, her head full of the tasks for the day, her curiosity vanished.

After a busy day Neena headed to the fifth-floor nurses' station to receive sign-out. Tonight would be the first time she would be on call. Starting this week a few of the students would be assigned to stay overnight every night.

This would allow them to observe how the responsibilities changed for the overnight on-call team and how care was delivered with fewer residents working. It seemed quite challenging but Neena was excited at the prospect. By five o'clock all of the daytime teams had endorsed their respective patients to the on-call team. It was an unwritten rule that all work would be completed by the daytime team so that the on-call team would only have to manage new issues that arose in the ensuing twelve hours.

Neena was surprised to note how quickly the nurses' station and hallways were suddenly devoid of doctors, residents, and students. Only the nurses remained since their shift didn't end until seven o'clock. She stood with the rest of the on-call team, which consisted of herself, Neel, Raj, Joe, and Duncan under Nurse Marge's ever-critical stare. Ron, the senior resident on call tonight, was walking quickly toward them waving copies of the sign-out sheets at them. They each took one while Ron barked out instructions. Neena fumbled for a pen in a pocket of her overstuffed lab coat. As she pulled one free from the jumble of items in her pocket several small, colorful items came flying out and showered the floor around her. Ron cocked a bushy black eyebrow at her.

"Babysitting," she explained embarrassedly and quickly gathered the small Lego pieces and stuffed them back into her pocket. She knew that these were tokens of high regard from Danny, who only shared his prized Legos with a select group of people.

Ron assigned a set of patients to each student and ordered them to make sure all of their assigned tasks were checked off as complete before five a.m. the next morning. Already turning away he tossed over his shoulder, "Dunk, you're in charge!" and stalked off down the corridor.

Dunk turned to the students. "As you can see, we are covering about forty surgical patients on two floors. And, if there are any emergency surgeries we will be asked to scrub in. Do each of you have your pagers?" They all checked the waistbands of their scrub bottoms and nodded.

"Neena and Joe, you can stay on this floor and split up the patients on

Five East. Neel and Raj, you can both head up to Six East. Follow up on labs that are pending and final radiology results. Check in on each patient on your list this evening and again tomorrow morning. If you get everything done and the OR is quiet tonight then head over to the call rooms to catch a little sleep." Dunk's pager suddenly started pinging and he quickly glanced down at the numbers displayed.

"That's Ron paging me to the ER," he said, already taking a few steps away from them. "They must need a surgical consult." He turned back briefly toward the students.

"Any questions? No? Okay. Good." Without waiting for their response, he turned away, quickened his pace, and soon he, too, was gone.

Neena and her classmates looked blankly at one another.

"I don't know about you all," said Neel, "but I have a lot of questions!"

He looked down at the pages in his hand.

"Do any of you know what all these abbreviations stand for? And what's with the stick figures? Is that Ron's idea of a joke?"

They huddled together and flipped through the sign-out sheets.

Neena tried to decipher the numerous abbreviations and diagrams on the sign-out sheet. She assumed the residents had tried to summarize in as few words as possible each patient's current diagnosis, labs, and treatments. Abbreviations such as "Rx" and "Xray" were familiar. But there was a veritable alphabet soup of unfamiliar abbreviations and acronyms. *What did Sx, Tx, Dx, NPO, BID, TID, QD, QOD, qHS, qAC, and PRN mean?* There also appeared to be horizontal stick figures in each patient's box with various numbers between the lines representing the limbs. And there was a horizontal line with three smaller intersecting vertical lines within which were jotted random-appearing numbers.

"Okay," said Neena. "Let's see if we can each pick one patient on this floor and try to figure out what some of these symbols and abbreviations mean." She went over to the chart rack and selected a name.

"You guys should each grab a chart as well. It will go faster if we all work together. Here is Smith, Dolores," she said, running her finger down their list until she found the initials D.S. Neena opened the chart and looked at the various color-coded tabs.

"There are order, progress notes, labs, and consult note sections," she said. "Let's start with the lab section first. It should be easier to match up numbers," she reasoned.

Joe, Neel, and Raj flipped through their respective charts until each had found the red tab which indicated lab results. Neena opened her chart and ran her eyes down the columns of tests and results. She compared them to the sign-out sheet and realized that what had looked like stick figures were actually a form of notation for various lab results. The values for such tests as hemoglobin or platelets occupied a consistent area defined by the spaces between the "arms" and "legs" of the stick figures, as did values for sodium, potassium, chloride, glucose, and creatinine within the other longer horizontal line with three smaller intersecting lines. Now it all made sense!

Before long the four students had managed to figure out most of the abbreviations and notations on their sign-out sheets. Neena and Joe remained at the Five East nursing station while Neel and Raj headed upstairs to the floor they were covering. Neena took the patients in the even-numbered rooms on one side of the hallway and Joe took the odd-numbered ones on the other side. It took Neena and Joe several hours to visit each of their patients, check the computer for pending lab results and document their notes in the charts. Although most notes written by surgeons or surgical residents resembled a form of shorthand at best and an alien script at worst, the students were still at the stage where they wrote legibly, which took them a proportionately longer time to finish.

At approximately eleven p.m., after six hours of diligent working, Neena finally finished all her scut work and realized she had missed dinner. Stopping at a vending machine she fished in her pockets for some change. She looked at the fistful of items in her palm. There was some change, some metal Parkway tokens, and a few bits of Lego. She selected the coins out of the jumble of items and inserted a few into the machine. Luckily the machine obligingly tossed out a bag of chips. There was a satisfying swish as Neena opened the bright yellow bag and popped a few chips in her mouth.

As she was savoring the crisp saltiness she heard a girlish giggle and a deeper voice murmuring somewhere close by. She stopped her noisy munching and stood still, head slightly tilted and ears cocked in the direction of the sounds. When the soft noises repeated themselves, Neena, despite her fatigue, decided to investigate. She peered cautiously around the vending machine down the hallway. At the end of another long hallway she saw two figures wearing blue scrubs and white coats. In the long coat was Dunk and the figure in the short coat was Victoria! Even from a distance Neena could see the furious batting of the girl's lashes. *What was Victoria doing here at this hour? She wasn't even on-call tonight!* Although Neena was not surprised to find Victoria flirting with Dunk, she was somewhat astonished to witness Dunk's apparent interest in Victoria. The girl was leaning against the wall with Dunk in front of her, his arms slightly flexed and his palms on the wall on either side of her. Neena watched in fascination, not untinged with disgust, as Victoria launched herself at Dunk and fastened her lips on his. Adding to her fascination was the impression that Dunk was not an unwilling participant. After a few seconds and with some difficulty, Neena dragged her eyes from the lip-locked pair. Neena wrinkled her nose and uttered a silent "ugh!" *Well, there is no accounting for taste*, she thought.

Neena trudged up the stairs to the on-call rooms, slowly munching on her chips. She was a little breathless as she alighted on the eighth floor and headed down another long corridor. A soft chime sounded and Neel and Raj emerged from the elevator behind Neena.

With a surprised look at Neena, Raj asked, "Why didn't you use the lift?"

"Dunno," she said, shaking her head wearily. "Guess I got used to following the residents up and down the stairs."

They all walked slowly down the hall together. Neel passed his hands over his bloodshot eyes. "I'm beat," he said. "But, looks like we can get a few hours of sleep before starting pre-rounds." His eyes brightened briefly at the thought of resting.

Since they had all been awake for almost twenty hours already, they nodded silently at one another and fumbled at the door of their call rooms trying to remember the code. Neena entered the women's call room and dropped heavily onto the bed nearest to the door. Without removing her lab coat or her shoes she fell back onto the bed, asleep even before her head hit the pillow.

Chapter 9

Within a few seconds, or so it seemed, there was a loud, high-pitched, beeping noise. Neena sat up with a start, banging her head painfully against the metal frame of the bunk bed above. Her first thought was that the fire alarm had gone off and she jumped off of the bed, rubbing her forehead with one hand and opening the door with the other. Her fellow residents emerged in a similarly confused status. Several fire alarms seemed to be going off at once. Blinking in the bright light of the hallway, Neena turned toward the nearest fire exit but was brought up short by a hand on her shoulder.

"Neena, where are you going?" said Neel.

"Fire," she mumbled and tried to pull him toward the fire door, but Neel resisted.

Joe pointed at the waistband of Neena's scrubs. "Turn your pager off." Looking down she blinked several more times trying to see through the dried-up contact lenses that were now stuck to her eyes. She pushed the small red button and the insistent noise finally stopped. Glancing up at the clock on the wall she was shocked to see that it was only 11:30 p.m.

"It's the OR," said Raj. "Come on, let's go!" They stumbled down the hallway but gained coordination and speed with each step. Neena noticed the friendly handyman slowly pushing his tool cart down the hall. As she ran past him she turned her head to say hello but this time he did not make eye contact. His usually pleasant face was lined with fatigue. Even in the short time she had been in the hospital, she had never known him to not smile at her. *Poor man must be tired*, she thought, since the hour was late. Neena squelched her own thoughts of sleep as abruptly as she had silenced her pager. By the time they reached the stairwell, they were running. They raced down the stairs, jumping the last two steps of each flight onto the next landing. Raj yanked the last door open and they suddenly erupted onto a dazzlingly lit white hallway. The double doors to the OR were on their left, and to the right Neena saw Ron coming toward them, looking more animated than she had seen him thus far.

"Patient is a forty-five-year-old man, MVA, requiring emergent orthopedic surgery," he said, sounding almost gleeful. "You are not going to believe what happened to him! Dr. Silverman is on his way and he agreed to allow all the students to scrub in, so move it!" He ushered them toward the lockers where they were to store their coats and other paraphernalia.

Suddenly, Neena realized the adrenaline running through her had pushed aside all vestiges of fatigue. Her heart was racing and she was wide awake. Neena pushed through the double doors and into the operating room's antechamber.

Neena felt a pang of remorse to be benefiting from another's misfortune but she also knew that, unfortunately, there was no other way to learn the art of medicine. She was still getting used to the intense and often harsh nature of medical education. The "see one, do one, teach one" strategy seemed awfully flawed to her. Thus far she had been able to successfully replicate most of the tasks and minor procedures she had witnessed. However, inexpertly removing a staple or two was not likely to compromise a patient's long-term outcome in any meaningful manner. But what about more complicated procedures like intubation, central line placement, and chest tube placement? These were usually procedures that were urgent and life-saving to the patient. What would happen if she had to teach another neophyte how to do their first intubation and failed? The thought made Neena feel weak in the knees. But, she decided to cross those bridges when she came to them and joined her teammates at the long bank of sinks.

Neena's second attempt at scrubbing in and suiting up was accomplished much more swiftly than the first. Soon she and her fellow students were standing along the far wall of the OR, in front of the light box, their hands folded carefully against their chests. An OR nurse extracted X-rays from the folder which Ron indicated and snapped the films into place. Neena looked eagerly at the series of films and tried to put some of her newly acquired knowledge from the morning to good use. Had it really been the same day since she had started her morning in the reading room?

There were many films of the patient's chest, abdomen, and lower extremities. Unfortunately, a thick white line was running diagonally across many of the images, making it difficult to evaluate the lower part of his body. Ron turned to the students, his now-familiar smirk firmly in place.

"Well?" he said, a challenge in his voice.

These images vaguely reminded Neena of something she had seen recently. Was it the heart size, or the lungs, or gastric bubble? The image of the coin in the child's esophagus sprang to her mind and she suddenly gasped.

"Is that long white thingy," she winced at her use of the least-medical sounding word in her vocabulary, "which seems to be lying across that man's leg actually going through his leg?" she asked in disbelief.

Ron turned to face her, his smirk momentarily replaced by surprise. He nodded grudgingly at her. "Well done, Neena," he said.

Now it was Neena's turn to be surprised. Not only had Ron uttered the nicest words she had ever heard him use thus far, but she had also nailed the diagnosis! Neena turned to look at her classmates who were gazing at the films with wide-eyed astonishment. Joe was the first one to recover and gave her a thumbs-up. When Neena turned back toward the films she was surprised to find herself suddenly standing next to Dunk who was slouching in that bored, elegant manner of his. Then the OR door banged open and Dr. Silverman entered with his brisk stride. As he expertly tied the ends of his surgical cap over his neatly combed hair, his keen blue eyes went at once to the X-rays on display. The team parted quickly down the middle to allow him access.

"Go ahead, Dr. Roberts," he said and turned to scrutinize the films. Ron launched into his presentation.

"The patient is a forty-five-year-old man who was in an MVA." The students all silently mouthed the words "motor vehicle accident." Ron continued, "He was in the front passenger seat in a car that was heading north on the GSP." Garden State Parkway, not to be confused with GSW, or gunshot wound, Neena quickly interpreted to herself.

"Just as his car was about to pass under a bridge, someone standing on the overpass above threw a metal pole onto the roadway. This pole rolled under the car, pierced the underbody and impaled his leg." Neena winced along with the rest of the students as they turned en masse to look at the unfortunate man on the operating table being prepped for surgery. Neena's awe at the unusual nature of this trauma was suddenly eclipsed by an overwhelming sense of pity. *This poor, poor man*, she thought, and blinked a few times to clear the tears that had sprung to her eyes. She would really have to conquer this tendency to cry over her patients, she thought to herself disgustedly.

The surgery was long and complicated as the surgeons worked to extricate the metal pole from the patient's femur. The harsh white light above the surgeons' heads brightly illuminated the surgical field. Neena swayed slightly with fatigue and closed her eyes briefly. When she opened them again she found herself in a sterile, blue-draped mechanics shop! Upon the gleaming metal trays she saw the light glinting off of hammers, saws, drills, and screws. Until now their education had been focused on subjects like pathology, microbiology, and physiology. They had never learned anything practical until this week. *These doctors are putting this man's leg back together with nuts and bolts,* Neena marveled. For some minutes now, the low murmur of the surgeons had become inaudible over the noises they were making with their instruments. A hammer was being wielded and created a harsh, metallic, monotonous beat. Thump-thump, thump-thump, clang, thump-thump, thump-thump, clang. *Almost like a heartbeat,* Neena thought. And rather than having the oil-stained hands of a mechanic, the surgeons' gloved hands were crimson with blood.

Suddenly, with each clang Neena's stomach started to lurch up and down. Her insides were churning. Up and down, back and forth, up and down, back and forth, until she could not think of anything but the waves of nausea which whooshed in her stomach. She could taste the salty spray of ocean waves and wondered if she had been transported to the shores of a beach in stormy weather. However, the realization dawned on her that it was likely the bile in her stomach which she was tasting. Suddenly another wave washed over her. This time of terror. If crying over a patient was unprofessional then how terrible it would be to vomit over one! She may get kicked out of the rotation and maybe even medical school! She took a small step back from the operating table and resolutely focused her gaze on the blank white wall ahead of her. She was NOT going to vomit, she told herself. Luckily, the thumping and clanging soon came to a halt and Neena was able to turn her gaze back to the operating table. She let out a sigh of relief and with a grimace thought that it was highly unlikely that orthopedic surgery would be on her list of future occupations.

Sometime around 4:30 a.m., Neena, who had remembered to take the elevator this time, stepped out into the long corridor at the end of which the call rooms were situated. *The hospital probably did that on purpose,* she thought grumpily. When she exited onto the eighth floor she stumbled headlong into a large metal box.

"Ow!" she cried, and bent down to rub her shin. *What on earth? Since when was there a metal cabinet in the middle of the floor?* When she straightened, she recognized the structure as the handyman's tool cart. Why would he have abandoned it here? This made no sense. In the distance she saw two tall people clad in blue scrubs, their heads still covered by the disposable blue surgical caps. They seemed to be inspecting something on the ground. It took her foggy brain several seconds to register the shapes of her classmates and then a pair of legs and sneakers sticking out on the floor. Her fatigue again vaporized as she started running down the hall.

"What's happened?" she called as she ran. "Is someone hurt?"

She skidded to a stop near the group and saw that it was Neel sitting on the floor near the call room. He was leaning against the wall and holding the left side of his head as if it was about to roll off his neck at any minute.

"What happened?" she repeated.

"I found him like this," said Raj. He and Joe were simply staring at their fallen comrade.

"Somebody get some ice!" Neena said. Joe turned abruptly and raced back down the hall to the nurses' station. Neena knelt down beside Neel and gingerly touched his arm.

"Neel? Neel, what happened?" Neel's eyes opened slowly and it seemed to take him some time to focus them on Neena.

"Something . . . hit . . . me . . . on . . . the . . . head," he said, producing one word at a time as if it cost him considerable effort.

Only then did Neena and Raj notice something large and metallic lying in the semi-darkness of the call room.

"This thing must have come loose and fallen out when he opened the door," Neena said. She tried to pick it up with one hand but it was so heavy she could not. She grasped it with both hands and brought a large brass object into the light.

"Oh my god! It looks like the door-closing mechanism. This is really solid and heavy. Neel, we have to get you checked out as soon as possible! You could have shattered your ear drum, fractured your skull, or dislocated your neck!" cried Neena, her voice becoming higher pitched and more frantic as each terrible possibility entered her brain. Like most medical students with little clinical knowledge, her initial differential diagnosis of any patient's condition usually started with the slightly catastrophic and, more often than not, ended with the extremely catastrophic.

Though he had closed his eyes again, the corners of Neel's mouth turned up slightly in a ghost of a smile. Neena's concern for Neel was briefly displaced by indignation.

"Neelesh Shah! This is no laughing matter!" she said, turning to look at Raj for support. Raj had easily subsided into a squat on Neel's other side and was now purposefully searching for a pulse.

"Neena, calm down," Raj said in a soothing voice. "His pulse is steady, he can open his eyes and he's talking. I am almost certain that these are not the signs and symptoms of a person with a dislocated neck." His tone was steady and did not hold even a hint of sarcasm, for which Neena was grateful.

"Yes, okay, okay, I guess you're right," she said. "But what should we do now?"

It appeared that Raj had already had some clinical experience since he confidently whipped out his ophthalmoscope and had jerked Neel's right eyelid up.

"Give me two minutes," he said. "I'm trying to check his pupillary reflex. Also, a careful fundoscopic examination may reveal signs of increased intracranial pressure," he recited as if from a textbook. It most likely was from their textbook, Neena thought.

"I think he has nystagmus!" Raj cried excitedly, as Neel's right eyeball rolled back and forth in its socket like a hard-boiled egg.

"Stop that!" said Neel, weakly pushing Raj's hand away. "I do not have nystagmus! That light is hurting my eye. I'm okay." He kept his right eye closed but now slowly opened his left eye.

Joe came running back with a plastic hospital bag full of ice chips labeled 'patient belongings'.

"Here you go," he said, and bending over Neel slapped the bag of ice briskly against Neel's head.

"Oww!" Neel yelped. "Take it easy!"

"Sorry, sorry," said Joe, backing away and allowing Neel to hold the ice to his own head. After a few minutes Neel lowered the ice and slowly released his grip on the left side of his head. Now that both arms were free, he used them to slowly push himself up straighter. Surprised and emboldened by the fact that his head still seemed to be firmly attached to his neck, he opened his right eye as well and tried to stand up.

"Are you sure about this?" Neena asked. "Maybe I should get you a stretcher, or at least a wheelchair." She started to turn away. But by this time, Raj had his hand tightly clasped around Neel's right forearm and pulled him gently to his feet. Neel swayed slightly but quickly balanced himself. Raj, who was as tall as Neel, was better positioned to examine Neel's head. He reported that there were no cuts or bleeding. Neel gingerly turned his head right, then left, wincing at this movement.

"Let's get you out of this lab coat," said Neena. "It must weigh a ton." She gently eased the coat off of Neel's left shoulder but it was clearly painful for him to move.

"You really should get examined by a real doctor, Neel. No offense Raj," she said quickly. Raj flashed that brilliant smile and immediately seconded Neena's suggestion.

Neel must have been feeling worse than he was willing to acknowledge since he agreed to let Raj take him down to the ER.

"Neena, at least go lie down for a few minutes," said Raj, leading Neel away. Neena simply nodded at him. Neena watched as Joe lifted the heavy brass door closer and placed it just inside the call room.

"Night, Neena," he said, turning away and pushing the door shut with his foot.

"Night, Joe." She was reaching for the knob of her call room door when she realized that Joe's door was still ajar. She tried to pull the door shut but it would not close fully. *Maybe the door will not close unless the door-closing mechanism is in place*, she thought. Then Neena looked down and saw one of the brass screws from the device caught in the doorway. She picked it up and shoved it in her pocket. Her only thought at this moment was to fling off her heavy lab coat and finally lie down.

Wednesday July 8, 1992

Chapter 10

Neena wearily opened her front door and entered her apartment exactly thirty-seven hours after she had left the day before. As soon as she had closed the door behind her she started shedding articles of clothing. She kicked off her shoes and socks and dropped her lab coat to the ground. It fell with a thud, due to her heavily laden pockets, but for once she did not spare a thought for the expensive diagnostic kit in her left pocket. Neena loosened the drawstrings of her scrub bottoms with one hand, turned on the hot water with the other, and pulled her scrub top over her head. Peeling off her bra and panties Neena let out a sigh as she stepped into the shower and the warm water coursed over her head and body. She was so tired that in the few minutes it took to shampoo her hair, rinse, apply conditioner and rinse again she couldn't remember if she had shampooed. So, she repeated the process. She emerged from the bathroom wrapped in her fluffy pink-and-white terry cloth bathrobe, looking like an Atlantic city summer taffy.

Neena suddenly remembered Idli and called out to her. The little cat had unfurled herself and was watching Neena from her perch on the sofa with a faintly critical air, one eye arched slightly higher than the other. Neena could almost hear the words, "Where the heck have you been?"

"I'm so sorry Idli! How are you doing, my little idli-piddly?" she crooned. She bent over to run her hand gently over the sleek head. Idli's haughty posture relaxed and she slowly melted into a furry bundle, offering her belly for a much-needed rub. Idli was easily affronted but she just as quickly allowed a few kisses and caresses from her mommy to coax her back into her usual silly, loving little self. Now that relations were restored between them, she jumped off the couch and raced into the kitchen, her tail twitching urgently. Idli sat down before her food bowl and meowed pathetically.

"You are a phony-baloney, Miss Idli," said Neena, laughing at the long-suffering, no-one-has-fed-me-in-a-week look. "You and I both know that Amy fed you last night and this morning. Look at your water bowl," she said pointing at the little ceramic bowl still half-full of fresh water. Amy, who was Chris and Melly's daughter, had volunteered to cat-sit as soon as she laid eyes on Idli.

"Don't you worry, Neena, I will take care of Idli when you're on call," she had said in a very authoritative manner, which Neena found to be sweet and comical coming from the body of a slim eight-year-old girl with delicate features, piercing blue eyes, and sun-streaked light brown hair. However, as the child of two physician parents, she was well versed in the intricacies of being "on call." And, as the oldest of Chris and Melly's kids, she was used to watching over her younger sister Katie and her little brother Danny.

"Besides," she had confided to Neena, "I always wanted a kitten but mom and dad thought that a dog would be more fun. I know Pinecone loves all of us but he's really more Danny's dog than anyone else's." Seeing her small wistful face Neena had felt a rush of affection for her young neighbor. As a child, Neena, too, had always wanted a pet. Neena had often explained to her parents that a cat would not be any trouble at all but her parents, worried about the expense and responsibility of a pet, could not be convinced. Therefore, adopting Idli had been one of her first major decisions after graduating college. Every time she looked at those inquisitive blue eyes and puffy, fluffy little body she couldn't help but be happy. So, she had readily agreed to accept Amy's cat-sitting services and often invited the little girl over to play with Idli. Neena quickly prepared both of their dinners and within a few minutes Idli was quietly munching on her favorite kibble while Neena, too tired to cook, settled down on the sofa with a bowl of Cheerios and milk.

Neena slowly chewed each mouthful of cereal. Although she was very hungry, she was too tired to chew faster. With each bite she reviewed the events of the day as various images flashed into her head, like looking through the red View-Master she had as a child. She remembered seeing Ron standing at the nurses' station this morning.

"How kind of you to join us," he had said, watching the student on-call team walking toward him. He had looked Neena up and down, from the toes of her slightly scuffed white sneakers to the top of her curly, frizzy head. One by one the rest of the team turned to face Neena, Raj, Neel, and Joe. Over the last week the residents and students had gradually separated into two groups. One group consisted of Ron, Victoria, and Dunk. These were the "cool" kids, or so they thought of themselves. The other group, which consisted of the average-Joes, was made up of Bill, Neena, Raj, Neel, and the appropriately named Joe.

Victoria inspected her fellow students' bedraggled appearance. Her eyes had lit up with a malicious gleam.

"Nice glasses," she said to Neena, "The '80s called and want them back."

Ron's smirk widened and Neena had felt her face grow warm with embarrassment. *Some things never change*, she thought. Whether it was in the sandbox, playground, school cafeteria, or now the floors of a hospital, human beings inevitably created a hierarchy and tried to put each other in their "place." But, Neena had to admit that in a teaching hospital a hierarchy of knowledge and experience was crucial to training successive groups of doctors as well as maintaining high levels of patient care.

Dunk had been lounging casually against the desk. "Now, now, play nice children," he had said, giving Victoria a wink and turning to grin at his team. Unlike the rest of them Dunk did not look as if he had been up most of the night. His hair was stylishly combed, his face clean-shaven and he had changed out of his scrubs into neatly pressed trousers and a crisp blue button-down shirt which exactly matched the blue of his eyes. Neena surmised that Dunk had gotten at least two more hours of sleep than the rest of them had. After the team had seen their patient installed in the SICU (Surgical ICU) earlier that morning, Dunk had been the first to head back to the resident on-call rooms. Not, however, before he had assigned additional scut work for the students to complete before they were free to rest. Neena had attempted to gather a few of her wayward locks and stuff them back into her hair tie. Out of the corner of her eye she had seen Neel, Raj, and Joe hastily tucking in their scrub tops and smoothing down their disheveled hair.

Mike added one last signature to the chart on the counter and now turned to face his team. As he glanced around his gaze landed on Neel, whose left arm was in a sling.

"What happened?" he asked. "Another accident?"

Everyone turned around to look at Neel who had positioned himself at the back of the group. Now, as everyone stepped away from Neel, he was left standing alone in a small circle of his teammates. A rosy flush crept up from his clavicles as all eyes focused on him. Neena sympathized with him as she realized that for all his easy-going ways that he, too, disliked being the center of attention.

"Uh, yeah," he stammered. "The door closer above the call room door came loose and hit me. I got checked out in the ER though," he added quickly as if anticipating Mike's next question.

Ron gave a slight snort. "This is the sorriest group of students I've ever seen," he said under his breath. Mike directed a quelling look in his direction.

"I'm fine actually," Neel insisted, and started to ease his arm out of the sling but Mike gestured for him to keep it on.

"Leave the sling on for today. You can sit at the nurses' station for now and get everyone's labs from the computer," Mike said.

"I know you had a busy night last night. However, the on-call team, residents and students alike, are still expected to be on time and to always be dressed professionally. During the day you are expected to change back into your street clothes, unless you are on call or in the OR. Understood?" he said not unkindly. Neena, Raj, Joe, and Neel nodded their understanding.

"Go on down to the cafe and get a cup of good coffee," he added, nodding at the sleepy quartet. "You're going to need it. Join us on the fifth floor."

Mike turned briskly back to the team as Neena and the three boys wheeled around and headed down to The Coffee Corner. The fragrance of freshly brewed coffee reached them as soon as they emerged into the lobby. Sniffing appreciatively, they hurried to get in line. As Neena waited her turn she glanced around and spotted an unlikely pair sitting at one of the small round tables. They had steaming mugs of coffee in front of them and their heads were together in quiet conversation.

"Good morning, Miss Helen," she said, smiling at the older woman. Then Neena smiled and nodded at Miss Helen's companion, who happened to be the sympathetic handyman she had seen several times over the last few days.

"Good morning, Doctor," said Helen with a warm smile. Then turning toward the handyman Helen introduced them to each other.

"This is my good friend, Edgar Robinson," she said. "Edgar, this is Dr. Neena Sundar, who has just started at LCH."

"Student-doctor," Neena corrected with a smile. "Good morning, Mr. Robinson."

"Morning to you as well, Doc," said Mr. Robinson. His smile was hesitant and not as easygoing as it had been all the other times she had encountered him.

"You sure do work long hours, Mr. Robinson," said Neena. "I am surprised to see you back here so early. I saw you late last night on the eighth floor."

"I could say the same to you," he said with a tired, kind smile. "But, I suspect you never left. I was covering the late shift for a colleague," he said, a small frown flashing briefly across his friendly face.

Despite several more cups of coffee, the rest of the day passed in a haze. Luckily there had not been any new admissions overnight and all the patients on the service were known to the team. Neena rounded on her patients and wrote SOAP notes for each of them. Neena had observed that the length of a doctor's progress notes was inversely proportional to the length of their white coats. The longer the coat, the shorter the note. At this point in her training, Neena's progress notes read like a five hundred-word essay, rather than the usual surgeon's note which was a three-line scrawl filled with acronyms and abbreviations.

Although Neena had anticipated some of the intellectual and emotional challenges of medical training she had not realized the physical component. Neena's feet ached and her legs felt wobbly. She had walked back and forth between patient rooms, the nurses' stations, laboratories, and radiology. Neena could not remember ever having been on her feet for so long. At least when she was walking or running during the day she relied on momentum to help propel one foot in front of the other. But having to stand perfectly still for hours on end during surgeries required something else entirely. If not for the novelty and fascination of surgery she did not think she could have done it. Neena herself had been surprised by her own strength and stamina over the past two days.

Neena had raced up and down the stairwells innumerable times over the past thirty-six hours. Now she was so tired she didn't think she could ever move again. Her eyelids closed and she pictured herself going around and around, up and down the stairwells all day long. With a final effort she decided to jump the last three steps. Neena waited for the soles of her sneakers to hit the cement floor of the last landing but instead there was nothing but space beneath her. She was falling! Suddenly her head bobbed against her chest and her eyes flew open. Neena shook off the dream and got slowly to her feet. She scooped Idli up in her arms and dropped the little cat on her bed. She lay down next to the furry bundle which promptly settled into the curve of Neena's body. With each stroke of the silky fur Neena felt the worries of the day being gently wiped away like an eraser on a chalkboard, so that the next day would be a clean, fresh start.

Thursday July 9, 1992

Chapter 11

Neena woke the next day before dawn to the persistent whine of her alarm clock and thought of, what else, but tape. By the time she was ready to leave, the smoky predawn gray was starting to lighten. Her car was parked under a streetlight and even in the gloom she could see that there was plenty of space to maneuver her car onto the road. With a sigh of relief she set off for LCH. The day was not as humid as it had been the last few days and there was still a coolness to the fresh morning air. The breeze from her window ruffled her newly straightened bangs and was as rejuvenating as her morning tea. Although Neena was not an early riser by habit, she found that she enjoyed the peace and stillness of these early morning hours.

Her scenic drive at an end, Neena drove through the entrance to Littlefield Community Hospital. As she headed toward the spot she had parked in since her first day at LCH she realized that it was already occupied. A quick glance around showed that almost all the spots in the front lot were taken. She roamed up and down a few more rows without success. What was going on? Who were all these people? Now feeling annoyed and a little worried that she would not have enough time to stock her box of supplies, Neena turned the car toward the rear parking lot. Fortunately, there were a few empty spaces and she quickly pulled into a slot. She left her windows open a crack in the hopes that the interior would only be a toasty ninety degrees or so when she returned that evening, rather than the searing one-hundred-plus degrees it seemed to have been these past few days.

Neena had never used anything but the main entrance thus far but she hurried to the back of the hospital, hoping to find a rear service entrance. Large double doors swung open and a delivery man pushed through with a metal cart filled with empty water cooler containers. Neena rushed toward the doors and assumed that as long as she headed straight toward the front of the hospital she would end up in the main lobby. However, once she went through the double doors she pulled up short at the blank wall in front of her. Two long corridors branched left and right. Where were the helpful gleaming plaques and signs? Neena turned to the left and quickly walked down the long hallway.

After several more turns, she finally recognized a corridor that she had been in before. She knew that the radiology reading room would be on the left and a stairwell to the lobby at the far end. As she approached the stairwell she passed the door to the billing department. She glanced quickly through the half-glass of the door and did a double take. She saw Ron speaking with a pretty brunette wearing a slim black pencil skirt and a white V-necked shirt that seemed far too silky and low cut for office wear. Ron and a pretty brunette? Neena had never noticed Ron flirting or even chatting with any of the nurses or medical students. Momentarily forgetting she was late for rounds, Neena edged closer to the door and noticed that it was slightly ajar. Most of the other desks in the office were not occupied at this early hour. Ron was leaning over a large metal desk, his meaty fists on the table in front of him. The brunette was standing on the other side with her chair pushed back against the wall.

"What's going on, Linda?" said Ron, waving a sheaf of papers at her. "Where is the rest?"

"These are the only ones I have for June, Dr. Roberts," said Linda. "There is nothing else and I know that no one could have removed anything from my desk. I keep them locked in this cabinet, and I am the only one with the key." She batted her dark lashes at him and her voice was placating but it didn't seem to have any perceptible effect on Ron. He was visible only in profile but his right eyebrow was tilted up at the edge. Neena could mentally fill in the rest of what she already knew to be a thunderous look. She had seen it many times in the last week.

Now Ron's voice was a low rumble, like an impending storm. "Where is the rest? Are you working with anyone else?"

Linda then lifted her chin defiantly and she met Ron's black eyes. "I think you are forgetting something, Dr. Roberts," she said. "As you know, I am very good at my job. I'm not certain that you really appreciate how hard I work and a girl does like to be appreciated." Shaking her head sadly she went on. "I don't think that even my boss understands how very hard I have been working these past few months." Linda tapped a chipped red fingernail musingly against her red painted lips. "Maybe I should make a detailed presentation for him about my latest achievements. He has a keen eye for numbers, when he's sober that is. Maybe I'll even get a promotion. As manager I could be so much more effective." She stretched the last word out for emphasis. "What do you think?" she said, a slight challenge in her voice.

"I think that it is you who are forgetting something," said Ron, his voice a low growl. "I assure you that I do know exactly how hard you are working. I have been keeping very close track of everything," he said slowly. "Again, I repeat, who else has reviewed your work? Answer . . . me . . ." With each of the last two words his voice rose louder and louder and he leaned closer and closer to Linda. "Now!" he finished with a thunderous roar. He brought his clenched fist down on the desk like a crack of lightning, causing both Linda and Neena to jump. Linda took a quick step back trying to retreat as far as possible from Ron. The back of her legs struck her chair and forced her to sit down with an abrupt thump.

"No one, Dr. Roberts, other than you and Dr. Goodwin. I swear." There was now a slight tremor in the girl's voice.

Neena was suddenly afraid. The last thing she wanted was for Ron to find her eavesdropping on this conversation. Whatever this was about, it was none of her business. Realizing that discretion was the better part of valor, she hastily backed away. Neena flung the door to the stairwell open and rushed through it. Suddenly she felt herself being wrenched backward. In rising panic she turned around, fully expecting to see Ron's beefy hand pulling on her lab coat. With relief she noted that the pocket of her lab coat was caught on the door handle. Neena managed not to cry out, pulled herself free, and raced up the stairs.

As she restocked the tape box Neena's mind kept returning to the disturbing scene between Ron and Linda. What had that been about? Why would Ron, a fourth-year surgical resident, need to worry about billing? She knew that all the residents were on a fixed salary so this didn't make any sense. Neena felt sorry for the girl in billing. Having been on the receiving end of Ron's displeasure often enough over the past week she knew how unpleasant the experience was. Picking up her tape box she walked as quickly as she dared down the gleaming corridor, slaloming between the wet floor signs toward the nurses' station. Nurse Marge and Victoria both glared at Neena, but Mike, who rarely missed a thing, did no more than spare her a quick glance. Neena, whose heart was still racing, willed herself to take deep breaths and calm down. She decided to delegate this unpleasant incident to the back of her mind for the time being and concentrate on the morning tasks. By the time the team reached the third or fourth patient Neena was breathing normally and her pulse had quieted down. She was even able to make a concise and coherent presentation when they reached the room of one of the patients she was following.

After approximately forty-five minutes, the team had circled back to the nurses' station and with a few final instructions Mike dismissed the residents and students so that they could attend to their individual duties.

"Remember," Mike said in parting, "today is Grand Rounds in the large lecture hall. It starts promptly at seven a.m. and I expect the entire team to be there. The nurses will page the resident on call if there are any emergencies."

That must be why the parking lot was full today, thought Neena. She was looking forward to her first surgical Grand Rounds. She was not sure what was "grand" about it but this was the name given to the weekly lecture given by each department in their particular specialty. She had heard that there would be Attendings, residents, and students in attendance at this lecture and that the guest speaker was often an expert from another hospital. However, Dunk had told them that once every four to six weeks a senior resident was selected to be the speaker. Neena was very glad that several more years stood between her and that dreaded day.

Neena remained at the nurses' station a few more minutes while she finished making careful notations regarding pending labs next to each of her patients. Her delicate nostrils suddenly picked up the unwelcome scent of body odor and she felt a sharp tap on her shoulder. Swinging around Neena let out a little squeak and took a step backward as she found herself facing Ron. He was frowning as he fished something out of his pocket and stretched out his hand to offer it to her. It was her hospital ID card! She usually pinned her ID card to the left breast pocket of her lab coat. Looking down she noticed the two empty pinholes in the fabric of her coat.

"Oh, um, thanks," she said, reaching out for the card. As her fingers closed over the plastic she felt Ron's grip tighten on it. Startled, she looked up at him.

"I found this in the stairwell near the reading room," he said, still holding onto the card. "What were you doing down there so early?" Ron asked.

As his words slowly penetrated her brain Neena opened her mouth but no words came out. The ID tag must have fallen when she opened the stairwell door and her coat caught on the handle. Did Ron know that she had overheard his conversation with Linda?

After what seemed like an eternity she finally said, "The reading room, right. I thought I'd get the final report on my patient's X-ray from last night," she lied, glad that her brain and mouth were now connected again.

Ron released his grip on the card but was watching her thoughtfully, his eyes slightly narrowed. Neena, whose face was an open book, fervently hoped that Ron would not be able to read her as well as her family and friends could. She busied herself with pinning her ID card back to her coat pocket, gave him a mumbled thanks and hurried away. Just before turning the corner Neena risked a quick glance over her shoulder. Ron was still there, staring intently, not at her retreating form, but at the large black-and-white clock that ticked loudly above the nurses' station.

Neena was rattled by her exchange with Ron. Her heart was thumping again and she had trouble concentrating on her tasks after leaving the nurses' station. It had not taken much time in his presence to realize how unpleasant he was. Ron was loud, arrogant, and rude. But now Neena thought him more than a little frightening as she remembered the menacing tone he had used with Linda. What was he doing there in the first place? And what did he want from Linda? Linda had mentioned Dunk as well. Not only were Ron and Dunk an unlikely pair but what had they to do with Linda? This did not make any sense to Neena.

Neena continued to worry about her encounter with Ron and had trouble accomplishing all of the tasks on her to-do list. But since it was almost seven o'clock she hurried to join her team for Grand Rounds. There was a sea of white coats milling around the lecture hall. She caught sight of Calvin, waving at her a few rows up and skirted around a few seats before sinking into the one he had saved for her.

"Thanks, Calvin," Neena said. She found herself sitting between Calvin and Neel, with Joe and Raj also in the row.

"How are you feeling, Neel?" she asked, turning to him.

"I'm okay," he said, and massaged the side of his neck. "Still sore but I'm able to move my shoulder and arm, and my head has stopped hurting. I hope Mike will release me from desk-duty today."

Neena leaned across Neel a little and addressed Raj.

"How about you? How is your head?" She noticed that the scratches on his face were fading and the bump on his forehead was smaller but had turned an unattractive shade of puce.

"I am feeling better," Raj said with a smile.

"I'm glad," she said.

The auditorium was frigid, even though it was likely going to be another scorching summer's day outside. Neena pulled the folds of her lab coat closer together and patted her left breast pocket to make sure that her badge was still in place.

Neel bent down and picked up something near his seat.

"Here, I got you this," he said, handing her a small Styrofoam cup. "You look like you could use this."

"Neel, the sign says no food or drink in the auditorium," Neena whispered. As a die-hard rule-follower, it would never have occurred to Neena to bring a drink into the auditorium even if she had been dying of thirst.

But, she gratefully accepted it and cupped her small hands around the comforting warmth of the beverage.

"Just look around. Everyone is trying to hide a cup of coffee under their lab coats. And you can't tell me you don't notice the strong smell of French Roast in the air," said Neel. He sniffed appreciatively and grinned at Neena.

She took a cautious sip of the hot liquid. "Mmm, thank you." Neena glanced at Calvin, who had already opened to a blank page of his notebook and had his pen poised to take notes.

"What is the lecture about today?" she asked as the auditorium filled up and the lights started to dim.

"Laparoscopic cholecystectomy," Calvin breathed. His eyes were shining and he was leaning slightly forward in his seat with anticipation. Neena laughed at his child-like enthusiasm.

"What's so exciting about that?" she asked, but he shushed her irritably and remained focused on the podium which was positioned to the right of the stage to allow a clear view of the large white screen behind it.

She turned to Neel and Raj and noticed that they, too, were both sitting up straight in anticipation. Neel turned to her, his green eyes almost glowing in the gloom of the auditorium. *He has beautiful eyes*, Neena thought in surprise as she looked at him. Like peridots. And Raj's were like topazes, and Cecilia's eyes were like sapphires, and mine must be like onyxes, she mused, momentarily distracted.

"What's so exciting? Are you kidding me?" Neel asked incredulously. "This here is surgical history we're witnessing."

Raj vigorously nodded in agreement and Neel continued, "The first laparoscopic cholecystectomies were done only a few years ago. I listened to a lecture on it a few years back, it was amazing! It was one of the reasons I decided to go to medical school. That's when I switched from mechanical engineering to biomedical engineering."

"I didn't know you majored in engineering," Neena said. She realized that she barely knew anything about her teammates and their journeys so far. She had assumed that most of her classmates had majored in biology, as she had done.

"Neel, what—" she started, but Calvin flapped his hand in their direction. "Quiet, guys! The lecture is about to start." Neena, with an effort that took her by surprise, wrenched her onyx eyes from Neel's peridot ones.

The Grand Rounds speaker was a Dr. Joseph Patterson and he had actually trained under those American pioneers of laparoscopic surgery, Drs. McKernan and Saye. He was tall and trim and didn't look a day over thirty, thought Neena. Dr. Patterson's lecture was punctuated by photos and even videos taken during the laparoscopies. There was one of him performing one of the procedures. It was amazing to see him operating without ever looking down on his patient. His eyes stared steadily at the TV monitor near the foot of his table while his hands manipulated his instruments inside of the patient. Dr. Patterson was a good speaker and Neena found that she too was really taken by this new surgical technique.

"To all our young future surgeons in the audience, now you can tell your parents that those countless hours you spent playing Pac-Man or Mario Kart were not wasted. You can rightly claim that you were practicing your hand-eye coordination for your future careers in laparoscopic surgery!" said Dr. Patterson, laughing. "Thank you all for your kind attention," he finished. The audience also erupted into laughter as well as applause.

"I see what you mean," Neena said to her companions. "That was amazing."

"I told you!" Neel said exultantly. As the lights came on the entire auditorium was abuzz with conversation. The students stood up and inched their way toward the stairs. Neena briefly lost sight of her team as she waited for a chance to insert herself into the stream of white coats climbing the stairs toward the large double doors.

"The others went ahead," said Raj as Neena emerged from the auditorium. "We thought you were right behind us."

"I was but then I was rudely brushed aside by a few of the I-am-so-important-all lesser-mortals-beware surgeon types." said Neena with a scowl.

Raj laughed and extended one long arm ahead of him indicating that Neena should precede him.

"Thanks, Raj!" she said, a giggle bubbling up from her lips and smoothing the furrows of annoyance between her thick black brows.

Neena and Raj headed back to the surgical floors. They had left their clipboards and notes in the surgical residents' lounge so they took a short detour to retrieve their things. As they approached the vending machine at which Neena had bought her snack two nights ago, she again heard hushed voices and giggling.

"Really?" she whispered. "It's eight o'clock in the morning! How does he have time for this?"

"What are you talking ab—" Raj started.

She put out a hand to slow her companion's steps and put a finger to her lips. Neena indicated that Raj should follow her as she crouched and carefully peered around the vending machine. His head cautiously appeared above hers.

Neena fully expected to see Dunk and Victoria entwined again. There was a couple up ahead and one of the pair was, indeed, Dunk. However, his partner was not Victoria, but the girl Linda, from billing. She had her arms twined around his neck and Dunk was nuzzling the side of her face.

"Boy, he sure does get around," said Neena softly. After a minute she said, "Okay, show's over." She gave a loud cough and bumped against the vending machine causing it to jangle slightly. Raj also coughed and they both tried to stamp their feet. By the time she and Raj approached, Dunk and Linda were standing a foot apart at the nurses' station.

"Hello, Dunk," said Raj with a grin.

Dunk turned around and greeted them nonchalantly. "Good morning, team." He raised his eyebrows at them. "Where are the rest? You're looking very happy this morning, Raj. That was a great talk, wasn't it?"

"Yes," said Neena. "We've seen a lot of interesting things this morning."

"Okay, well, are you here to get your stuff? Hurry up then and get up to the sixth floor," he ordered and then dismissively turned away.

Neena noticed Linda's eyes following Dunk as he walked down the hall. What was going on here? Had Ron been angry with Linda because he suspected she was seeing Dunk? Is Ron jealous of Linda and Dunk? Whatever it was that Linda was doing with Dunk, it certainly didn't look like "work," as Ron had accused her of.

"Come on," Neena said to Raj. "And wipe that silly smile off of your face. What are you, a prepubescent eleven-year-old?"

Raj continued to smile and raised his shoulders in a shrug.

"Grow up!" Neena muttered irritably, and stalked off toward the lounge.

Although Neena and Raj returned to the sixth floor in record time, when they arrived they were met by an irritated-looking Ron. He was tapping his foot impatiently and looking pointedly at his watch.

"Nice of you to show up," he said, scowling at each one of them in turn. He pointed at his watch face. "Do you realize it's almost eight-thirty?" Ron's gold watch glittered in the harsh light of the nurses' station. And, Neena noticed that he was wearing a gold chain around his neck. These flashy accessories did not go with his stubbly face, unruly hair, and scuffed shoes, Neena thought. She was feeling quite unkindly toward Ron this morning. She noticed, with a satisfaction unbecoming to her usually charitable nature, that he had an ordinary, old Bic pen in his breast pocket with a cap that had been chewed on.

"What's his problem?" asked Calvin, jerking a thumb toward Ron's back once they'd received their orders for the morning and he had walked away.

"Oh, he seems to be his usually sunny self," said Neel, glancing up briefly from the chart he was reading. He pulled a pen from his left front pocket and started making notes on his to-do sheet.

Neena, hugging her clipboard against her chest, leaned slightly toward the others and said in a lowered voice, "I think he may be in a lover's triangle."

Joe and Calvin snorted in derision and started pulling their patient charts from the cart next to them.

"Lover's triangle? Get outta here! Who with?" asked Neel, surprised into looking up from what he was doing.

"A pretty brunette, Ron, and Dunk." The students all looked at Neena in disbelief.

"Come on, stop pulling my leg," said Neel.

"She hasn't touched your leg, Neel," said Raj seriously.

"Very funny, Raj," said Neena. "No, I tell you I saw Ron with her earlier this morning. Her name is Linda and she works in an office near the radiology reading room. I was passing by the door when I heard them arguing. Ron asked her about Dunk and he was really mad! He had such an ugly look on his face that it scared me a little. He almost caught me eavesdropping but luckily I made it into the stairwell before he came out. And just now Raj and I saw Dunk kissing the same girl!"

Calvin noticed the slight crease of worry on Neena's forehead. "Did Ron say anything to you?" he asked.

"No, he didn't, but I didn't like the look on his face," she said.

"Ha!" said Neel. "Do you think anyone likes the look on his face?

Especially a pretty girl?"

"Well, he is a surgeon," said Raj. "And she may be hoping to marry a doctor."

"Yeah," Neel agreed. He added, nodding at the boys. "We are prime matrimonial prizes, my friends. So watch out for all those predatory females!" Faced with an outraged stare from Neena he threw up his hands placatingly.

"Neena, I'm just joking!" protested Neel.

"You guys are such Neanderthals," said Neena. "You're probably right though. But it is mind boggling that any girl would even consider Ron if she could choose Dunk instead. I mean, Dunk is handsome and popular. And, he's already rich, isn't he? And Ron is just a big brute. He always reminds me of a bull in a china shop. Okay, let's get going. I don't know about you but I have at least six patients to see and dozens of labs to follow up. See you all later for lunch?" They all nodded and dispersed, each student heading purposefully in a different direction.

At twelve o'clock Neena headed to the cafeteria. Their lunchtime lecture was canceled today since they had already had a didactic lecture in the morning. Usually during lunch the team met in the conference room and either Mike or Ron, or occasionally, the Attending on service, would give a talk on the basics of clinical medicine. It would be a relief, Neena thought, to sit at a table to eat lunch rather than to balance a paper plate on her lap, attempt to eat neatly, listen to the speaker and be ready in an instant to answer the questions that were regularly lobbed at them. Neena found it challenging to digest food and knowledge simultaneously. However, if there was one thing that the last week had taught her, it was that doctors had to avail themselves of any and all bio-breaks whenever time permitted.

Chapter 12

Neena's stomach gave an anticipatory rumble as her nostrils detected the delicious aromas coming from the cafeteria. LCH's cafeteria lived up to the expectations of a fancy, private community hospital. There was a sandwich station, a salad bar, hot food counter, coffee bar, and a dessert station! The last few days it had been quicker to grab one of the premade cold sandwiches and a bag of chips to eat during the noontime lecture, but today Neena was looking forward to a real meal. She took a tray from the gleaming silver stand and a bright white plate. She proffered it to the smiling woman in a crisp white uniform behind the counter and pointed at several of the trays in front of her in quick succession. The woman served her a heaping portion of baked ziti, several meatballs, and sauteed broccoli. Neena helped herself to a warm roll, a glass of water and a small piece of decadent-looking chocolate brownie. Neena remembered her old high school cafeteria and shuddered at the memories of greasy chicken nuggets, which were composed of more fried batter than chicken, soggy pale french fries, ketchup as the "vegetable option" and small white Styrofoam bowls with yellow-gray chunks of fruit salad.

As usual, Calvin was the first one to spot her and she followed his chubby waving arm to a circular table in the back of the dining area. She put her tray down in front of the empty chair next to him.

"Hey, Neena," mumbled Joe around a mouthful of food. Neel, who had just taken a huge bite of an enormous cheeseburger, only smiled and nodded at her.

"Hi!" said Neena to the group, smiling impartially around the table. She took off her lab coat, which was surprisingly still a pristine white, and hung it on the back of her chair. She was well aware of one of the Laws of Attraction which stated that every speck of bright red sauce had an instant and powerful affinity for any piece of white clothing.

Raj, who seemed to have made great inroads on his plate of roast chicken and vegetables doused in hot sauce, stood up as she arrived. "Hello, Neena," he said, politely, resuming his chair only once Neena had sunk down into hers.

Neel, who was now wiping ketchup off his chin with a napkin, elbowed Raj in the leg.

"Dude, sit down. You don't have to stand up for Neena. You're making the rest of us look bad," he said.

"I thought it was an American custom," Raj said.

"Maybe in the eighteen hundreds," Neel replied, opening his mouth very wide for another bite of his burger.

"Well, then I think my mother read too many British regency romances when she was younger," he said, smiling. "I think she was trying to instill some Western manners in me. In India men don't usually stand up when a woman enters the room."

Neel's Adam's apple bobbed as he swallowed strenuously. "Now that's what I'm talking about!" He looked at Neena with a challenge in his eyes. Neena stuck her tongue out at him in the universal American gesture of childish rebuke.

"Don't listen to him, Raj," Neena said. "With your cool accent and your lovely manners"—she directed a quelling gaze at Neel who was still grinning—"the girls are going to be lining up for you. And you're a doctor to boot!"

Raj's light brown cheeks assumed a pinkish hue.

"That's very kind of you to say," he said, picking up his fork and knife again.

Neel looked between Neena and Raj, a speculative gleam in his eyes. Neena raised her eyebrows at him and favored him with another glare. He wisely popped a few fries in his mouth and said no more.

Neena decided to ignore Neel and spread her white paper napkin across her lap. "Mmm, this smells so good and I'm starving," she said. Just as she picked up her fork, she spotted Cecilia, tray in hand, looking around the cafeteria.

Neena called to her friend, "Ceclia! Over here!" Cecilia, smiling in relief, headed toward them, her tray held skillfully aloft in one hand and her clipboard and branded water bottle in the other.

Instantly, all the boys, Neel included, were on their feet, shuffling around to make space for Cecilia, demonstrating again her friend's power to glide gracefully through any crowd. *She is a force of nature*, thought Neena. Neel grabbed a chair from a nearby table and inserted it between himself and Raj. They all greeted Cecilia enthusiastically and as soon as she had put her tray down and took her seat the others did so as well.

"Hmph, "said Neena to Neel, giving him a pointed look for the speed at which he had stood up when Cecilia approached.

"What?" he asked. "We had to make room." But he gave her a sheepish smile to acknowledge his contradictory behavior. She noted that his cheeks were slightly flushed and decided not to pursue the inconsistencies of his chivalry.

"What are you doing here?" asked Neena. "I thought the medicine team always ate in their conference room? Did you have Grand Rounds today as well?"

Cecilia, who had been drinking thirstily from her water bottle, wiped her mouth with the back of her slim white hand, rendering an elegance to even that crude gesture.

"No, ours is tomorrow," she said. "The conference room was not available today so our chief resident let us loose for an hour." Cecilia shook open her paper napkin and placed it on her lap. She, like Neel, had opted for a cheeseburger and fries, and reached over for the bottle of ketchup. As Cecia took a huge bite, Neena noted that both Raj and Neel smiled and nodded approvingly.

Neel, stretching his long arm across Cecilia to reclaim the ketchup bottle, winced and let it drop onto the table.

"What's wrong?" asked Cecilia, her delicate eyebrows drawn together in concern.

"Nothing, I'm fine," said Neel, rubbing his left shoulder. "Just a slight accident."

"What accident? First Raj and now you too?" Cecilia put her napkin down and turned her attention to Neel.

"I guess we haven't spoken since Sunday brunch," said Neena as she told Cecilia about Neel's accident outside the call room.

Cecilia ran her hand along the left side of Neel's neck and shoulder, prodding enthusiastically at one-millimeter intervals. "Does that hurt?" she asked. "How about that?" Even from across the table Neena could see that Cecilia's slim fingers were pressing none too gently into Neel's bruised shoulder. Judging from the pained expression on his face it was clear that Neel's shoulder was still quite tender. So, was he permitting Cecilia's "tender" ministrations out of politeness or perhaps he was simply enjoying Cecilia's attentions? Neena wasn't sure but seeing that there were now a few beads of sweat on Neel's forehead she decided to put a halt to the physical examination.

"Cecilia, I don't think anything is broken and he did get checked out in the ER yesterday."

"Hmm, yes, I think you're right. I don't feel any bony irregularities along his clavicle," Cecilia said, pressing firmly on Neel's left clavicle. Oblivious to the wince on his face she gave Neel's shoulder one final pat, and turned back to her plate.

Neel slowly let out the breath he had been holding and used his napkin to dab at his forehead. He looked at Neena and mouthed a "thank you" at her. She acknowledged this with a faint smile. Neena wondered how long it would take her and her classmates to master the art of the physical exam. So far poor Neel had been the one to bear the brunt of both Raj's and Cecilia's clinical evaluations.

Cecilia swallowed a bite of food. "You guys are certainly accident-prone. Or maybe it's The Curse of the Surgical Rotation?" she said seriously.

"What curse?" asked Calvin.

"Haven't you heard? Every seven years at this hospital one of the surgical teams always has the most terrible luck. Someone has almost always gotten sick or injured or made a horrible mistake."

"Yeah, right," Joe scoffed.

"No, it's true!" Cecilia insisted. "I heard it from a fourth-year student who heard it from one of the interns."

"What kind of things happened?" Neena asked.

"Well, I heard that the last time the curse struck a medical student got hit by a car while crossing the street, a resident was knocked unconscious after slipping on a wet floor in the surgical wing, one student fell down an elevator shaft, and an Attending was electrocuted with the Bovie during a surgery!" They all looked at Cecilia incredulously. After a moment she burst into a peal of laughter that sounded like wind chimes on a breezy summer day.

"I know. It's so ridiculous, right? But that's what I heard," Cecilia said again, giving Neena a wink. Neena, along with the others, had joined in the laughter. However, slowly she stopped laughing and the smile faded from her face.

"Neena, what's wrong?" asked Cecilia.

"Well, Raj was pushed into oncoming traffic and Neel was knocked unconscious," she said.

"That's right!" said Calvin.

"I wonder who's gonna fall down the elevator shaft?" Joe mused.

"Stop that!" Neena said. "We don't want any self-fulling prophecies."

Neel let out a bark of laughter. "You're crazy," he said. "There is no such thing."

Neena's black curls bounced emphatically as she shook her head. "There absolutely is such a thing," she protested.

"What's meant to be, is meant to be," said Raj sagely. "Our destinies are already written in the stars and we are only fulfilling what the fates have intended for us." Neena nodded seriously at him. Her belief systems were a complex mix of Eastern and Western cultures. She was naturally affected by many of her parents' cultural superstitions. But, she also strongly believed that she had some agency over her destiny. After all, even though Mr. Das had seen her future as a physician, she still had to expend the time and energy to realize that destiny.

Neena returned her attention to her meal and as was her habit, took a bite of everything on her plate. She started with a forkful of pasta, then a piece of meatball, and then a broccoli floret. Having come full circle she started again with another bite of pasta. She chewed for a few minutes and then realized that her tablemates, other than Calvin and Cecilia, were all staring at her.

"What's wrong? she asked. "Do I have sauce on my face?"

She hurriedly wiped her mouth and chin with her napkin.

"No," said Neel. "I've just never seen anyone eat like that. Do you always go clockwise?"

Joe and Neel laughed and Raj suppressed a smile.

Calvin gallantly came to her defense. "Neena is very methodical and detail-oriented no matter what she's doing," he said. "You should see how organized her notes and study materials are. When it comes time to study for an exam I always try to sit at her table in the library. She has flash cards, mnemonics, color-coded notes, and snacks!" said Calvin appreciatively.

This only made Joe and Neel laugh harder. Neena threw her napkin at them.

She speared a bright green broccoli floret and waved it at them.

"Ha ha, very funny, guys," she said. "Thank you, Calvin. You can always study with me."

"It's nice to see a girl with a healthy appetite," Raj said soothingly.

"Hmph," said Neena, but she smiled. Despite being teased she had enjoyed her meal. Neena pushed her plate back and picked up her brownie. It was velvety soft and full of small chocolate chips. "What do you guys think of Dunk?" she asked

"He seems cool," said Neel, reaching for the large peanut butter cookie that was the only remaining item on his previously loaded tray.

Joe nodded his head. "Yeah, he's all right. I like that he's laid back and not arrogant like most rich guys."

Since Calvin, who was busily eating his dessert, had not answered, Neena gently joggled his elbow.

"What do you think?" she asked again.

"Of what?" he mumbled around a mouthful of lime-green jello.

"Duncan. What do you think of him?"

"I dunno. He's okay, I guess. I don't really like these surgical types."

Neel looked up at this. "Hey, what do you mean? I'd like to be a surgeon. Are you saying you don't like me?"

"I'm considering that as well," said Raj seriously.

Joe wiped his mouth and threw his crumpled napkin onto his tray. "Me three," he said.

"Aww now, that's not what I meant to say. I didn't mean you guys," Calvin protested. A delicate blush spread over his round, smooth cheeks, making them look like a pair of pink lady apples. "Well, at least not yet," he added truthfully, if not very diplomatically.

Neel laughed. "Okay, fair enough. Let me know what you think after a few years."

"Never mind that," said Neena impatiently. "I only asked because I don't think he likes me very much. He assigned me so much scut work that night we were on call after the poor man's surgery. That's why it took me so long to get back to the call rooms."

"You had a lot of scut work on Tuesday night after the surgery?" asked

Raj. "He didn't give me much."

Neel, wiping cookie crumbs from his mouth, nodded. "He gave me some scut. I thought it was going to take me longer than it did which is why I got to the call room first. But thinking about it now, maybe I should have taken my time. Then that hunk of metal would have landed on someone else's head."

Neena looked sharply at him.

"Yes, it would have landed on Raj," she said.

"Oh, yeah," said Neel a little sheepishly. "Sorry, Raj. But it's a good thing you came upstairs when you did. I don't think I was lying there with my head bashed in for too long."

"It was simple bad luck for you, Neel," said Raj. "But, you were lucky you were not seriously hurt."

Neena turned to look at Raj. *It certainly had been bad luck*, she thought. If Raj had been the first one to open the call room door the brass door closer would likely have fallen on him. The object was so heavy that a direct hit on the head would have caused a significant injury. Was Raj the one with the bad luck, then? Last week he was pushed off the curb into oncoming traffic and this week he could have possibly sustained a serious head injury.

Neena stood up and quickly put on her lab coat, which thanks to her forethought, did not have even a speck of red sauce on it. She thrust her hands into her bulging pockets to check that the contents were still intact.

"Ow!" she said, pulling her hand out of her pocket. There was a small crimson bead of blood blossoming on the tip of her right index finger. She sucked her finger and taking the napkin Raj quickly proffered, pressed it firmly over the small puncture wound.

"What do you have in your pockets that's so sharp?" he asked.

Neena carefully fished all the items out of her pocket. She pulled out her stethoscope, pocket notebook, penlight, a few coins, a handful of the small Lego pieces she had forgotten to return to Danny, and lastly, a shiny brass screw with a very sharp point on it.

"Why do you have a screw in your pocket?" asked Joe.

"It must be the one I picked up outside your call room. Maybe this screw came loose and then the door closer became unstable?"

Joe held out his hand and Neena deposited it in his palm. He took a quick look and gave it back to her.

"It looks brand-new," he said. "The mechanism was also bright and shiny so it may have been recently replaced. I guess whoever installed it didn't tighten it enough."

"I guess so," said Neena slowly as she turned the screw over in her palm. The screw was bright, shiny, and brass like the door closer and looked brand-new other than the head of the screw which had a few deep gouges in it. Perhaps the handyman had had trouble screwing it in? Could it have been Mr. Robinson who installed the door closer? He was the handyman she had seen most frequently in the last week on the surgical floors. In fact, he had been leaving the floor two nights ago when she and the team had come to the call rooms. But he had seemed like the conscientious type to her. He worked long hours and she had noticed, with approval, that his red tool cart was sparkling clean, and had bins on top which held screwdrivers, mallets, paint brushes, as well as other tools, all neatly sorted. He didn't seem to her to be the type of person who would do shoddy work. But she now also remembered that on that night he hadn't flashed his usual friendly smile, or even acknowledged her at all for that matter, as he had always done on the other occasions on which they had crossed paths. And, the next morning when she had bumped into him in The Coffee Corner talking with Helen, he had seemed worried as well. Maybe he had heard about Neel's accident that morning and felt that he was to blame? But then why had he looked so concerned earlier that night before the accident? Neena felt that something was not quite right with this picture but she didn't have time to puzzle it out now. However, her methodical mind filed this incident away in her mental filing cabinet under the label of "interesting and/or strange events" for future consideration. She looked at her watch and started stuffing the items she had tossed on the table back in her pocket.

"Come on, guys, lunch is over. Let's go!" Neena picked up her tray and took off.

As Neena strode through the room she spotted Ron, sitting at a table in what looked to be the cafeteria's overflow area. She was a little surprised since she had never seen him eating but was not surprised to note that he was sitting alone. There was something odd about his behavior though. He was shoveling food into his mouth but almost never glanced down at his plate. Although his mouth was fiercely chewing it was clear that it was his eyes that were devouring something in a corner alcove. Neena followed his gaze and her eyes alighted on Dunk and Linda sitting at a little table for two. Their heads were close together and, like in a romance novel, they appeared to be "gazing deeply into each other's eyes." Linda fingered a delicate gold chain on her neck from which a gem sparkled while Dunk held her right hand lightly with his left one. His other hand was idly playing with a bracelet on her wrist. As he turned it over and over, tiny sparks of light winked from the bejeweled (diamond?) tennis bracelet. Neena could see a rosy glow on the girl's cheeks and the coy fluttering of her dark lashes. Suddenly, Dunk's eyes moved around the room and Neena found him looking directly at her. Embarrassed at having been caught staring she hastily averted her eyes, but not before she had caught his lazy wink and sardonic smile.

As she looked away her gaze alighted on another one of her teammates sitting alone. Victoria, unlike Ron, had not touched a morsel of the food on her plate. However, just like Ron, her laser-sharp gaze was fixed on Duncan and Linda, sitting cozily together at their table for two. Victoria's lean face was pinched and her lips were tightly compressed. *Wow, this is not a lover's triangle*, thought Neena, *it's a quadrangle*. Judging by the looks on Ron and Victoria's faces this situation was not likely to end well. But, she reminded herself that it was none of her business and filed this incident away for future review as well. Neena deposited her tray on the conveyor belt and before the rest of the group at her table had even stood up, she was gone.

Back at their table, Neel looked at Calvin. "Is she always this bossy? And fast?" he asked, as he followed the blur that was Neena's curly head making its way quickly toward the exit.

"Yup," said Calvin. "But you'll get used to her."

Neel and Raj exchanged quizzical looks and each gave one of those manly shrugs that clearly said, "Women!"

When Raj picked up his tray he saw that Neena had left a few of her coins and Legos behind on the table. He hurriedly scooped them up and shoved them into his own pocket. Then Joe, Calvin, Raj, and Neel hurried to dispose of their trays and rushed after Neena.

As Neena stood waiting for the elevator she patted her left breast pocket again to check that her ID was pinned firmly in place. She was relieved to see that it was, but when she removed her hand she noticed a small crimson circle staining the white of her coat. Her finger had started to bleed again.

"Fudge," she muttered in annoyance. It seemed that the Law of Attraction was indeed a force to be reckoned with.

One of the diners looked up and followed Neena's progress with a calculating eye. Although intellectual curiosity was valued in the medical field, was it really good for one's health? After all, hadn't curiosity killed the cat?

Chapter 13

Neena slowed her little gray car and searched for a parking spot along the street near Patel's Pantry. Although it was only past six o'clock, the rays of the evening sun shone brightly against the glass windows of the storefronts. Neena spied the distinctive orange, white, and green-striped awning of her favorite Indian store-cum-takeout eatery. During the warmer months of the year the Patel's showcased their fresh produce under the colorful awning. Large, woven trays were filled with an impressive variety of fruits and vegetables. Along with the expected apples, bananas, and tomatoes, there were also more exotic offerings of ripe orange mangoes, wiry brown coconuts, tiny green chili peppers, and long thin spears of okra. Neena imagined that a giant hand had used the woven trays to scoop the rainbow-colored produce like candies from a large glass jar and arranged them all on the long, wooden tiered tables.

The portly form of Mr. Patel was visible half a block away. He appeared to be spritzing the produce with water from a spray bottle to keep them cool and fresh in the summer heat. In his bright orange apron he closely resembled one of the pumpkins that would soon be displayed on doorsteps and porches in the fall. However, from an old black-and-white photo displayed in the store she knew that he had once been much leaner and fitter. In the photo Mr. and Mrs. Patel were standing in front of their store with a banner hanging from the awning proclaiming its grand opening in large block letters. Mr. Patel was in an apron (presumably orange) with the sleeves of his shirt pushed up over his muscular arms and Mrs. Patel was slim and straight in a printed saree that fell in graceful folds to her feet. Now, his rounded form was a testament not only to his wife's excellent cooking but to the bounty and prosperity he was enjoying in his adopted country. Neena chuckled at the thought of the giant hand trying to pick up the rounded form of Mr. Patel to place him among the fall pumpkin display.

The side of the road was crowded and Neena marveled at the precision with which the cars were parked, bumper-to-bumper, with scarcely a few inches in between to maneuver. Momentarily ignoring the admonishments of her rule-loving self she decided to briefly double-park while she ran in to collect her prepared food order. Heat still radiated from the sidewalks and warmed the thin soles of her black leather flats. Mr. Patel looked up as she approached.

"Hello, Neena beti," he said, using the affectionate term, which meant child or "little one" in Hindi, as a part of his warm greeting. "How are you this fine evening?"

"Hello, Uncle," Neena replied, in turn using the respectful appellation for any older man that was commonly used in South-Asian culture. "I am well, thank you. How are you?"

"Me, I am well as always, as you can see," he said, patting his belly and laughing.

"You look as strong and healthy as ever," Neena agreed, also laughing, as she stepped into the coolness of the store. At the soft tinkle of the bell above the door Mrs. Patel looked up from the jars of spices she was arranging.

"Hello, Aunty," Neena said.

"Hello, beti! I have been waiting for you. Your favorite Bindi masala and Tadka dal are packed and ready. Go eat it before it gets cold. You are too thin!" she admonished, wagging a slim hennaed-finger at her. "You must eat some more so that you have energy to work all day and night at the hospital."

"Yes, Aunty, thank you, I definitely will," Neena promised with a smile. After quickly settling her bill Neena carried her food back to her car and hurried home. As she walked up the flagstone pathway Neena automatically looked up at the large picture window to see Danny and Pinecone, there as usual, smiling, waving, and wagging at her. Neena returned Danny's smile and waved at the duo. Idli was the next one to welcome her as she let herself into her apartment. She bent down to caress the soft white head that pressed against her ankle.

"Hello, Idli baby. How are you today? Did you miss me?" Neena could have sworn the little cat nodded before briskly setting off toward the kitchen, her plume of a tail swishing as she walked. She stopped in front of her food bowl, looked pointedly at it and then at Neena.

"Yes, I know, I know. You're hungry. Well, since I have a treat for dinner I think you should have one too, don't you?" she asked and received a soft meow in response. Taking this as an affirmative Neena opened a tin of specialty cat food and spooned it into her bowl. Idli licked quickly but daintily at her food, emptying the little bowl within a few minutes. As she settled down to clean her face and whiskers Neena deposited her package on the counter and headed to the bathroom for a quick shower.

Neena selected a pair of loose white cotton pants and a summery light blue sleeveless top from her closet. After tying her damp hair back with a ribbon, she tucked into Mrs. Patel's food. As she scooped up a bit of spicy okra on her plate with a piece of roti, the doorbell rang. She quickly popped the food into her mouth and stood up. She was preceded to the door by the fluffy form of Idli.

"Hi, Raj. I'm almost ready!" said Neena as she opened the door. She waved her hand casually toward the sofa. "Come in and take a load off."

Raj looked a little puzzled. "I am not carrying anything," he said, turning his empty palms up for her inspection.

"Oh, I'm sorry, Raj. That's just an American expression which means to 'have a seat,'" she explained with a smile.

"Ah, as in take a load off one's feet?" Raj said, as understanding dawned. "I am still learning to understand the American accent and all of your quaint expressions."

"Yes, there must be a lot of culture shock," Neena said sympathetically as Raj sat down on the sofa.

Glancing around, she called, "Idli!"

"Very kind, but no thank you. I've already eaten," said Raj politely.

Neena giggled and pointed behind the door. "I wasn't offering you idlis, Raj. I was calling MY Idli." She indicated the fluffy white creature sitting bolt upright and staring intently at them with a pair of piercing blue eyes. Idli gracefully sauntered forward.

Raj gave an unexpected shout of laughter.

"Hi, Idli," he said and reached down to pet the little cat which was winding between and around his ankles. Idli, having allowed Raj the number of caresses she deemed sufficient for a new acquaintance, swished toward her water bowl.

"Idli! What a fantastic name! Do you play that trick on all of your first-time guests?" Raj asked.

"I do get a kick out of seeing people's reactions," Neena admitted. "Obviously it only works on people who know what idlis are. But," she said, quickly remembering her manners, "if you'd like some food I have plenty." She indicated the remaining food on the table.

"Thank you, but I have just eaten," Raj said again. Though she was a very hospitable person, Neena was slightly relieved and quickly cleared the table, putting the food back into the fridge. She was usually able to get several meals out of her orders from Patel's Pantry but she was sure that if this had been Neel, rather than Raj, all her leftovers would have not-so-magically disappeared.

Neena slid her small crossbody bag over her shoulders and grabbed her keys from the porcelain bowl on the top shelf of her bookcase. Outside, Neena stopped short when she again found her little gray car tightly boxed in by two larger cars.

"Sugar!" she muttered, turning to Raj in dismay. He looked at her quizzically and started to open his mouth but then changed his mind.

"Is this your car?" he asked. From the look on her face he surmised that it was.

"It does seem to be a very tight fit but I'm sure you can extricate it," was the encouraging response.

"Hmph," said Neena as they got into the car. The heat from the little car hit them like a blast from an oven.

"Feels like home!" Raj joked, quickly cranking the window handle to let the air escape. Inch by inch, shifting gears backward and forward, Nina attempted to extricate her car. Tiny beads of sweat formed on her forehead with the effort of turning the manual steering wheel. After a few minutes, and with very little progress, she put the car in neutral and shook her arms to loosen her aching muscles. Neena blinked rapidly as a bead of sweat dripped into her eye. She glanced over at Raj who had been watching her performance in polite silence. He reached into his pants pocket and offered her a crisp white handkerchief. She accepted it gratefully and patted her warm face.

She smiled ruefully and shook out her cramped hands. "Sorry, I just need a little break. My arms feel like jelly."

Raj smiled sympathetically back at her. Then, stretching his long arms he leaned across her and grasped the steering wheel, his large brown hands briefly covering her small ones.

"What are you doing?" Neena asked, removing her hands from under his.

"It's called teamwork," Raj said. "You shift gears and I will help you turn the wheel." Neena was skeptical but did as he said. As Neena worked the clutch, brake, accelerator, and gear stick, Raj turned the steering wheel. With his help Neena was able to gradually nose the little car out of the tight parking spot.

"Wow!" Neena said, wiping her forehead again with the handkerchief. "Thank you! You made that so easy! It would have taken me so much longer." She proffered the handkerchief back to Raj but he shook his head.

"You are welcome. Super job, Neena!" said Raj, relaxing back into his seat and looking as if this exercise had not taxed him in the least. He waved away the handkerchief.

"You keep it," he said. With a little nod of thanks Neena stuffed the handkerchief into her pocket.

"I'm impressed that you are able to do this daily by yourself. Soon your biceps are going to be bulging," he said, smiling. She was slightly surprised at his teasing since his manner toward her had been rather formal thus far. But, Neena was glad to see him looking more at ease and hoped he was acclimating to his new country. When his face relaxed she thought he looked rather handsome, despite the mustache. Neena glanced pointedly at her skinny brown arms and then at Raj's long well-muscled arms. He laughed. "Hmm, maybe not bulging, but I think you're probably stronger than you look," he said. *Yes*, Neena thought, as she swung her car into the road, *that is certainly true*. Due to her size people often underestimated her strength, both literally and figuratively.

Chapter 14

As the little gray car slowed near the wrought iron gates, a second car, which was quickly approaching from the opposite direction, came to a sudden stop. The driver's eyes widened in surprise as the rays of the setting sun clearly illuminated the two occupants. What on earth were these two doing here?

―

Neena had found Mr. MacMillan's address in a local map and had memorized the route. They drove further into the suburbs, enjoying the warm summer breeze drifting in from the car's open windows. The well-tended, yet small, lawns from Neena's neighborhood gradually gave way to larger and larger expanses of green. Through the trees and bushes on the heavily landscaped yards, Neena and Raj caught a glimpse of large brick or stone-faced houses. However, when Neena turned onto Bougainvillea Boulevard the lawns were no longer visible as the homes on this street were shielded from the road by large stone walls, punctuated by equally large wrought iron gates. After driving by a particularly long stretch of a high stone wall, Neena stopped the car and checked the house number displayed on a polished brass plate.

"Here it is," she said. "3215 Bougainvillea Boulevard." She eased her little car onto the small stretch of stone driveway in front of the iron gate and leaned out of her window to press the button on a discrete panel. Within seconds a crisp male voice requested them to state their names and their business.

"Um, this is Neena Sundar? Mr. MacMillan hired me as a nursing aid and he is expecting me? My classmate, Raj is also with me?" Neena said. As usual, when she was nervous, she spoke in interrogatives. She glanced at Raj who only raised his thick black eyebrows. After one or two long minutes the large intricately shaped iron gate silently swung open and Neena drove through. In her rearview mirror she saw the gates shut swiftly behind them. The driveway was long and meandering, bordered by rows of large trees, which created a leafy canopy overhead. After driving for what seemed like a quarter of a mile the car emerged from a curve in the road and the house was suddenly before them.

Neena's mouth formed a perfect "O" as she stared at the structure in front of them. It was not a house but a mansion made of light gray stones which now glowed creamily in the evening sun.

Raj's eyes opened wide. "Now I see why Neel called it billionaire's boulevard!"

The car crunched along the gravel courtyard and around the large stone fountain in the center. Neena pulled to a stop and they got out, both still staring at the elegant three-story Georgian home. Four imposing white columns flanked the large entrance. Neena and Raj approached the glossy black-painted double doors, accented by shining brass hardware. Other than the tinkling of the fountain, all was quiet.

Raj glanced over at Neena and then bent his head toward hers.

"Maybe you should close your mouth?" he whispered, flashing his quick smile at her. Neena promptly complied. She stepped forward and pressed the doorbell firmly. They could hear a musical chime echoing through the house. The door was soon opened by a trim man of medium build and indeterminate age in a neat black suit.

"Good evening," he said sonorously, with a slight lilt. Everything about him appeared crisp and efficient from the top of his neatly combed curly black hair, to the bottoms of his gleaming black shoes. The man's dark blue eyes were sharp as he appraised Raj. Then he gave a small incline of his head and stepped back to allow them to enter. Raj gave a slight nod of his head in response and followed Neena inside.

"Uh, hello, good evening," stammered Neena, fidgeting with her purse and keys. Her voice echoed slightly from the high-vaulted ceiling. The large round foyer was tiled in white marble edged with a decorative black border, and there were several marble niches displaying beautiful Greco-Roman sculptures. The expansive entryway felt cool and airy after the warmth of the day.

"Please, come this way," the man said. "Mac is in the morning room." He led them down one of three long hallways leading from the foyer. The walls were a delicate eggshell blue with white crown molding and elegant raised-panel wainscoting. A plush strip of oriental carpet in muted tones ran the length of the hall, absorbing the sounds of their feet. The man paused at a set of doors at the end of the hallway and tapped lightly.

"Mac?" he called.

When there was no answer the man tapped again and opened the door slightly.

"Mac?" he said again. When the door opened fully, Mr. MacMillan's head raised with a snap and he opened his eyes. Presumably he had been dozing.

"A Miss Sundar and Mr. Raj are here to see you, Mac," the black-suited man announced, stepping aside so Neena and Raj could enter. Mr. MacMillan looked a little dazedly at them and then cleared his throat

"Please come in," he said softly. Mr. MacMillan was propped up by pillows on a large chintz-covered sofa, with a light blanket over his knees and more pillows elevating his legs. They entered the large bright room which was furnished with clusters of sofas, chairs, and tables arranged in small groups. He looked much paler than the last time she had seen him.

"Thank you for coming, Neena." His tone was friendly but not as strong as she had remembered. The last time she had seen him he had had a little stubble on his cheeks but today there seemed to be several days' worth of growth on his face, giving him an older and more haggard look. *He really must not be feeling well*, she thought. His blanket started to slip off as he attempted to stand up. However, Neena strode over to him, and waved him back down.

"Hello, Mr. MacMillan, please don't get up," she said with a friendly smile and hurriedly straightened the blanket. He offered her his hand and Neena shook it gently. Before letting go of it she automatically positioned her fingers on his wrist to take his pulse. She was in full nursing-aide mode now. She glanced at the second hand on her watch and counted. Her dark, neatly shaped eyebrows arched as she frowned slightly. Although his pulse was strong it was quite rapid. Perhaps it was the surprise of being woken up suddenly? Or maybe he was in pain?

"How are you?" she asked, a look of concern on her face.

"I've been better," he acknowledged with a wan smile. "This surgery has taken more out of me than I had expected. But, I felt sure that I would be able to get more rest at home than I would in the hospital."

"Yes, I am sure you will be more comfortable at home. I have heard it said that hospitals are not a place to rest, which is unfortunate," Neena said.

"It certainly was good to sleep in my own bed," Mr. MacMillan said. "But, my care at LCH was excellent so I can't complain. Though it did seem that someone or the other was popping into my room every five minutes!"

"I know that I was definitely one of those 'others,'" Neena said with a smile.

"I am so glad you came when you did. Those staples were driving me mad! You had them out in a wink."

"I don't know about 'a wink' but I am very glad I was able to remove all of them. Though I am sure I caused you some discomfort in the process."

Mr. MacMillan waved his hand at her. "Not at all, not at all. I was thankful for your steady hands and light touch."

Finally, his warm brown eyes moved past Neena and settled on Raj, who had been standing quietly near the door.

Neena suddenly glanced at Raj, then anxiously back to Mr. MacMillan who was gazing intently at Raj.

"This is my classmate, Raj, um, just Raj," she said in some confusion. "I'm so sorry. I should have checked with you first but Raj just came along for the ride, I hope you don't mind?"

His gaze focused back on Neena and he nodded slowly. "That's perfectly fine, Neena," he said softly and looked back at Raj who took a few steps forward and smiled hesitantly at Mr. MacMillan, clearly uncertain of his welcome.

"Good evening, Mr. MacMillan," he said. "I perfectly understand if you are not comfortable with me being here and I am happy to wait outside for Neena."

"No, no, not at all. Welcome, Raj. It was good of you to accompany Neena." Now Raj advanced quickly into the room with his right hand outthrust. The older man reached out his own hand and firmly clasped Raj's. Holding the handshake for an extra second or two he looked searchingly at Raj.

"Mr. MacMillan?" Raj asked uncertainly, looking at their clasped hands. Mr. MacMillan suddenly released Raj's hand and gave a little shake of his head, as if to clear his mind.

"So sorry," he murmured softly. "You remind me so much of someone I used to know." His voice trailed off. Quickly recollecting himself, he continued, "Please have a seat." He pointed to the sofa opposite him and two large overstuffed arm chairs which flanked the sofas. "Anyway, the more doctors the better, right?" he said with a small laugh.

Neena perched on the edge of the sofa and Raj settled into one of the arm chairs.

"Patrick?" Mr. MacMillan called to the man in the black suit, who had been waiting patiently in the doorway. "Please bring in some refreshments for our guests."

"Of course, Mac," said Patrick, and silently withdrew from the room.

"Oh, that's really not necessary, Mr. MacMillan," Neena protested. "I am here to work, not to be entertained."

"Nonsense! I'm sure you will both appreciate a cool drink as I hear that it is quite warm outside." Neena thought that it was almost as warm inside as it was outside since the entire back wall of the room was made up of a series of French doors. Heat from the lingering warmth of a scorching July day radiated through the glass. She was glad of her loose cotton shirt and pants, which allowed what air there was to circulate about her limbs. She glanced at Raj who seemed quite comfortable in the heat.

Mr. MacMillan turned back to Neena.

"As I was saying, it was your steady hands and light touch which assured me that you would be the perfect person for this position as my nurse's aide. I would like your help with changing my bandages, assisting me with my physical therapy, and other minor tasks."

Raj had been quietly listening to their conversation.

"Pardon me for interrupting," he said, rather stiffly. "Mr. MacMillan, I'm sorry for asking this, but why do you want Neena's help when you can clearly hire any number of professionals to help you?" He fixed his steady gaze on the older man's face.

Neena, surprised by the bluntness of his question, turned to him. "Raj!" she said, in a low but urgent tone, in an attempt to shush him.

"It's quite alright, Neena," said Mr. Macmillan. "I am glad to see your young man is looking out for you."

"Oh, no! He's not my . . ." started Neena.

"No, no it's not like that," Raj also protested simultaneously. "We just met a few days ago on our surgery rotation."

"My good friend Cecelia convinced Raj to come with me," Neena explained, with a slightly embarrassed smile. "You see, she and Raj and Neel, another classmate of ours, were all just a teensy bit worried about me driving here by myself so then Raj offered to accompany me. Please don't be offended!"

"Ah, I see," said Mr. MacMillan, looking at Raj thoughtfully. For an instant, Neena thought that his soft brown eyes clouded slightly but then they immediately brightened again. "I am not in the least bit offended, my dear. In fact, I think that is perfectly reasonable and I commend your friends' good sense." He gave Raj a small approving nod.

"Yes, Raj, you are absolutely correct. I am able to hire any number of nurses, therapists, and caregivers. You see, I have always been a great supporter of all educational endeavors. When I see a young person who is enthusiastic, skilled, and kind," he inclined his head toward Neena, "I feel I should do my part to encourage such a person, one who is not only working toward a goal but is also trying to pay their way. To be perfectly honest, I hoped that a position in my home would be a little less onerous for Neena, and better paying," he said, looking at both of them in turn.

"I see," said Raj, looking more convinced. His face and shoulders lost their rigidity and he once again relaxed against the comfortable cushions.

"That is very kind and generous of you, sir," said Neena.

"Not at all," said Mr. MacMillan. "Like I said, you are doing me a great service. The last nurse's aide was a perfect dragon," he added with feeling.

"Her name wasn't Marge by any chance, was it?" Neena asked, as she and Raj exchanged a conspiratorial smile.

A light tap at the door was followed by the appearance of Patrick, now bearing a large tray upon which was a pitcher of lemonade, several tall chilled glasses, and a plate of cookies. Setting it down on the low wooden table between the two sofas he proceeded to fill the glasses and handed one to Neena and then to Raj.

"Neena, Raj, please help yourselves to a cookie. Or, as my Scottish cook would say, a biscuit. Her shortbread is quite delicious."

Raj and Neena, who had been sipping their lemonades, now both politely reached forward to take a cookie from the plate. Neena enjoyed the buttery goodness of the cookie which was complemented by the sweet, cold lemonade.

"I brought you something warm to drink," said Patrick to Mr. MacMillian. Mr. MacMillan, however, was looking hopefully at a glass-topped table behind the sofa filled with cut crystal decanters and bottles.

"Now you know that is against doctor's orders, Mac," Patrick said reprovingly.

"I know, I know," said Mr. MacMillan with a small sigh.

"But," Patrick went on, "Dottie has made you a nice cup of warm milk with a little sugar and cardamom." He handed Mr. MacMillan a cup from the tray.

With another sigh Mr. MacMillan resignedly accepted the large white ceramic mug and said, "Thank you, Patrick."

He cupped his hands around the warmth of the mug and took a sip. "Mmm, that's very nice. Please thank Dottie for me." He took another sip and turned to Neena and Raj. "She has been experimenting with various spices. I do love the scent of cardamom."

Raj nodded in agreement. "Yes, my mother makes the most delicious cup of chai with cardamom and other spices," he said wistfully.

"I know how to make chai," Neena said. "I will make you some the next time you visit," she offered.

After only a few sips Mr. MacMillan placed the almost-full cup of milk back on the saucer.

"I believe I've had enough," he said to Neena, and there was a fine tremor in his hand as he handed it to her. She took it from him, careful not to spill the remaining milk on the expensive-looking oriental carpet.

Ha, she thought, *then I'd literally be crying over spilt milk.* When she looked back at Mr. MacMillan, he was leaning back against the pillows with his hands clasped in front of him. His eyes were slightly hooded and the laugh lines around his mouth had tightened.

Neena, who was feeling quite refreshed after her snack, quickly put her empty glass down, wiped her fingers on a napkin, and tucked a wayward black curl behind her ear.

"Are you in pain Mr. MacMillan? Can I get you some medication?" Neena asked. Then, before he could answer, she decided for him. "I think that would be a good idea before we change your dressings, don't you?" She looked inquiringly at Patrick.

"I'll be right back," said Patrick and walked toward a door along the far wall.

"Now, Mr. MacMillan," Neena said, sitting up straight and using her most businesslike tone. "Where do you keep your medical supplies? Would you like me to do this evening's dressing change here?"

Mr. MacMillan gave a little shake of his head as if clearing away the cobwebs of discomfort. He looked at her, his brown eyes again alert, and with a smile said, "The first thing I'd like you to do is to call me Mac. Being called mister and sir makes me feel a hundred years old."

"Um, okay," said Neena, feeling slightly uncomfortable at using such an informal mode of address to an older gentleman. He was not old, per se, she thought, but he was much older than she, and Neena was used to using respectful titles for older adults. She couldn't very well call him "uncle" as she did older Indian males though, could she?

"The supplies are in my study which is in the adjoining room," Mr. Mac-Millan pointed in the direction Patrick had gone. There was a discrete door on the wall behind him which blended into the wood paneling. "You will find a cart in there that should have everything. If you need anything else, please let Patrick know and he can get it for you."

Neena stood and suddenly Raj also jumped to his feet.

"I will help you," he said and they both started toward the back of the room. With his long strides he was already at the door and opened it for her.

"Thanks," said Neena. This large corner room had sweeping views of the back and side lawns. A row of tall evergreen trees along the side of the property blocked the rays of the setting sun and had already started to throw elongated shadows across the lawn. As a result, the study felt relatively cooler than the morning room. Tucking a few more of her stray curls into her ribbon Neena looked around the room. Tall windows were flanked by royal blue velvet drapes, edged with gold trim. They were held open by decorative wooden holdbacks whose intricately carved *fleur-de-lis* blended seamlessly into the carved wooden chair rail that bordered the room. The room was very masculine with dark wood floor-to-ceiling paneling and a large mahogany desk. A computer monitor and keyboard were placed on one corner of the desk. Although the twenty-first century was less than a decade away, Neena didn't know of many people who owned their own computers and she looked at it with the wariness which she felt toward all strange machines. The only incongruous note in the otherwise elegant room, was the seemingly haphazard stacks of documents, periodicals, and computer paper which covered the desk, some of them tilting quite precariously. Neena raised her eyebrows in surprise. Everything she had seen so far of the house was very neat and meticulously maintained. Patrick, who had turned away from a corner table, was holding a small bottle of pills. He shrugged at Neena's reaction to the mess and shook his head.

"Yes, my fingers practically itch to put things in order but Mac absolutely forbids anyone to touch anything on his desk. Surprisingly, he is usually able to find exactly what he's looking for in an instant. I really don't know how he does it. Anyway," he said, "I'll give him his pain medication while you get your supplies together." He indicated a gleaming metal cart.

Neena immediately did a quick survey of the supplies and was pleased to see that there was every size and shape of gauze, as well as neatly arranged bottles of sterile water, hydrogen peroxide, and betadine. There was a metal tray lined with a folded sterile drape upon which tweezers and scissors were neatly arranged. And, to Neena's amusement, there was plenty of tape!

"We can use this to carry the supplies," said Raj, holding up a small white basket.

They selected all the items they thought would be needed and soon the basket was overflowing.

"Here," she said, "let me take those boxes." She reached for the pile of cardboard boxes containing gauze of various sizes and shapes. "And you can take the rest of the supplies."

"Whatever you wish, madam," said Raj with a flash of his white teeth. He gave her a small salute, picked up the tray and headed toward the door. *My, he is getting comfortable*, thought Neena, surprised at his cheeky comment. Neena picked up the cardboard boxes and followed him. As she passed Mac's desk her elbow inadvertently grazed a stack of newspapers. The uneven tower cascaded off the desk and landed with a clink on the floor. Startled, Neena turned suddenly and all of the boxes of gauze flew out of her grasp. She muttered an oath and looked around in exasperation.

Neena quickly gathered the boxes and placed them on the seat of a nearby leather club chair. Luckily, the newspapers had fanned out as they fell and their order was easily discernible. She squatted down and gathered them together into a neat pile, moving with duck-like steps around the corner of the desk. As she picked up the last folded newspaper, she noticed a silver-framed photo underneath. As Neena straightened to replace it on the desk, she paused as a vaguely familiar face looked up at her from the photo. A pretty young woman with blond hair was holding a young child's hand and laughing down at him. A breeze had sent long tendrils of the woman's hair flying behind her and the curls of the tow-headed boy were also ruffled. The child's softly rounded cheeks suggested that toddlerhood had not long passed. The sun shone off their golden heads and the photographer had captured them mid-skip on a grassy path. The little boy was not looking at his mother, as Neena presumed the woman to be, but was looking straight into the camera with a mischievous smile that brought a sparkle to his bright blue eyes. That smile and those eyes were strangely familiar.

As Neena stared at the photo her vivid imagination slowly morphed the image of the little boy into an older, taller version, with a lean jaw replacing the gently curving baby cheeks. When her mind's eye added the piercing blue eyes and the infectious grin to the image she gasped in surprise. This child looked exactly like a younger version of Duncan Goodwin! Those eyes and that smile were quite distinctive. Could this be a photo of Mr. MacMillan's son and wife? And, if so, why was Duncan's last name Goodwin and not MacMillan? But, if Neena remembered his chart correctly, Mr. MacMillan's social history and family history had stated he was unmarried with no children. And, he had never mentioned a wife or children. There was a strong resemblance between the woman and the child but Mr. MacMillan's features were not reflected in the little boy's face. Neena carefully replaced the photo frame in a small space she had cleared on the desk, and with a thoughtful expression gathered her supplies and returned to the sitting room.

Neena, with Raj's assistance, made quick work of Mr. MacMillan's dressing change. Raj positioned himself next to Neena and handed her the items she needed in a quick and accurate manner. Neena kept up a steady stream of chatter as she worked, glancing frequently at Mr. MacMillan to determine if he was in pain. She noticed that Mr. MacMillan's gaze was mostly fixed on a point above her right shoulder, though at times his eyes were closed. She gave a gentle pat to the final piece of tape and straightened.

"All done, Mr. MacMillan," she said

"Mac," he corrected, looking at her with a gentle smile.

"Mac," she said, rather awkwardly. He laughed at her discomfiture. "You'll get used to it in time." *I don't know about that*, Neena thought to herself, but returned his smile. "Get some rest, mister—um, I mean, Mac. I will see you on Saturday."

"Thank you, Neena. Yes, see you then. Raj, it was very nice meeting you. It was good of you to accompany Neena."

"It was my pleasure, Mr. MacMillan," said Raj. "I wish you all the best." He gave a small nod of his head. At the door, Neena glanced back at Mr. MacMillan and found that he was gazing intently at them. She gave him a final wave before pulling the door closed.

As Neena pulled out onto the gravel drive she looked in her rearview mirror for a final glimpse of the stately mansion which now glowed a soft pink in the setting sun. It had certainly been an interesting experience, she thought. She was grateful for Mr. MacMillan's (she could not yet think of him as Mac) generosity and kindness in employing her. Although she would miss her clients in the nursing home, this position with Mr. MacMillan did mean less work for a higher wage, which would give her more time to study. The drive back was accomplished in complete silence as both Neena and Raj were engrossed in their thoughts. She dropped Raj off at his home and was soon back in her own cozy little apartment. She changed quickly and shook out the clothes she had just discarded. Raj's handkerchief fell out of one of the pockets and floated to the ground. She would have to launder it before giving it back to him, she thought as she picked it up from the floor. Neena puzzled over a row of tiny embroidered letters in one corner, R.M.M. She squinted myopically at it for a few seconds, then with a flick of her hand she tossed the handkerchief into her laundry basket and flung herself into bed. A little white paw emerged from the quilt and Idli meowed reproachfully. "Oh, I'm so sorry, Idli," Neena cooed. "Go back to sleep baby-cat." She curled around the small, soft bundle, dropped a quick kiss onto the little furry head, and promptly fell asleep.

Friday July 10, 1992

Chapter 15

The next morning, Neena, shrugging into her white coat, walked quickly into the lobby of LCH. She smiled at the volunteers sitting behind the polished information desk.

"Good morning," they chorused when they saw her. Today there were only two of them. Miss Helen in a pale pink pinafore and the aptly named Miss Lavinia in a pale lavender one. Neena could not remember the name of the other member of their trio.

"Good morning," said Neena as she hurried to The Coffee Corner for a much-needed dose of fluid and caffeine. Due to an unforeseen delay in her morning routine Neena had not had time to prepare her usual cup of tea. Upon returning from her shower Neena had found her basket of hair ribbons, which she usually kept on top of her high dresser, scattered all over the floor in a riotous profusion of color. Sitting on the bed, far removed from the colorful chaos, was Idli.

"Oh, Idli-cat! What have you done?" Neena cried as she quickly gathered the tangled mess of ribbons and thrust them into the basket. No answer was forthcoming but Idli, her little chin at an arrogant tilt, calmly turned limpid blue eyes at Neena and looked for all the world as if she had not moved an inch. Unfortunately for Miss Idli's defense there were multiple strands of ribbons entwined tightly around her little paw. Neena's annoyance was tempered by amusement at Idli's haughtiness and determination not to look at the state of her paws. Clicking her tongue, Neena set about the delicate task of unraveling the ribbons which were ensnared in Idli's tiny, sharp nails. Once she was successfully extricated, Idli jumped gracefully to the ground and headed purposefully toward the kitchen and her breakfast. Neena glanced at her bedside clock. "Shoot!" she muttered and raced to get ready.

Neena now hurried to join the surprisingly short line at The Coffee Corner and she soon had a steaming cup of the rich fragrant brew with generous dollops of cream and sugar. As she headed through the lobby toward the elevator, Neena stopped and quickly ducked behind a stand of brochures. Ron was barreling straight toward her! She knew he would be furious if he caught her loitering in the lobby drinking coffee. When she took a cautious peep from her hiding spot, she saw Ron angrily wrenching open the door to the stairwell. Once he had plunged through the doorway she walked as quickly as she could to the elevators, being careful not to slosh her hot drink.

Once on the fourth floor, Neena took a few last gulps of her coffee before tossing it into the waste bin. She retrieved her box of tape from the residents' lounge and quickly restocked it. She then climbed two additional flights of stairs to meet her team on the surgical wing as usual. At the door to the sixth floor, Neena hugged the large unwieldy box to her chest with one hand, balanced it on a raised knee, and fumbled for the door knob. Just as she managed to maneuver through the door, she collided with a firm, yet yielding surface. Neena let out a squeak of alarm as the box started to tip away from her. However, she immediately found herself steadied by a gloved hand which firmly grasped one of her upper arms while a second hand stabilized the box. Above the box she met a pair of startled eyes, partially hidden under a thick fringe of blond hair.

"Whoa, there!" said Duncan, as he took the box from her.

"So, sorry!" said Neena. "Thanks, Dunk. This box is so big I can barely see over it." She rubbed her upper arm where Dunk had grabbed her in a vice-like grip.

"Aren't you a little late?" he asked, returning the box to her. *So much for chivalry*, Neena thought. Dunk flipped the hair out of his eyes and arched one bleach-blond eyebrow at her. His bright blue eyes gleamed sardonically. Neena suddenly decided that she disliked Dunk's facial expressions and manner of speaking. In a way, she preferred Ron's straightforward anger—unpleasant though it was—to Dunk's mocking tone. At least when Ron was sneering, glaring, or bellowing, one knew exactly which emotion he was conveying. Neena, whose face and nature were an open book, found Duncan's hooded eyes unsettling. He leaned casually against the wall and proceeded to remove his gloves. He rolled one into the other and with a lazy flick of his wrist tossed the bundle neatly into a nearby receptacle. *It was a slam dunk*, she thought, and stifled a giggle.

"What's so funny?" he asked, his tone suddenly sharp. Neena was a little startled at hearing him speak in anything other than his usual lazy drawl.

"Oh, nothing," she said quickly. "The way you tossed your gloves into the bin. It was a slam dunk," Neena explained. "And your name being Dunk, it just seemed funny."

"Dunk, yes," he said, his characteristic smile back in place and waved a languid hand indicating she should precede him. Neena took a firmer grip on her box and marched down the hallway toward the nurses' station. She was glad to note that she must not be too late since Ron was himself just joining the group. She was relieved not to have been greeted by Ron's impatiently tapping foot and his all-too-familiar sneering greeting of, "Nice of you to join us."

Dunk raised an inquiring eyebrow at Ron, who looked away and began organizing his papers.

Suddenly, Victoria was standing next to Neena. "What were you two doing?" she asked in her frostiest tone, her pale blue eyes practically glacial. *Yikes*, thought Neena. *She looks like she could turn me into an ice sculpture.*

"I was getting my box," said Neena, dropping said box onto the floor and shaking out her tired arms. "What did you think?" She suddenly turned a shocked gaze on Victoria when she realized the import of Victoria's question. Did Victoria think that Neena had added herself to the list of rivals for Dunk's affections? Did she think that Neena and Dunk had just had a private tete-a-tete? *Ugh*, she thought, with a mental shudder. Not only was Duncan not her type but she would never want to be around someone so sarcastic, snarky, and smart-mouthed. Thinking of Duncan's mocking tone she suddenly heard a sly, taunting voice in her head. "Whaddya do?" it said. "Kiss a white boy?" This was followed by peals of laughter from a group of middle school boys. She had been twelve at the time and during the last class of the day their teacher had offered everyone a box of powdered donuts as a treat. Neena remembered hastily wiping the powder from her lips and even now cringed at the embarrassment of that long-ago incident.

Pushing her unwelcome and unbidden memory aside she smiled sweetly at Victoria and whispered, "Don't worry, Vicky, he's not my type." Victoria turned away in a huff, her dirty-blond ponytail swinging around to hit Neena in the face. Neena, batting the hair off her cheek, added, "Anyway, Dunk was with a patient." Ron, who's hearing must have been acute, looked up at this and then straightened as Mike strode quickly toward them.

"Let's get started," said Mike as he faced his team and handed out the day's patient lists. Neena noted with dismay that the pristine white sheets had dozens of small black squares of action items just waiting to be ticked off. *More scut*, she thought resignedly, and suppressed a sigh as she reached out to take her copy. She added the sheets to those on her clipboard, placed it on top of the box, then heaved everything into her arms. As usual, she was the last duckling in line and she hurried to catch up with her classmates, all of whom seemed to be squawking animatedly.

Their morning rounds were completed quickly and efficiently as the

A PRE-MED(ITATED) MURDER

junior members of the team were now familiar with the routines. The students and residents once again gathered around Mike at the nurses' station, awaiting his further instructions and the arrival of Dr. Silverman. Marge's large untidy head suddenly loomed up behind Mike, causing Neena and several of the students to hastily take a few steps back. A meaty hand tapped Mike's shoulder and he turned around. Although Mike was a tall man, Marge still managed to look down her bulbous nose at him. Neena was impressed that Mike did not at all seem perturbed by the towering, glowering form of Nurse Marge.

"Good morning, Marge," said Mike, with a smile that softened Marge's austere features. Her other hand clutched the phone, which she now shook under Mike's nose.

"You have a phone call, Dr. Windsor."

"Thank you, Marge," he said as he pulled the receiver to his ear. "Yes, sir. We will see you then, sir. Thank you, sir." Neena surmised from the number of "sirs" that Mike was talking to an Attending.

"That was Dr. Silverman," Mike confirmed, as he turned back to the team. "He is not doing rounds this morning but will be here a little later as we do not have any surgeries scheduled this morning. He requested that we be ready with all patient results before that time." Mike ran his pen quickly down his list of things to do. "So, here's what we're going to do, team. We will head down to the radiology room now to review all the films from last night rather than waiting until Dr. Silverman arrives. All right, let's go!" He strode briskly toward the stairwell and pulled the door open. Neena quickly set her tape box down, and tucking it under one of the counters, she hurried to join her teammates. Mike, holding the door open, gestured for the team to precede him.

"You three," he pointed at Victoria, Neena, and Calvin, who happened to be standing at the front of the group. "Head down first and pull all the jackets we will need to review." They nodded and clattered down the stairwell at high speed, which was the only speed acceptable for the surgery team. Neena started to feel a little dizzy after she rounded the landing of the second floor. With Victoria close on her heels, she felt the need to jump the last two steps of each flight of stairs just to prevent the other girl from stepping on her. *Two more floors*, she thought as she clutched her clipboard tightly under one arm and ran her other hand lightly along the handrail to keep her balance.

As they approached the basement door, which led to the reading room, they heard a muffled scream and then a large crash. They ran into the hallway and Neena came to an abrupt halt, causing Victoria to run into her and Calvin to collide with Victoria.

"Oh my god!" said Neena softly.

There was another thin scream, followed by a thud. Neena turned back to find student-doctor Victoria Cabot in a dead faint on the scuffed tiled basement floor. In fact, there were several bodies sprawled on the floor before them. To the left was the crumpled form of one of the elderly volunteers, and Neena recognized her as the one who had been missing from the lobby this morning. Her lemon-colored pinafore and soft white curls made her look like a discarded daffodil. The metal cart which she had been pushing had been upset and piles of mail and inter-hospital manila folders were strewn about her. To the right, Neena registered splashes of red, a filmy red silk blouse, a hand with bright red painted chipped nails, and smudges of red on the floor near the body. The face of the woman was swollen and suffused with a purplish-red hue. She would have been unrecognizable except Neena had seen those nails before. She gazed in horror at the very dead-appearing Linda.

"What's going on?" Mike's voice was sharp, as he pushed through the crowd of stupefied medical students. Stepping over Victoria and pushing Neena against the wall Mike took in the scene before him.

"Calvin! Call the operator and announce a code blue, basement, radiology wing," he said, quickly falling on his knees next to the elderly volunteer.

"Ron, Raj, Neena, and Bill over there." He pointed to the young woman with one hand while his other hand was searching for a pulse along the elderly woman's neck.

"Neel, Duncan, and Joe, you're here with me," he said as he rapidly took out his stethoscope and inserted the earpieces.

The students were jolted from their stupors and rushed to do as they had been bid. Ron was already on the floor near Linda's head, his hand searching for her jugular pulse. Neena, who had crouched down beside the body, saw that on the front of the neck there was a thin, almost surgical-looking laceration. Small crimson droplets dotted the pallid whiteness of the skin.

"Start CPR!" Ron barked at Neena. She quickly positioned herself over Linda's body with the base of her right hand over the mid-sternum and her left hand clasped over her right. Elbows tightly locked and leaning over so that all her weight would be concentrated over her outstretched arms, she started pressing down while counting out loud.

"One, and two, and three, and four, and five and—" said Neena in the sing-song manner she had practiced during her ALS course. She caught a tiny spark of light out of the corner of her eye and looked up from her labors. She watched as Ron, penlight in hand, lifted Linda's eyelids to check her pupillary reflexes.

Suddenly, a beet-red countenance, alarming due to its beast-like unibrow and blazing dark eyes, was inches from her face.

"Are you taking a break?" Ron roared at her, the veins on either side of his face bulging.

Neena hastily resumed. "Six and seven and eight and—" She paused when she had counted to fifteen and sat back on her heels. She only now noticed Raj, who was squatting behind Linda's head, holding an ambu-bag with a mask. As soon as she stopped compressions he immediately placed three fingers of his left hand around Linda's jaw and gently, yet firmly, lifted her chin up to straighten her airway as much as possible. He then curved his other two fingers around the mask he placed over her nose and mouth, holding it in a tight seal. With his right hand he slowly and surely compressed the bag.

"One . . ." he said, his eyes fixed on Linda's chest. As her chest rose and fell with the first breath he pressed the bag again. "And two." Raj removed the mask and sat back on his haunches.

Neena, again with hands clasped and elbows locked, was ready, and looked toward Ron, who was once more checking for a pulse. He shook his head and nodded brusquely at Neena to resume compressions.

"One and two and, three and, four and, five and—" she continued counting.

After she had done three rounds of compressions there were beads of sweat on her forehead and she was relieved when Bill, a fourth-year student, tapped her on the shoulder to indicate he would take her place while Raj forced two more slow, measured breaths into the limp body. By this time, someone had found a crash cart and Ron was placing the defibrillator on the floor next to the patient. With one quick jerk, he ripped the shirt off of Linda, exposing a lacy black bra. Then Ron whipped out his red-handled trauma shears and ruthlessly cut through the center of the bra, allowing Linda's alabaster white breasts to fall to either side. That bra, sexy and alluring, should have been ripped off in a moment of passion, thought Neena, as tears pricked her eyelids. Now, it was only an impediment for the defibrillator. Neena quickly blinked back tears as she watched Ron pull out the wires and briskly slapped electrodes onto Linda's chest. Neena heard the sound of feet pounding down the stairwell getting louder and suddenly one of the ER Attendings stood breathless in the doorway. Ron looked up and gave a rapid and succinct history.

"Female, mid-twenties, found unconscious, with obvious injury to the neck, possible strangulation. No pulse, CPR was started, four rounds so far." While he was speaking he placed both paddles in position on the patient's chest.

"Clear!" he bellowed, and everyone stepped away. Neena watched as Linda's body convulsed and then settled back to the floor with frightening flaccidity.

Ron, Raj, Bill, and Neena continued their efforts to resuscitate Linda, with the Attending now running the code. Mike and the rest of the team had easily resuscitated Miss Yellow Pinafore from her faint and sent her on to the ER for observation. Now they also crowded into the room and Neena moved to one side as another one of her classmates took over the compressions. There was an unnatural silence in the room, punctuated only by the noise of the code. Each sound fell on Neena's ears with the painful intensity of a hammer hitting an exposed nerve. As if on a loop, she heard the Attending calling out an order, the monotonous counting of "one and, two and, three and—" and the soft whoosh of the ambu-bag. Then there was the whine of the defibrillator charging, the urgent call to "clear!" followed by the soft thud of Linda's body falling back to the floor again and again. Finally, after what seemed like an eternity, the Attending glanced at the clock on the wall and ordered the team to stop its efforts. In a flat voice he pronounced, "Time of death 7:28." Then he turned and left the room as quickly as he had entered it. Now there was utter silence in the room and the team listened to the receding sound of the Attending running back up the stairs until the stairwell door slammed shut. Neena sat frozen on the ground near the dead girl.

Mike was in the process of standing up when suddenly his arm shot out and he took hold of Neel's hand, which was poised above the ET tube, apparently about to pull it out.

"No! Leave it in," he cautioned. "Everything is to be left in place."

Neel hastily withdrew his hand. "Sorry, I didn't know," he said, with a miserable glance at the still form before them.

Mike straightened, brushed off the knees of his trousers and turned to the team, a grim look on his face.

"Back to work, everyone."

Ron picked up his penlight and stethoscope, stuffed them back into the right-side pocket of his lab coat and straightened. Then he suddenly stooped down again and rapidly, almost furtively, scooped up a few alcohol pads, tongue depressors and a pen. His beefy fist was closed tightly over the items. Again, Neena noted a small glint of light. She watched as he shoved the lot into his left-side pocket, fumbling with a bit of chain that was wrapped around the chewed up cap of his pen. When Neena looked up she found Ron's intense dark eyes fixed on her face. His thick black eyebrows underlined the deep grooves that scored his scowling forehead. After a few frightening seconds she dropped her eyes and focused on his thick neck instead, unable to bear the intensity of his gaze. He jerked his thumb toward the door and grunted at his team to follow Mike.

Dunk, who had been leaning against the door frame in his habitual slouch, was the first to respond. He straightened and looked around at the students, each of whom appeared to be rooted in place.

"You heard him, come on, let's go!" he said, and clapped his hands loudly, startling them out of their reveries. Bill, Joe, and Neel obediently followed Duncan out of the room without even a backward glance. Neena noted that Victoria, whom no one had bothered to assess or assist, had wakened from her faint and was now in a sitting position. She watched numbly as the other girl staggered to her feet and gave an irritated "Hmph!" Glaring at her retreating teammates Victoria walked slowly toward the stairwell.

Raj gently put down the ambu-bag he was still holding, careful not to dislodge it from the ET tube, and stood up as well. "Neena," he said, extending an arm down to her. She was staring at Linda's frozen white countenance. As she averted her eyes, she noticed that an open tube of cherry-red lipstick had rolled under the desk. The image of Linda vainly painting her lips for what, unbeknownst to her, would be the last time, made Neena's stomach churn. After Ron's initial quick summary to the Attending no one had spoken again of the mechanism of injury. The surgical team had encountered countless patients who were victims of accidental and non-accidental injuries. And, they had witnessed numerous deaths in the OR, the SICU (Surgical ICU) and the wards. But MURDER? Victims of murder usually did not need the services of a surgeon, thought Neena. Who could have done this? She was filled with revulsion, pity, and fear for what she had just witnessed.

"What? Oh, yes," she said slowly. She took his hand and allowed him to pull her to her feet. When their hands unclasped there were red stains on both of their palms.

"Where did that blood come from?" Raj asked sharply.

Neena's eyes flew to the dead girl's neck. The thin line of dripping crimson beads had now darkened into a macabre henna-like pattern.

"That can't be blood. Maybe it's lipstick?" she said, and indicated Linda's gray-white face, against which the peri-oral streaks of bright red gave her the ghastly appearance of a clown bleeding from the mouth.

"Look, you have something red on the side of your coat as well." Raj said, pointing. Neena looked down at the red smudges on her once-pristine white coat.

"Where . . ." she trailed off as she looked down at the floor where she had been sitting. There were multiple linear and circular smudges of lipstick on the gray-blue linoleum floor near the body. Had Linda still been holding the lipstick as she fell to the floor? Were those marks made as her arms thrashed during the final moments of her life? As Neena continued to stare at the floor, vague shapes started to emerge. Directly beneath where she had been sitting were the blurred yet identifiable shapes of two letters written, not in blood, but in crimson lipstick. They read: "D R".

Chapter 16

It was a somber group which assembled at the nurses' station awaiting Dr. Silverman's arrival. Neena's teammates were either sagging against the counter or slumped in one of the rolling chairs. However, the brisk click of Dr. Silverman's stride brought everyone to attention.

"Hello everyone," said Dr. Silverman, his voice quiet and serious. "I've been apprised of the incident this morning." He nodded slightly in Mike's direction.

"Although we see the face of death on a regular basis in our jobs, stumbling onto a crime scene is something altogether different. I commend all of you on the presence of mind you all demonstrated and your valiant attempt at resuscitation." His gaze moved around each of the faces surrounding him.

"Thank you, sir," said Mike, as the rest of the team simply nodded.

"Mike has just spoken with the detective in charge of this investigation and each of you is requested to meet with him in turn so that you can make your official statements."

"Yes," said Mike. "The detective is in the resident's lounge and will be meeting with you all individually. He asked that for the time being you not speak amongst yourselves regarding this tragic incident." He inclined his head toward the hallway where a uniformed policeman had suddenly appeared. "This officer will take down everyone's information and keep you company while you wait."

At this, Neena's eyes widened in alarm and her heart started to race. What was going on here? Were they all being treated as suspects? Then she slowly let out the breath she had been holding when she realized that there was no possibility of any of them being involved in the murder. After all, they had all come upon the dead woman at the same time, hadn't they?

The officer approached the edge of the group with a clipboard. He handed it to Calvin who peeled himself off of the wall and took it with as much reluctance as Neena felt. His pen raced rapidly across the page and he passed it quickly to the next person. The clip board was passed along from person to person like a hot potato. When it was Neena's turn she looked at the neat columns and filled in her name, address, phone number, and position at the hospital. She signed her name in the last column and shoved the clipboard at Neel. She felt the sudden desire to wipe her fingers on her coat as if she was somehow tainted by the implications of filling out that form. Once all of them had filled in their data, the officer quickly scanned the list of names.

He looked up and pointed at Victoria, who happened to be the first person his gaze alighted upon.

"You!" he boomed, causing Victoria to squeak in alarm. "Who are you?"

Neena was grudgingly impressed to see that Victoria, even in times of stress, remained true to herself.

"I am student-doctor Victoria Cabot, of the Boston Cabots," she said.

He arched a bushy eyebrow at her in disgust. "I don't care if you're from the Boston Red Sox," he proclaimed dismissively. Neena heard a few suppressed snorts emanating around her and had some difficulty herself in holding back the giggle that bubbled to her lips.

"Detective's waiting for you. He wants to see the students first and work his way up to the senior-most of you. The rest of you stay put until your name's called." Neena and her team exchanged worried glances but the small moment of hilarity had certainly helped, if ever so slightly, to lighten the mood.

Within a surprisingly short amount of time Victoria strode jauntily back to the nurses' station. Her nose was firmly back up in the air and her face wore the usual haughty sneer.

"Wow, that was fast!" Neena blurted out before she could stop herself. It had not taken Neena long to realize that to initiate any conversation with the other girl only resulted in a frustrating, if not demeaning, encounter.

Victoria looked down the long length of her nose at the group.

"Of course. My background is irreproachable and there was nothing whatsoever that I could contribute to the investigation," she informed them with a smug smile. As she passed by Duncan, Neena saw her give him an almost imperceptible shake of her head and a confidential pat on the arm. She saw Duncan's eyebrow lift inquiringly. Neena wondered what Victoria was trying to tell Duncan. Had Victoria withheld her knowledge of Duncan and Linda's relationship from the police? Perhaps Duncan did not know that Victoria had seen him cozying up to Linda in the cafeteria a few days ago.

Neena was the next one to be called upon. She wondered if, since she and Victoria were the only women in the group, the officer was adhering to the gallant tenet "women and children first." *Well, better to get it over with sooner than later*, she thought to herself.

Her tentative knock on the door was immediately answered by a brisk male voice and she promptly entered the room.

"Come in!" he said again, and waved her into the room.

A man was seated behind the small, gray metal desk which was reserved for the use of the senior residents.

"Take a seat," he said, indicating the chair opposite him. Neena found that her fear and hesitancy had immediately been replaced by irrepressible curiosity. Her only prior knowledge of detectives came from the pages of her mystery novels. Neena had expected to see a middle-aged, crusty (whatever that meant), cigar-smoking, ill-groomed man wearing wrinkled trousers and a trench coat. She was completely taken aback by the vision, yes vision, sitting in front of her. No wonder Victoria had emerged so jauntily from her interview with the detective. Neena had felt that Victoria always operated on the assumption that all men were subject to her beauty, charm, and money. Neena was willing to give Victoria a point for her wealth but absolutely nothing else.

Neena, who had always been fascinated by beauty in all its forms, stared at the man in front of her. His face had the symmetry of a Grecian sculpture. His black hair shone, as if he was wearing a cap, above the perfect rectangle of his very intelligent-appearing brow. Although his intense dark brown eyes were framed by a fringe of impossibly long dark lashes, his every pore oozed masculinity. The chiseled lines of his jaw bracketed a pair of firm yet sensuous lips.

"Ahem," said the sculpture, and Neena tore her gaze away from his lips, feeling a rush of embarrassment warming her cheeks.

"Oh, hi, um sorry, yes, Detective?" she stammered, pressing her cold hands to her flushed face.

"No need to apologize, Miss, um," he glanced down at the form she and her team had filled out. "Neena Sundar? I know you've been through a traumatic experience." His dark eyes looked sympathetically at her and she felt her face grow warm again. He was already making this interview incredibly difficult. He was not only beautiful but he was nice too? How was she ever going to utter a coherent sentence?

"My name is Detective Brian Flannigan and I'm from the county police station since Littlefield is, uh, too little for its own police force," he said, smiling at his own joke.

Neena gave a small nervous laugh. She took a few deep breaths, sternly ordered her frivolous mind to behave and tried to gather her wits.

"I understand that as a third-year medical student this is your second week of clinical rotations?" Neena nodded in agreement.

"And, prior to beginning your surgical rotation, had you ever visited

LCH?" he asked, picking up his pen and hovering over the yellow-lined pad in front of him. Neena shook her head in denial and watched his pen scratch across the surface of the pad.

"Had you ever met the victim prior to today?" Neena started to shake her head but stopped herself.

"I've never met her, but I did see her in the hospital last week," she said, pleased to find that she had formed an intelligible sentence and that her voice was steady.

"I see," said Detective Flannigan. "Can you tell me where you saw her?"

"I was leaving the radiology reading room, which is in the basement, and rather than use the elevator I thought I'd use the stairwell at the end of the hall. As I passed by, I saw Linda sitting at her desk in her office."

The detective's head snapped up. "How do you know her name?" he asked sharply, lifting his pen.

"I, um, she was talking to someone and I heard her referred to as Linda," Neena said, starting to feel a tingle of fear at the base of her spine.

"So, she was talking to someone in her office then, not on the phone?" he asked quickly. Neena nodded and then shook her head. Her thoughts were all in a whirl. Now she had to tell him about Ron, she thought unhappily. Ron had looked so angry just at the suspicion that she had been in the stairwell at the time of his argument with Linda. What would happen if he found out that she had actually heard a significant amount of that heated conversation in Linda's office? And, even worse, that she had reported that fact to Detective Flannigan? Neena could feel the tingle of fear making its insidious way up her spine. Pretty soon it would reach the base of her neck and she knew that if it entered her brain that she would be struck dumb. An ember of panic now emerged and unfortunately acted as an accelerant.

"Miss Sundar?" said a voice. A hand reached across the table and gently shook her arm. "Are you okay?"

Neena felt the cloud of smoke clearing her vision and she blinked at the detective.

"What has frightened you?" he asked gently. "Whatever you know or think you know, it would be in everyone's best interest if you could tell me."

"I am afraid," she said in a small voice.

"Are you afraid of the person you saw speaking with Linda that day in her office?" Neena nodded miserably. "I can only help you, and help get justice for Linda, if I have all of the facts." He stood up and walked over to the water cooler in the corner of the room. He brought back a small plastic cup of water and pressed it into her hands.

"Take a sip," said the detective and Neena obediently did so. She would need much more than a few sips to quench the inferno of panic that had consumed her, but she knew he was right. Detective Flannigan returned to his chair and picked up his pen.

"Okay," he said gently. "Whenever you're ready." Two pairs of dark brown eyes regarded one another. Neena gathered her thoughts and once she opened her mouth the words came tumbling out. She told the detective about Ron's argument with Linda, Ron considering Neena with suspicion when he returned her badge, Duncan and Linda together at the nurses' station and then in the cafeteria. She described the anger she saw on Ron's face as he was watching Duncan and Linda. And finally, she reported seeing Duncan and Victoria in a passionate embrace and then finding Victoria also staring angrily at Duncan and Linda in the cafeteria.

"I don't know what's going on," Neena concluded. "I thought that they were all in a lover's triangle or quadrangle. But do you think Ron would commit murder over that? And he was the one who led Linda's code. He seemed genuinely upset and worked so hard to resuscitate her." She lifted her hands in a helpless gesture and let them fall back into her lap.

Detective Flannigan put down his pen. "People have killed for much less," he said. "And ambivalence can be terrifying." He stood up and came around to her side of the desk. "Thank you for trusting me with this information," he said. "I know this will be difficult but I urge you to go about your usual routines. I will make sure we have eyes on Dr. Roberts. I will be in touch if

I need anything else." Neena nodded silently. He had behaved in such an intelligent and sympathetic manner that she felt comforted by his words. As she exited the room, she allowed herself one last lingering glance at the handsome detective.

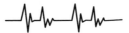

A pair of eyes watched her thoughtfully as she walked quickly down the hall. What did she know? Had she pieced together the seemingly disparate facts? This was a complication that could not be left to chance.

Chapter 17

Neena groaned with frustration and fatigue as she circled her car around the streets near her apartment for a third time. She finally located a spot several blocks away and began the complicated process of parking. When she was finished, her arms felt all jiggly and it took her a few minutes to roll up her window and get out of the car. Although she would usually feel nervous walking home in the dark, tonight she was too tired to feel any trepidation. Slinging her messenger bag across her body she trudged toward home.

What a day it had been! The twin shocks of finding a dead body coupled with the failed resuscitation attempt had been more than enough to process. After the unprecedented and traumatic start to the day she could not remember how the remainder of the day had passed. But somehow, she and her team had made it through. She was thankful that she was not part of the on-call team that evening and felt sorry for Joe and Calvin. The saving grace had been that even after only ten days on the job numerous aspects had already become rote. She had listened to hearts and lungs, prodded bellies, and examined surgical wounds. She dutifully documented her findings in the charts and noticed that already her notes were shorter and more concise. But not quite surgeon-esque, she decided, since they were still clearly legible.

And then there was the interview with Detective Flanigan. Neena felt her heart skip a beat each time she thought of it, and she did not think it was due to the vision of the beautiful detective's face. Had she really implicated Ron in Linda's death? Surely there was a reasonable explanation for his argument with Linda? What could that have been about? What connection could he have with a secretary in the hospital? Suddenly the image of Ron racing through the hospital lobby that morning sprang to her mind. At the time she had simply assumed Ron had been too impatient to wait for the elevator and had planned on climbing the stairs to the fourth floor. But she now remembered that that same stairwell also led down to the basement! Had Ron gone down the stairs rather than up them? Did he go to Linda's office? Perhaps they had had another argument and this time it had turned violent. Neena could only too easily imagine Ron strangling the slim young woman with his bare, beefy hands.

When Neena arrived at the nurses' station that morning for rounds, she had been relieved that Ron had not been waiting there, tapping his foot in annoyance and barking out his usual surly greeting. She had seen him arrive after her and Duncan. In the time it had taken Neena to retrieve her tape box and then take the stairs up two flights she would have thought that Ron would have already arrived at the nurses' station, especially given the speed with which she had seen him go barreling into the stairwell. There could be an innocent explanation for this, couldn't there? Perhaps he stopped to see a patient or went to the men's room. His late arrival didn't necessarily mean that he had been busy murdering Linda in the intervening time.

A shudder went through Neena's thin frame and she hoisted her messenger bag more securely over her chest. Her head bent and her thoughts in a muddle, she gasped as suddenly the lights in Patel's Pantry went off and she was plunged into the inky shadows cast by the awnings. She was still a few blocks from her apartment and decided to pick up her pace. Another block and she would be in the residential area where the homes all had bright porch lights and numerous street lamps illuminated the sidewalk.

Then, suddenly, Neena came to an utter standstill. Two images were seared in her brain, side by side. They reminded her of one of her beloved children's magazines, *Highlights*, which had kid-friendly articles and several pages of activities. Her favorite had been the one in which two seemingly identical pictures were on opposing pages but in fact one of them contained several changes to the scene. Sometimes a three-legged dog would be substituted for the typical canine in the other picture, or the American flag was spangled with fourteen stars rather than thirteen. She loved this activity and with her attention to detail she was usually able to spot each difference in record time. Now there were dueling images in her brain of Linda's body, before and after the resuscitation. She remembered the sparkle of light from Ron's hand. She had assumed that it had been his penlight both times. She saw the dark line encircling Linda's thin neck with dots of blood along the chain that was embedded in the bruised flesh, like garnets on a delicate strand of gold. But the second image at the end of the code showed Linda's neck beaded with blood but now with no necklace! *Aha!* she thought, and with great satisfaction Neena mentally circled this feature. Were there any other discrepancies in the two pictures? *Yes*, she thought. Not only was the chain missing but the gem that she had seen resting on Linda's chest in the cafeteria was also missing. Could that have been the source of the glimmer she saw in Ron's hand? Had Ron pocketed Linda's chain and diamond pendant? Was he simply an opportunistic thief or was there another reason he had taken the necklace?

She would think about it more later, she promised herself as a new wave of fatigue washed over her and the strap of her messenger bag chafed against her neck. The old blue bag was so laden with textbooks and notebooks that it felt heavier with each passing second. She reached up to move the strap away from her neck when, to her utter disbelief, it started to tighten! Neena automatically tried to pull down on the thick nylon strap around her neck but there was no relief in the tension. She reached higher up and felt a pair of hands pulling on the strap and encircling her neck. Panic started to grip her. *Oh my god, I'm being mugged! Is someone trying to steal my notes?* Doubling her efforts she gripped each of the hands with one of her own. The fingers were lean and strong, but the flesh felt unnaturally cool and smooth to her touch. She plucked frantically at the fingers but she was unable to find a purchase. She pulled harder and felt a snap like a rubber band. Was her assailant wearing surgical gloves? Under the inexorable pressure she tipped backward and her feet no longer touched the ground. As her breath caught in her throat and her vision became blurred, she thought to herself, *Haha, medical school is literally cut-throat.* But her final thoughts about her imminent demise were not ones of fear or sadness, but of indignation. How dare this happen to her when she had not yet become a doctor!

The strap that had tightened so rapidly now just as quickly slackened. Neena thought maybe she had already died, but then her knees and palms struck the cement and searing pain shot through her. *I thought there would be no pain after death*, she thought irritably, jarred out of her dream-like state. She heard thumps and thuds behind her and wondered hopefully if her assailant had also fallen. Then there was the sound of rapidly receding footsteps. She felt a pair of muscular arms gathering her up and turning her over. Now, bright lights were pricking at her eyelids and a voice harsh with fear was yelling in her ear. "Neena! Neena!" it called. A large hand supported her head and shoulders while another smaller hand gently loosened the top button of her blouse. The voice, now louder and more desperate, demanded again, "Neena, wake up!" She felt a light touch on the side of her face, and another voice, softer and higher, added its entreaties, "Neena beti, please answer me!"

When Neena opened her eyes, she found herself bathed in the glow of light filtering through the brightly colored awnings of Patel's Pantry. Two anxious faces hovered over her. A band of orange cut across Mr. Patel's face. With his dark bushy eyebrows squinched together and his even bushier mustache quivering he reminded Neena of a worried-looking tiger. The slighter form next to him, swathed in yards of pale green cotton, swayed gently in the breeze, like a delicate palm frond. Mrs. Patel's hand moved anxiously over Neena's person and her eyelashes fluttered as she blinked away tears.

"I'm okay," Neena tried to say, but only heard a faint croaking noise emanate from her mouth.

"Shh!" said Mrs. Patel. "Don't try to talk." She turned urgently to her husband. "Pick her up, Darshan."

"Shouldn't we call the police or an ambulance?" he asked, his black bushy eyebrows now tilting up in inquiry.

"Her pulse is strong," said Mrs. Patel, her cool fingers pressing lightly against Neena's wrist. "And we can't just let her lie on the pavement. Chalo, chalo," she urged.

"Hmph," said Mr. Patel as he hoisted Neena easily into his arms and stood up. The sudden movement caused her head to spin and she quickly let her eyelids close. Her neck was throbbing and her head pounded with each beat of her pulse. *At least I have a pulse*, she thought to herself. As a wave of fatigue washed over her, Neena reluctantly allowed herself to be carried away into a sea of darkness.

Chapter 18

Bright lights again pricked her eyelids and Neena tried to squeeze them shut but someone determinedly pulled them up to examine her pupils. Neena felt the prick of a needle in her arm. *I guess Mr. and Mrs. Patel called an ambulance after all*, she thought as her stomach lurched with the motion of the vehicle and the whine of the sirens caused her head to ache. It hurt to breathe and Neena felt a rising panic again.

"It's okay," said a firm, soothing voice. "You are okay." A mask was placed gently over her nose and mouth. Her breathing eased a bit and she dozed off and on during the ride to the hospital. She was jarred awake when the stretcher was placed on solid ground and there was a flurry of activity around her as soon as she was wheeled into the ER. Nurses, techs, residents, and medical students surrounded her but all their faces were unfamiliar. The intense attention overwhelmed her. She squeezed her eyelids shut to contain the tears that were welling up. However, one small tear slipped past and slowly trickled down her cheek. Neena felt the gentle touch of a tissue as someone wiped her face. She opened her eyes and found herself looking into Cecilia's big blue eyes, dark with worry.

"Hi, you," said Cecilia, holding Neena's hand.

"Hi, you," Neena whispered back.

Calvin was holding Neena's other hand and patting it nervously.

"You're awake," he said with a relieved sigh. His dark brown eyes were wide and his round cheeks looked like deflated balloons.

Cecilia's hands fluttered over her. She wiped one of Neena's cheeks and then the other. She straightened the sheets, checked the taping around the IV, and straightened the sheets again. Mike entered the bay. "Okay, you two," he nodded at Calvin and Cecilia. "Give me a few minutes to examine Neena," he said. Each of her friends stood up and reluctantly let go of her hands.

"I'll be right here if you need me," said Cecilia, before stepping away. Neena nodded and the corners of her lips turned up in a small smile. With a deft flick of his hand Mike closed the curtains around Neena's stretcher.

"Hi, Neena. I'm sure you didn't imagine yourself being on this side of the doctor-patient equation, did you?" he said with a kind smile. "If it's okay with you I will do a quick exam." Neena gave him a reluctant nod of assent. He went on, "As you know, we usually start with taking the patient's history first but I know it may be hard for you to speak right now. Besides, I did get some of the history from your friends, the Patels. And the detective is on his way to interview you anyway so it's best you save your voice for him. Let's start at the beginning, shall we?" he asked, taking out his pen light. His face looked grim as he examined her neck. Although his touch was gentle it still caused Neena to wince.

"I'm sorry, Neena," he said. "I know that must hurt. Can you open your mouth?" Neena obediently opened as wide as she could but that was painful as well. When he took out his stethoscope Neena noticed that he rubbed it briskly in his palm before placing it gently over Neena's chest. *I'll have to remember that little trick*, she said to herself. Mike's exam was quick yet methodical. Just as he was finishing up the curtains parted again and with a slight shock of surprise Neena recognized the Attending who had supervised

Linda's code earlier in the day.

"Dr. Levine," he said by way of introduction to Neena and then nodded at Mike who immediately launched into his presentation.

"The patient is Miss Neena Sundar, twenty-four years old, who was assaulted earlier this evening. She sustained injuries to her neck and was noted to have brief LOC (loss of consciousness) as per the couple who found her at the scene. Her exam now is within normal limits other than the obvious contusions to her neck. Her vitals are stable, CXR and EKG are negative and screening labs are normal. She has IV access and I've ordered maintenance fluids for now. I would recommend observation for another hour or so, after which she can be trialed on P.O. (per os, or oral intake) clears and then full liquids. If she tolerates P.O. and continues to remain stable then I believe she can be discharged." Neena found it amusing to hear Mike presenting her history and physical to the Attending in exactly the same manner that the students presented patients to him, although in a far more succinct and professional manner. *I will get there eventually*, Neena thought to herself.

Dr. Levine nodded at Mike and turned to Neena. Whipping out his stethoscope he did a quick yet comprehensive exam, flipped through her chart and then stared for a few minutes at the cardio-respiratory monitors she was attached to.

"You are a very lucky young woman," he said. "Everything looks fine but you'll have quite a nasty bruise on your neck for a while and your throat will be sore for a few days. I agree with Dr. Windsor. Just to be safe I'd like to keep you here for observation for a few hours. Sound good?" Neena inclined her head slightly. "Mike," he added, "there's a detective waiting outside. He can speak to her for a few minutes but don't let him exhaust her, she needs to rest."

"Yes, sir. I will keep an eye on her. After all, I need her back on my team as soon as possible." He smiled at Neena.

Being a patient in the hospital had given Neena a new perspective. She felt a new-found sympathy for the patients who had to endure endless questions and exams from a series of medical professionals, starting with the least experienced and, moving with excruciating slowness, to the Attending. In her case, however, her teammates had given her the professional courtesy of not subjecting her to their inept ministrations.

A nurse came in to place another pillow behind her back and helped her into a more upright position. Neena tried to rub the sleep from her eyes with the edge of her hospital gown. She heard the brisk tap of shoes approaching her bay. Then Detective Flannigan's soft melodic voice said, "Knock, knock," outside of her curtain. Neena hastily patted her curls down and bade him enter. As she looked again at his face, she realized with a smile to herself that often even the direst of situations could also have a silver lining.

Saturday July 11, 1992

Chapter 19

Neena gingerly laid back against the soft cushions of her sofa and closed her eyes. It was a relief to finally be home again. It had taken almost the entire day before she was discharged from the ER. Detective Flannigan's interrogation had taken a long time since she had had to speak slowly and in whispers. Although Mike had tried to hurry the detective along, Neena had been determined to complete the interview. Now she felt as if all of the muscles, tendons, and even the bones which were keeping her head firmly attached to her body, were aching and protesting. Had it really only been thirty seconds before Mr. Patel had come to her rescue? It had seemed more like thirty hours as each excruciating second had ticked by. She felt a dizzying sense of relief and gratitude as she thought, for the umpteenth time, of the miracle of simply being alive today. There was a thud on her chest and her eyes flew open.

"Idli-cat!" chastised Cecilia. "Leave mommy be. She needs to rest."

Neena shook her hands in protest as Cecilia attempted to detach the furry white mass from Neena's worn fleece sweatshirt.

"It's okay," she croaked softly and allowed Idli to settle back onto her chest. The little cat extended her soft pink paws and immediately started making biscuits. Neena found the soft rhythmic movements soothing and she ran a light hand over the little creature's back. She heard the gentle rattle of crockery as Raj appeared next to Cecilia, carefully carrying a cup and saucer.

"I've made you some chai, Neena," he said. "I hope you don't mind but I found your spices and added some cardamom and cinnamon, as well as a few cloves. My grandmother always advised me to put a clove in my cheek for a toothache so I thought it would help your throat as well. It's not too hot and I've added a lot of sugar."

She mouthed a "thank you" and started to sit up. Cecilia propped her up with a pillow. Despite the warm summer's day Neena shivered involuntarily, causing Cecilia to immediately tuck a blanket around her. She also attempted to put a few more pillows under Neena's feet.

"I'm okay, Ceci," she said softly, smiling and waving her hands at her friend, declining the pillows Cecilia was getting ready to slip under her legs. Neena held the cup to her lips and took a cautious sip. The sweet, fragrant liquid slid down her throat and warmed her insides as softly and gently as the fleece blanket with which Cecilia had covered her body.

"Ah!" cried Neena, as a loud crash sounded from the kitchen, causing her to slosh a little tea into the saucer.

"Neel!" yelled Cecilia, turning toward the kitchen. "What are you doing?"

"Sorry, Neena!" Neel replied from the kitchen. "Everything's okay, nothing broken."

"Really, Neel, how can you hope to be a surgeon if you're such a klutz around the house?" Cecilia rolled her eyes at Neena and the tight lines around Raj's mouth relaxed a little.

"I'll have you know that I caught the vase before it crashed due to my exceptional reflexes and hand-eye coordination," Neel said, emerging with a large glass vase filled with daisies.

"Those are beautiful, Neel. That was so thoughtful of you. Thank you,"

Neena said in a hoarse whisper.

Neel looked sheepish. "Um, well I just put them in water," he admitted. "They were already on the doorstep when I arrived."

"Oh, then who?" Neena asked. Neel fished in his pockets, pulled out a small folded piece of cardboard and handed it to her. Neena quickly read the few lines written on it.

"They're from Mr. MacMillan," she said, looking at the bold script wishing her well and signed: Mac. "How incredibly thoughtful of him. How did he even know I was hurt?"

"You were supposed to work there this morning, Neena," Raj said. "And when you didn't arrive he called your home and then called the hospital to see if you were on call. Mike spoke to him."

"Oh, shoot!" Neena said. "I completely forgot. I feel so bad." She tried to push the blanket aside and was about to swing her feet onto the floor when Cecilia intervened.

"Oh, no you don't! You are not going anywhere today. Mr. MacMillan will be okay. You're in no condition to do anything today." Cecilia lifted Neena's legs back onto the sofa and tucked the blanket even more tightly around her, hoping, it seemed, to secure Neena firmly in place.

Neena felt terrible. It was not in her nature to miss work or appointments. But, she had heard the phrase, "physician, heal thyself." And, if she could not take care of herself then how could she set a good example for her patients? As a child she had frequently seen parents who insisted to their kids, "Do as you are told, not as I do." Neena thought that actions, as well as words, set powerful examples for children. It was one of the many mental notes Neena had on file for herself in the event that she was ever a parent in the future.

"Yes," she said with a heavy sigh. "You're right." She settled back against the cushions and sipped more of her tea. She gestured to Neel who was still holding the vase of flowers. "Neel, can you please put them over there, on the top shelf of the bookcase? Unfortunately, as much as I love the flowers, they are actually quite dangerous for cats. Cecilia, can I re-gift you these daisies?"

"Sure, I can take them to my house," Cecilia said, her eyes anxiously watching Neena's every move. Neena swallowed her last sip of the tea, noticing that the pain in her throat was perceptibly better.

"Raj, the tea was wonderful. My throat does not hurt as much right now," she said.

"I'm so glad," said Raj, his dark eyebrows drawn together and his face now somber. Neel's face also bore uncustomary lines around his mouth and his green eyes did not shine as brightly as they usually did.

"What's wrong with all of you?" Neena asked in alarm. "Are you okay?" At this, a faint smile played on Neel's lips.

"We're worried about you, you silly girl!" said Cecilia.

Raj nodded in agreement. "I cannot believe that you were attacked and almost strangled just a block away from your house. And your parents still don't know?"

Neena shook her head. "No, I can't tell them. They will be so worried."

"Well, of course they will be worried," said Cecilia.

"I know, but there's nothing that they can do now, so there's no reason to tell them. I didn't die right?" Neena passed her empty cup and saucer to Raj. Then she added, "If I was dead then I would tell them. Okay? Happy?" Neena's three friends exchanged glances.

"Maybe she hit her head when she fell?" suggested Raj.

Neena held out her scraped palms for him to see. "No, I fell on my hands and knees. Why?"

"Never mind," Cecilia said quickly. "I am so glad you are okay." Her voice quivered slightly and she leaned forward to give Neena a gentle hug.

Idli leaped from Neena's chest and headed purposefully toward the door with her plume of a tail swishing. A few seconds later there was a tap on the door.

Neena sat up and pushed her curls back from her face. "Now, who could that be?" Cecilia opened the door and ushered Mr. and Mrs. Patel inside.

"Neena beti, how are you?" asked Mrs. Patel in her soft, accented voice. She walked quickly over to Neena with her hands outstretched, her eyes warm with concern. Bending over the sofa she took Neena's hands in hers and gave them a gentle squeeze. Her dark brown eyes, framed by long dark lashes, searched Neena's face. Mr. Patel, his arms full of brown paper bags, loomed over his wife. He also gave Neena an appraising glance.

"You are looking much better than yesterday," he said gruffly and bustled into the kitchen with the packages. Neena giggled. "Yes, I am sure I must." Then she sobered, "Thank you, Uncle. You saved my life," she said simply, turning to look at him.

"Hmph," he said and with his back to her began to place containers of food on Neena's little table.

Cecilia also turned toward Mr. Patel. "How did you come to Neena's aid so quickly? It must have been only seconds after the attack."

He turned back towards the living room. "What do you Americans say, 'right time, right place?'" Neena noticed the quick glance that he shared with his wife.

"That's for sure!" said Neel. "How did you manage to stop the attacker, Mr. Patel?"

"Yes, how did you do that?" said Neena. Neena belatedly realized that Mr. Patel may have also suffered injuries from the attack. She turned anxious eyes toward him. "You didn't get hurt, did you?"

Mrs. Patel patted Neena's hands reassuringly. "Now, now, don't you worry, my dear. Darshan, in case you didn't know, was once a boxing champion, and even made it to the All-India competition," she said, looking proudly at her husband.

Mr. Patel patted his rotund belly. "How could they know there is still some muscle under all of this?" he said, smiling. Both Raj and Neel both looked impressed, however. "Can you teach us some of your moves?" asked Neel.

"I would be happy to," said Mr. Patel, looking at the boys. Then his gaze fell on Neena and Cecilia. "Maybe, these young ladies should learn a trick or two as well, eh?"

Cecilia impulsively threw her arms around Mr. Patel's bulky form and gave him a hug. "Thank God and Mr. Patel."

"Harrumph," he said, a warm color spreading from his cheeks toward his bald pate. He turned back toward the table and continued to empty the seemingly bottomless brown bags.

"He doesn't like to be praised," said his wife. "But I agree with you, Cecilia, thanks be to all the lords in heaven." She placed a hand briefly on Neena's curly head as in a blessing. Then, clearing her throat softly, she straightened, the folds of her saree falling in graceful pleats to the floor. "Now, who's hungry?" she asked with a smile, looking at each of the young faces around her. Neena had noticed Neel's frequent glances toward the kitchen and it seemed that Mrs. Patel had too.

"I am!" replied Neel, and he sniffed appreciatively at the delectable aromas now wafting through the room.

Mr. and Mrs. Patel quickly passed around heaping plates of food.

"Eat, eat," said Mrs. Patel. "And then take more! I want only empty dabbas to come back to me," she warned, wagging a slim finger at them.

Neel, his mouth full of food, gave her a thumbs up.

"Thank you, Mrs. Patel," said Neena, accepting a plate filled with a kaleidoscope of tantalizing curries. "Please tell me how much I owe you."

"No, no, no! No money is needed. You just eat and get strong," she said, folding the paper bags and placing them neatly behind the garbage can. Steadfastly refusing any payment and waving away their choruses of "thank yous," Mr. and Mrs. Patel departed, promising to come back frequently to check on Neena.

Chapter 20

Neena folded her legs to make room for Cecilia on the couch and the boys sat on the rug, picnic style. Neena noticed that Mrs. Patel had only served her those dishes which were soft and smooth. Suddenly feeling quite hungry, Neena mixed some of the bright yellow dhal flecked with mustard seeds into the fragrant white rice on her plate. To her relief, the warm, creamy mixture slipped easily down her bruised throat and she was able to eat more than half of the food on her plate. Neel, having emptied his first plate, was now making great in-roads into his second. Neena looked over at Cecilia who was not eating but simply pushing her food around on her plate.

"What's the matter, Ceci?" she asked. "Don't you like it?" She placed her own half-eaten plate on the table and turned to Cecilia. Neena knew her friend had a good appetite and she had never, ever known Cecilia to turn down Mrs. Patel's food.

"What?" said Cecilia, startled out of her private musings. "Oh, no. I'm sure it's delicious as always. I'm just not that hungry." At this, Raj, who had been scooping up a morsel of potato curry, looked up.

Cecilia looked around at her three friends. "I can't swallow a bite, Neena. I think the shock of what happened to you is just hitting me. Actually, now that I come to think of it, each of you has been hurt in some way over the last week. I mean, what is going on here?" she asked.

Raj looked at Cecilia and then at Neena.

"It is quite disturbing," he agreed. He popped the piece of roti and potato into his mouth and chewed thoughtfully.

"What do you think, Neel?" asked Cecilia.

Neel swallowed strenuously, his Adam's apple bobbing up and down in his slim throat. Putting his empty plate aside, he wiped his hands and mouth on a paper napkin before answering.

"It's true. Like you said, a lot of strange things have happened to Raj, Neena, and me recently." Then he shrugged. "I guess it's just a bit of bad luck."

"A bit of bad luck?" scoffed Cecilia. "A bit of bad luck is spilling coffee all over your white coat or missing the bus or forgetting your keys. I think being pushed into traffic," she nodded at Raj, "and getting koshed on the head," she cocked an eyebrow at Neel, "or being strangled," she waved one of her delicate expressive hands at Neena, "are more like a lot of very bad luck!" Her usually soft melodic voice, now tinged with anger and worry, sounded thin and sharp.

Neel leaned forward to pat Cecilia on the hand.

"Cecilia, it's all okay. We are all okay," he said soothingly. But Cecilia looked far from soothed and pulled her hand away.

"No, it's not okay!" she said, shaking her head so vigorously that the barrette she had used to pin back her bangs flew to the ground and her silky blond hair spilled onto her face. Cecilia swatted irritably at the strands and tried to tuck her baby-fine hair behind her ears.

Raj cleared his throat and said, "I think Cecilia is correct. Not only are the events unusual, but they have also been extremely dangerous. And, any one of these accidents could have been deadly. Not that what happened to Neena was an accident," he corrected himself hurriedly. Cecilia nodded and gave him a grateful look.

"Okay," said Neena slowly. "So, let's talk about it. What do we know? And, could any of these events be related? Do you think someone has it in for third-year medical students?"

"What do you mean?" Neel scoffed. "Are you saying you believe in the surgical rotation curse? Come on, Neena! You can't be serious?"

"To be exact, it is called The Curse of the Surgical Rotation," she corrected. At this Cecilia's eyes lit up with her ever-ready humor, and even Raj, whose lips had been set in a straight line under his neatly trimmed mustache, relaxed into a smile.

"Okay, fine. I don't really believe in the curse but this really makes no sense! What possible connection can there be?"

"I think that what happened to me and to Neel could really be considered accidents, Neena," said Raj. "After all, the pavement was crowded when I walked home after the soccer game and there was a large man behind me. Perhaps he slipped and bumped into me. But he also pulled me back to safety. He was a complete stranger. Why would he want to hurt me? And if his purpose was to hurt me, why did he then proceed to rescue me? And as for Neel, I think the brass door closer simply became loose and that was definitely simple bad luck."

Neena shook her head slowly. "No, I am not so sure. Neel, can you please pass me my lab coat?" Neel, who had been sitting cross-legged on the floor, rose in one fluid movement. He retrieved Neena's white coat from the hook by the door and handed it to her.

"Thank you," she said and started rummaging through her pockets. "Aha! Here it is!" She held up the small brass screw for all of them to see.

Neel gave it a cursory glance. "Yeah, so what? Like Raj said, the screw came loose."

"No, take a closer look," Neena said, passing the screw to Neel, who now turned it over in his palms several times before passing it to Raj. When both Raj and Cecilia had had a chance to inspect the brass screw, Neena looked at them expectantly.

"Well?" she asked. "What do you see?"

"I really don't see anything, Neena," said Cecilia apologetically.

"Me, neither," agreed Neel. "Other than a few scratches on the head of the screw it looks brand new."

"I don't see anything else either Neena," said Raj slowly. Then he looked up at her. "But then is that your point?" he asked.

"Yes!" said Neena triumphantly. "That's it exactly! I noticed that the door closer over the women's on-call room was gray metal and appeared to be old. But, the brass door closer on your call room door and the screw both look brand new! Why would such a new mechanism malfunction? You wanna know what I think?" she asked.

"If we said 'no' would that stop you from telling us?" teased Neel. Neena rolled her big black eyes at him but continued as if he had not spoken.

"What I think is that this screw was deliberately loosened. That would explain the scratch marks on the head of the screw. The handyman that's been around, Mr. Robinson, seems way too experienced to be doing such a shoddy job."

"Oh my god!" said Cecilia. "Why would he do that? Why would anyone do that, for that matter?"

"Maybe he hates medical students?" suggested Neel.

"No, I don't think so," said Neena, her curls bobbing. "He was very friendly and has such kind eyes. Whenever I've seen him he almost always gives me a smile or a thumbs-up."

"Yes," agreed Raj. "He's been very friendly with me as well. He always says hello and was kind enough to ask me how I was settling in." He gave them all a rueful smile. "I suppose I really must have looked more clueless than I even actually thought I was. Not that I have found many clues in the last week, but at least I don't get lost more than once a day now!" They all smiled at him.

A thought flashed into Neena's mind and she opened her mouth in a silent "O."

"Neena, what is it?" asked Raj sharply.

"I was just remembering our first night on call. That day I saw Mr. Robinson several times and he was always smiling. He even witnessed my battle with Nurse Marge as I tried to get a staple remover from the supply closet," she said. "And, when I emerged victorious, he winked and gave me a thumbs-up. But that night, when we were headed to the emergency surgery, I saw him in the hallway pushing his cart. He passed right by me but he seemed lost in thought and didn't even look at me, much less smile. What if he suspected someone had been tampering with it? After all, Mr. Robinson is like a fixture in the hospital and I bet most people don't even notice he's there."

"But why would anyone do that?" asked Cecilia. "It seems so random. Anyone could have gotten hurt. If someone had purposely done this, how would they know when the mechanism would fall?"

"Hang on!" interrupted Neel. "Are you saying that someone tried to deliberately bash my head in? Who? Why? I think I'm a pretty harmless kind of guy."

Cecilia, who was caressing the furry mass which had settled on the sofa between herself and Neena, smiled at him. "You are as innocent as a kitty cat, Neel," she assured him. Neel raised an eyebrow at her.

"Well, I don't know how innocent Miss Idli is," said Neena. "You should have seen the trouble she got into yesterday with my hair ribbons!" But she also looked affectionately at her feline friend. She went on, "So, if not you, then who? Duncan, Joe?"

"Maybe it's Raj," suggested Neel, punching Raj playfully on his arm.

"Raj? Come on Neel, he's as innocent as a newborn lamb! Besides, he's only been in the country for a week. How could he have made an enemy so quickly?" Neena asked.

"Maybe this is an international thing and someone followed him from India!" Neel countered.

Now Raj punched Neel in the shoulder. "Come on, man, are you crazy? I led a studious, blameless life thus far in India," he said. "Well, mostly blameless," he amended.

"Mostly blameless, huh?" said Cecilia with interest. "Care to fill us in on the 'mostly' part of that?"

Raj, looking slightly flustered, hurriedly went on. "We are getting off the subject, team."

Neena looked at Raj and imperiously held up a slim finger.

"Hmm, I don't know Raj. Let's think about this a bit more. Cecilia, can you please hand me that pad of paper and a pencil? I'm gonna make a chart!" Cecilia's worried face relaxed a little and she obediently handed her friend the requested items. The lines of tension on Neel and Raj's faces also eased a little.

"Ha ha ha," she said. "You can laugh all you want boys, but once you see the power of my charts you are going to be singing a different tune."

Cecilia patted her friend on the arm "To know her and her charts is to love them," she assured the boys. "I soon became a convert, let me tell you. I don't make them but luckily Neena is very generous about sharing."

Neena had flipped to a fresh new page on the yellow legal-sized pads she loved to use for her copious notes.

Neel held up his hands placatingly. "Okay, okay!" he said. "Go on, Neena, show us what you got."

Neena held up the pad for all of them to see. "Just for argument's sake, let's say these events are not accidents. Let's think about them as symptoms that we have to use to formulate a diagnosis. It's like a medical mystery!" she said, her eyes now gleaming. She quickly divided the page into four large rows. "So, let's write a SOAP note."

"That's a great idea," said Raj, nodding with approval. "So, what do we have for the subjective?"

She tapped the pad with the point of her pencil. "Hmm, subjective. How about we list all the strange things that have happened over the past ten days. Raj, I think your accident was one of the first occurrences, right?"

Raj nodded. "Yes, and then Neel had his accident."

Neena's pencil raced over the page. She brushed a stray curl off her forehead. "Okay, what next?" she asked, looking at her friends.

"What about the incident in the basement?" asked Neel. "None of us was injured, but a woman was killed."

"Yes, definitely!" said Neena, busily scribbling. She wrote "Linda's murder" as the next entry on the left.

Cecilia chimed in, "You should think back to any and all interactions you've had in the hospital since the first of July. Was anyone angry at you or did you hear any arguments? Did you see anything odd or strange?"

Raj looked at Neena. "Well I don't like to gossip but this may be important in light of what happened to that poor girl yesterday," he said hesitantly.

"Go on, Raj," Neena encouraged.

"Neena, do you remember us coming across Duncan and the girl who was killed on Thursday morning, after grand rounds? I may be wrong but they seem an unlikely pair. I somehow can't picture Duncan being interested in a secretary, though she was quite pretty." In her mind Neena could see dueling images of Linda. One was "before" and the other "after." The pretty, dark-haired young woman with fluttering eyelashes and gems winking on her wrist and breast was no more. In a few swift strokes the sharp pen of fate had transformed Linda into a macabre caricature of herself. Her porcelain white breast had been bared with professional efficiency for all to see and the carefully applied ruby red lipstick was now horribly smeared, distorting the once-pretty mouth into the morbid grin of rigor mortis.

"Yes, I agree with you, Raj," said Neel, smoothing a paper napkin between his fingers and stirring Neena from her grim reverie. "Duncan seems like the type of guy who'd want someone with money or prestige."

"I also saw Linda and Duncan sitting together at a table in the dining room," Neena added, and immediately started to put another entry into the subjective box of the SOAP note. "It almost looked to me as if they were on a date. Dunk was holding her hand and playing with the tennis bracelet she was wearing. Linda was batting her eyelashes at him and seemed to be hanging on his every word."

"Really?" asked Cecilia in surprise. "I've never seen Dunk with any girl.

I don't think fending Victoria off counts. Do you?"

"It doesn't, but now that you mention it, I also saw him and Victoria kissing in the hallway! He wasn't doing much fending then."

Cecilia gave a little gasp. "No! You must be joking!" she said in disbelief. "What is this, General Hospital? Okay, in the interest of being thorough, we should add this to the subjective. But this is stranger than any soap opera I've ever seen."

"Yes," agreed Neena. "Soap opera..."

Her voice trailed off.

Chapter 21

"Ron and Victoria," said Neena. Then she added, "Duncan and Linda."

"Joe and Calvin," offered Neel, causing Neena to turn to him.

"What do you mean?" she asked, sounding slightly irritable. "What do they have to do with anything?"

"I dunno. I thought you were doing some sort of free-association exercise."

"No, stop, you're distracting me," said Neena, shaking her head as if to clear her thoughts.

"It may help if you use full sentences," suggested Cecilia. Raj, looking slightly confused, nodded his head.

Neena looked up at her friends. "Yes, yes. Okay. Ceci, I was actually answering your last question."

"What question?"

"You just asked, 'What is this, General Hospital?' It got me thinking about Ron, Dunk, Victoria, and Linda. There is some strange dynamic going on there. The day that I saw Dunk and Linda sitting in the dining room, I also saw Ron and Victoria."

"You saw Ron and Victoria eating lunch together?" asked Neel.

"No, they were each sitting alone at separate tables. But what was striking was that both Ron and Victoria were just staring intensely at Dunk and Linda. Neither of them took their eyes off of the romantic tete-a-tete. Ron was glaring."

"What a surprise," interjected Neel with a snort.

"Yes, he was shooting daggers at them. And Victoria looked so pale and frosty, it's a good thing Dunk and Linda didn't look in her direction. I'm sure they'd have turned into ice sculptures."

"So, you don't think that Duncan and Linda noticed Ron and Victoria?" asked Raj. Neena shook her head vigorously, black curls bouncing.

"Well, I don't think so since they were so engrossed in each other. The only time I saw Duncan look away from Linda was actually when he looked at me," said Neena, sounding slightly surprised at this recollection.

"What did he do?" asked Neel.

Neena reached for her glass of water and took a sip. The cool water soothed her throat. "Nothing really. Gave me that stupid wink of his."

"So what?" asked Neel. "I don't think Duncan gives a hoot who sees him. Do you? And why would Ron care about who Duncan is seeing? I've never seen Ron even talking to a woman who wasn't a patient, resident, or med student."

"Maybe he's already married?" asked Raj. While Neel and Cecilia gave Raj skeptical looks, Neena tried to consider his suggestion. *He is so charitable*, thought Neena. She had noticed that he usually gave people the benefit of the doubt and was the rare person who tried to see the good in everyone around him.

"I really don't think so, Raj," said Neena. "I'm sure we'd have heard of it by now."

"Hmm, okay," he said, stroking his mustache thoughtfully. Neena was momentarily distracted.

If only he didn't have that mustache, thought Neena. *He'd be quite handsome.*

"Okay, Neena, how's your chart coming along?" asked Cecilia, causing Neena to tear her gaze away from Raj's facial hair.

Neena held up the pad for the others to see. The subjective section was filled in nicely with her neat printing.

Cecilia tapped on the next box, labeled objective, with a neatly manicured finger. "Okay, what actual evidence do we have?"

Neel looked up. "We have the door closer that fell and the missing screw with the scratches on it." Neena nodded encouragingly as she started writing. "Yes, yes, good. What else?"

"And, we have Linda's body," he added. Neena's pencil faltered briefly and she looked around at her friends' sober faces.

After a brief pause Cecilia said, "So we know that Duncan knew Linda very well. Was he there when you found her? He must have been so upset to see her like that!"

Neena, Neel, and Raj exchanged puzzled looks.

"I didn't see him until the end," said Neel. "I think Ron led Linda's code. Right?" He looked toward Raj and Neena for confirmation.

Raj nodded. "Yes, initially it was Ron, Neena, me, and Bill, the fourth-year student. Then the Attending arrived. I don't really remember when the rest of you joined in."

"Mike, Duncan, Joe, and I were working on the older lady. The volunteer from the front desk. Miss umm . . ." Neel looked at Neena.

"Miss Barbara, I think it was," supplied Neena.

"Yes, Miss Barbara. But luckily, she had only had a syncopal episode, not a heart attack or anything. She must have hit her head pretty hard when she landed so that probably accounted for her brief loss of consciousness. She came around when we started examining her. The code-blue team arrived pretty quickly and as soon as they had lifted her onto the stretcher the rest of us came into the room."

"So, Duncan was helping with Miss Barbara?" Neena asked.

"I wouldn't say he was helping since there wasn't that much to do actually.

I think he was just watching," Neel looked toward Neena.

"Did you see what his reaction was when he saw Linda?" continued Cecila.

"No, not really. I wasn't looking at him. But, I don't think he came into the room, did he?"

Neena shook her head. "No, I didn't see him. It was Bill and me doing CPR, Raj was ventilating, and Ron started defibrillating."

Raj leaned against the bookshelf and stretched out his long legs. "Yes, true. I think it would have been incorrect for new team members to interrupt in the middle of the code unless one of us needed to be relieved."

Cecila, who was still toying with her food, had a troubled look on her face.

"Ceci?" asked Neena, tapping her friend gently on the knee.

"Hmm, what? Oh, sorry. This just doesn't sound right to me," she said. "A girl he was recently kissing and spending time with ends up dead and he doesn't do anything? He didn't say anything? He didn't react at all? He simply watched?"

Again, Neena, Raj, and Neel looked at each other. Then they nodded their heads.

"Yes," said Neena. "I think that's what happened." A slight shiver ran through her slim frame. Duncan's reaction seemed disproportionately understated considering Linda was more than a casual acquaintance of his.

"Are you cold, Neena?" asked Cecilia worriedly.

"No, no," Neena reassured her. "Dunk's reaction is kinda chilling. Don't you think?" This didn't prevent Cecilia from pulling the blanket further up Neena's small frame and securely re-tucking the ends that had come loose.

Cecilia nodded. "Yes, it is."

"Maybe he was in shock?" said Neena.

Raj nodded. "Yes, that must have been it. Otherwise, his reaction was quite inhuman."

Neena suddenly picked up her pencil and started writing quickly. Another picture of Linda, lying on the scuffed linoleum floor, rushed unbidden into

Neena's mind. It was again a duo of macabre before-and-after *Highlights* diagrams over which Neena was hovering with a large imaginary red crayon poised in her hands.

"Raj!" she cried, startling everyone. "Do you remember the red lipstick marks on the floor next to Linda? What did they say?" she asked excitedly.

"Red lipstick?" he started to say, then came to a sudden halt, as realization dawned. He and Neena locked eyes.

"Doctor!" they both said simultaneously.

"Doctor who?" asked Cecilia.

"Next to her body, written in red lipstick, were the letters D and R," explained Raj.

"There was?" asked Neel. "I didn't see it."

"No, you wouldn't have," said Neena. "It was on the floor near her right hand and I was kneeling over it when I was doing CPR. And then after the code I think I sat right on it." She reached over and held up her lab coat so they could see the bright red streaks for themselves. "It looks like blood, right? That's what Raj thought when I stood up. But, there wasn't much bleeding from Linda's injury and that's when we looked around and saw the writing."

"What are you saying?" asked Cecilia in a hushed tone. "That Linda, as she was being strangled, was trying to identify her killer?"

"Yes," said Raj, nodding slowly. "I think that's exactly what she did."

"But D and R?" said Neel incredulously. "In a hospital? That sure does narrow down the list of suspects!"

"Well, it does, rather," said Raj. "So, it wasn't a workman, orderly, nurse, or student. This most likely rules out a random act of violence. Linda knew her killer."

The warmth of the summer evening suddenly dissipated and Neena pulled the blanket tighter over her shoulders. Even Cecilia could not suppress a delicate shudder.

Raj started ticking items off on his fingers. "Okay, let's summarize the evidence. Number one, we found the faulty door closer and screw. Number two, Linda's body. Number three, the writing on the floor. Anything else that we can consider as an objective finding?"

Neena, who had continued writing, ended with a flourish. A prominent exclamation mark punctuated her last phrase.

"You've thought of something, Neena?" asked Raj.

"Yes," she said, her dark brows drawn together in a frown. "And, it's not good."

"What is it?" asked Cecilia anxiously.

"It's Ron," she said slowly. "Last week, on the morning of surgical grand rounds, I had to park in the rear parking lot and got lost in the basement. I finally found the stairwell near the reading room. You know the one?" They all nodded. "Anyway, the last door at the end of the hallway was open and I heard Ron's voice talking to someone. Talking is not the right word. He was yelling."

Neel had been folding and unfolding his paper napkin. He stopped and looked at Neena. "Who was he yelling at?" he asked.

"Linda."

Cecilia's hands also stole up to cover her mouth. "Oh, my!"

Neel looked at Cecilia and Neena in turn. "What are you saying? Just because he yelled at her doesn't mean he killed her."

"He was so angry! Linda was talking about her work and he was upset about it. But why would he be upset about that? When I peeked through the door Linda was backed up against the wall and she looked frightened."

"Could she be working for him? But doing what?" asked Cecilia.

"That doesn't make any sense," said Neel.

"No, it doesn't," agreed Raj.

Then he looked sharply at Neena, his thick, dark brows drawn together. "But, Neena, aren't you forgetting another significant piece of evidence?"

"Um, I don't think so. What else is there?"

"You."

"Yes, me," she said slowly, and reluctantly put her name under the objective findings. "What if it was Ron who attacked me?" she asked.

"Ron! Why would he do that? You couldn't have possibly done anything to warrant such a level of hatred!" protested Raj.

"You never know, Raj, still waters run deep," said Neel seriously. Cecilia gave him a withering glance.

Neena shook her head slowly. "What if Ron killed Linda? Even though his motive is not clear to us it doesn't mean that he doesn't have one. That morning in the stairwell I was pretty sure that he didn't see or hear me. When he started to sound ugly I turned and ran up the stairwell. But my coat pocket caught on the door handle. For a minute I thought it was Ron!"

"Yikes!" said Cecilia. "That does sound scary. But, Neena, it still doesn't give Ron a reason to hurt you."

Neena put up her hand and continued. "What I didn't realize is that when my coat got stuck, my ID badge fell. After rounds, Ron's big fat finger actually did tap me on the shoulder. When I turned around he had my ID in the palm of his hand. He obviously found it in the stairwell and knew I had been there. He asked me what I had been doing there so early in the morning."

"What did you say?" asked Cecilia.

"Well, it took a few seconds for my brain and mouth to reconnect. But then I babbled about checking on a final X-ray report for one of our patients. Luckily, he didn't ask me who! He had such a strange look on his face as he finally let go of my badge."

"Okay," said Cecilia. "Don't panic. Just add this to the chart and let's focus on Ron. What else do any of you know about him?"

Raj shook his head. "I don't know anything else. It's been less than two weeks since I arrived here. Perhaps the rest of you have heard some rumors about him?" He looked over at Neel.

"I was just told that he was unpleasant and to steer clear of him if at all possible. Like I can be on the same team and do that," said Neel, now tearing his napkin into small squares and folding them.

"What about you, Cecilia? Even though you're in IM now, have you heard anything?"

Cecilia put her untouched plate of food down and turned to consider the question. "Well, I also heard that he was unpleasant. And, not very fair to the female students." She looked at Neena. "Didn't he make you hold that lady's 100-pound leg during surgery for no good reason?"

Neena's eyebrows came as close to a frown as she could manage. "Yes, he did! He's a bull! A bullying bull, that's what he is," she said.

"That certainly was brutish behavior," said Raj soothingly. "But you proved him wrong. I'm sure he was just waiting for you to drop that leg."

"Yeah, and I would have too if you hadn't helped me under the drapes," said Neena with a grateful look.

"You're such a gentleman, Raj," said Cecilia with approval.

Neena was interested to note the look Neel aimed at Cecilia. Usually, Neel's face was amiable and relaxed. In the short time in which she had known Neel she had never seen him angry or upset. *He's annoyed because he thinks Cecilia is flirting with Raj,* she thought. She looked over at Cecilia. Her bright blue eyes were sparkling and her face had a rosy glow. *She really is so lovely,* thought Neena. *No wonder he's jealous. I really think I should give him a little nudge.* She resolved to have a friendly chat with Neel.

Chapter 22

"People, we are getting off track!" Neena reproved. She tapped on the next unfilled box on the chart she was holding. "What is our assessment?"

"Assault, murder, and theft?" volunteered Neel.

"Hmm," said Neena thoughtfully. "I think those are still objective findings."

"We have evidence but nothing points to a specific person," said Cecilia. "I think we should move on to the plan. What can we do to figure out who is behind all of these incidents and if they are actually all related?"

"I think it's Ron," said Neena. "How can we prove that Ron is guilty?"

Raj looked up at that. "What happened to your country's legal motto, 'innocent until proven guilty?'"

Cecilia gave him a small nod of approval. "Raj is right, Neena. No matter how much you dislike the guy, that doesn't mean he's a murderer."

Neena's brows furrowed in concentration. She was certain she had witnessed an important detail. Now where had she been at the time? What had she been doing? One of Neena's tried and true methods of memorization was to concentrate on certain facts or details in certain locations. She remembered walking home last night and she had just passed Patel's Pantry. What had she seen? Images from her favorite childhood magazine, *Highlights*, had flashed through her brain and she remembered coming to a standstill. In her mind's eye she was looking for substitutions or omissions between the images.

"Linda's necklace was missing!" Neena blurted out. "When we first came upon Linda's body, I saw a necklace deeply embedded in her skin but by the end of the code the necklace was gone! There had been a glimmer of light which I attributed to Ron's penlight but I think that he may have stolen Linda's chain and the diamond pendant."

Cecilia asked, "Why would he do that?"

"Well, maybe he used it to strangle her? And, he removed it so that his fingerprints wouldn't be found?" said Neena.

"Wouldn't the coroner be able to determine the mechanism of injury? It would be known that the necklace caused the injury," said Neel, still absent-mindedly tearing bits from his paper napkin and folding them into tiny squares.

"Yes," agreed Neena. "But what if he was trying to distract attention from himself and try to make it look like a robbery? I mean, why would he want to steal a necklace from a crime scene?"

"Okay," said Cecilia excitedly. "How do we prove it?"

"We need to find that necklace," said Neena. "Where could it be?"

"Where did you last see it?" asked Raj. "To be honest, I didn't notice Linda's necklace at all. That was a good observation, Neena."

Neena squinted in concentration. Another memory flashed before her eyes. "I remember seeing Ron scoop up a handful of items from the floor and stuff them in his pocket before we left. There was a chain of some sort wrapped around the tip of that chewed-up Bic pen he carries around. So, the last memory I have of the chain, and presumably the diamond pendant, was of Ron trying to stuff it into his pocket."

"Well, let's check his lab coat pocket and his locker then!" said Cecilia excitedly. She reached for her plate of food and took a few bites. Now that her worry about Neena's health had been replaced by curiosity about the murder, she seemed to have regained her appetite.

Raj shook his head. "Why would he leave it in his pocket? All he had to do was throw it into a waste bin. Or even better yet, into a red medical waste bin. No one is likely to be searching through one of those."

"Maybe he took it home with him?" suggested Neel.

"Why would he do that?" asked Neena. "That makes no sense."

Neel arched his right eyebrow at her in an annoying fashion. "It makes just as much sense as him secreting it in his locker in the hospital," he retorted.

"Now, now, children," chided Cecilia. "Be nice."

"Do you know where Ron lives?" asked Raj reasonably.

"Good question, Raj," agreed Neel. He looked between Neena and Cecilia. "Well, do you?"

Neena and Cecilia exchanged a sheepish look at the "gotcha" question.

"No, we don't, Neel," answered Cecilia. "So, like I said, let's start with the residents' lounge, the chief resident's desk, and his locker."

Raj still looked skeptical. "That doesn't seem right, Cecilia. That's an invasion of his privacy." He pronounced the word "privacy" in British fashion.

"I think murder could be considered the ultimate invasion of one's privacy!" said Neena, stressing the American pronunciation.

Cecilia nodded vigorously, causing wisps of hair to fall over her face again. She blew them away. "You say po-TAH-to, I say po-TAY-to."

Neel shrugged. "Yeah, I guess so. But I think you should talk to the detective first, before you and Cecilia go haring off to dig through Ron's things."

"Okay, yes, we will certainly discuss it with him," Neena said hurriedly. "But, I don't feel right about accusing a senior resident without some proof. Can you imagine the fallout if we're wrong? You can just kiss your A in surgery goodbye!"

Both boys exchanged looks of consternation. Neena crossed her arms over her chest and leaned back against her pile of cushions.

"Right, that's what I thought," she said with a look of triumph and determination writ large across her thin, expressive face.

Neel's busy fingers stilled and he cupped them under the small bunches of paper in his palm.

"Okay," he said, sitting up straighter. "You win. Go on, you two, let's hear it. We can at least try to rule Ron in or out."

The girls proposed and discarded various schemes with lightning speed. After several more minutes of debate, they came to a decision. Neena carefully documented the details into the plan section of her SOAP chart. She and Cecilia agreed that Monday would be the day since both of their teams were on call that evening.

The boys, who had been silently watching the rapid exchange of ideas between Neena and Cecilia, now exchanged bemused glances.

"I don't know that this is much of a plan," protested Neel. "It seems a bit simple."

"The simpler the better," said Neena. "That way there is less chance of things going wrong."

"I can imagine many ways that this could go wrong," said Raj with concern. "At least let us help you," he entreated.

Neena and Cecilia looked at one another. Cecilia gave a shrug of her slim shoulders.

"Okay, why not?" she said. "We could use a pair of lookouts."

Raj and Neel looked uncertainly at each other, then nodded reluctantly.

"Lookouts," agreed Neena. "Just don't interfere, okay?" she said in her bossiest tone.

For the first time all day Neel laughed. "Well, I guess you're feeling better," he said as he stood up. Gathering their plates and cups, Neena's friends made quick work of putting away the leftover food and stacking the dishes in the dishwasher.

"Neena," asked Cecilia, "how are you feeling now? Would you like me to stay with you tonight?"

Neena shook her head. "No, Ceci. I am feeling much better. I'll be okay. I just want to go to sleep."

"Are you certain?" Raj asked. "One of us can certainly stay with you." Neel also nodded in agreement.

Neena got up from the sofa and looked at her friends' faces, all three of which were lined with fatigue. "Thank you, but that's really not necessary. You've all kept me company since last night. Please go home and get some sleep."

Cecilia held up a hand to hide a yawn. "I think it's okay for us to go now," she said, nodding at the boys, who were also suddenly yawning as well. She gave Neena a quick hug and reached up to the bookcase for the vase of flowers. "Thanks for these, Neena," she said.

"Idli thanks you for taking them," said Neena, with a fond look at her little cat who had snuggled into the warmth of the spot Neena had just vacated.

"Take care, Neena," said Raj as he headed for the door.

Neel, who had been placing something on the bookshelf, suddenly turned and enveloped her in a tight hug. He released her just as quickly. "Be careful, Neena," he said gruffly and pushed past Raj. Neena felt slightly shocked at this display of emotion. After all, she had not really known Neel well until this past week.

"I guess he cares after all," she said jokingly as she tried to hide her embarrassment. Neena could feel the warmth creeping into her cheeks.

"Hmm," said Cecilia, a speculative gleam in her eyes. She exchanged a glance with Raj who gave a faint smile and a slight shrug.

"Come, Cecilia. We should let Neena rest," said Raj, and gently guided Cecilia to the door.

"I will check on you tomorrow," promised Cecilia. Neena, whose face had split into a wide yawn, nodded at her friend. As soon as she closed the door she heard Cecilia's voice. "Lock the door!" she admonished. And, just as Neena was reaching for the chain, she heard Cecilia call, "And the chain!" Only when Neena had bolted the door and slid the chain firmly across did she hear her friend's footsteps recede. Stifling another yawn, she turned to the bookshelf to check that there were no leaves or flowers left behind. Where the vase had been there was now only a pile of small, intricately folded, white paper flowers.

Monday July 13, 1992

Chapter 23

Neena stepped out of the elevator and glanced anxiously at her watch. *Oh my goodness!* she thought, it was almost time for sign-out. It was a quarter to five and she could feel her pulse increase beat by beat with each tick of the second hand. Tonight was the night she and her friends meant to search Ron's locker and desk for any incriminating evidence. Neena and Cecilia had decided to put their plan into action just after evening sign-outs since this was usually a hurried time of the day when everyone who was not on call was eager to thrust their daytime responsibilities onto the on-call team and rush out of the hospital to enjoy their free evening. One by one, her teammates, emerging from various patient rooms and corridors, converged on the nurses' station. Taking a deep breath and a firmer hold on her clipboard she marched purposefully down the hall.

Calvin's round cherubic face looked up from the chart he was scribbling in.

"Hi, Neena," he said, his smile fading a little as he took in his friend's expression.

"What's wrong? Did something else happen?"

Neena hastily tried to relax her face and bared her teeth at him in what she hoped looked like a smile. "What? Oh no. Nothing, everything's good. Um, why do you ask?" she said and began sorting through the papers on her clipboard while avoiding Calvin's gaze.

Calvin gave her an exasperated look. "Are you serious? Did you think I'd forgotten that you were almost strangled a few days ago? How are you feeling? Are you okay? I know you're on call today but I can switch with you if you're not up to it. I don't mind, really."

Neena was annoyed, not with Calvin, but with herself, for having to deceive him. There were already too many people to keep track of tonight and she did not wish to involve him as well. She put her clipboard down and looked into his anxious brown eyes. "You are very sweet to offer to do my call tonight. Thank you, but I think I can manage." His pursed lips and skeptical glance brought a smile to her face. She placed a hand on his sleeve. "I'm fine, Calvin, really I am. I would tell you if I wasn't."

"Hmm, okaaay," said Calvin. "But, I think you should . . ." Neena never heard what Calvin thought she should do since suddenly they found Nurse Marge looming above them, her hand extended imperiously. Calvin hastily shut the chart he was holding and thrust it into Marge's outstretched hand. She greatly disliked the charts being out of their numbered slots and was constantly snatching them away from the students like a harried waiter clearing plates from a table of boisterous diners.

Neena and Calvin picked up their clipboards and arranged themselves alongside their team members just as Ron charged toward them, his hands full of sheafs of paper. He slapped the stack against the acting intern's chest. Luckily, Bill's dexterous hands caught the bundle and he quickly passed them out to the team. Just as Neena was lifting the metal clasp on her clipboard to insert the new sheets she felt a hard shove to her left shoulder.

"Ow!" she said, rubbing her shoulder as her clipboard bounced onto the gleaming tile floor, releasing all her papers and coming to rest under the sole of Ron's grubby white sneaker.

"Oh, did I do that? Sorry, Neena," said a high simpering voice, and Victoria pushed her way to the front of the group, her ponytail swinging to and fro. She took the sheaf of papers Bill held out to her, elbowed him aside, and ended up right next to Ron.

She batted her sparse, straw-colored lashes at him. "Hi, Ron."

"Hmph," grunted Ron. He pushed Neena's clipboard back toward her with the toe of his shoe. Neena bent over to catch it and then tried to gather up her papers. She nodded gratefully at Neel and Calvin who each passed her a handful of her notes. She shoved them back into the clipboard and stepped back to her spot in the semicircle.

Ron positioned himself in front of the nurses' station and glared impartially at the team. *At least it's not just me he favors with that look*, thought Neena. Mike walked briskly around the nurses' station and stood next to Ron. Mike's calm, handsome face was in sharp contrast to Ron's dark scowl. *They look like the angel-doctor and the devil-doctor*, thought Neena. She wouldn't have been surprised to find a pair of horns nestled among the dark thicket of Ron's head.

The day's census was surprisingly low and sign-outs were completed in record time.

"Okay, people, see you tomorrow morning," said Mike. He nodded at the on-call team. "I will not say the Q-word," he said with a smile. "But, have a good night." He turned to leave.

"Oh, Mike," said Victoria, sidling up to him. "That appendectomy you did today was just amazing," she gushed, batting her eyelids at him. "I have so many questions I wanted to ask you. I'll just walk down with you, shall I?" And before Mike could respond she started peppering him with questions and matched him stride for stride as he headed toward the elevator.

"What's the Q-word?" asked Raj. "Does he mean qui—" The end of his sentence was drowned out in a chorus of shushes by the rest of the on-call team to avoid hearing the dreaded word.

Joe shook his head at Raj. "Are you crazy, man? No one ever says the Q-word when they're on call. It's just asking for a bad call night. It's like you're never supposed to wish an actor good luck. That's why they say 'break a leg.'"

Raj held up his hands in a placating gesture. "Sorry, sorry. I did not know. Well, in that case let's hope for a dull evening for a change. Maybe we can all get some studying done."

"Yes, we all have a lot of work to do," said Neena, looking pointedly at Raj and Neel.

Duncan, who was also on call tonight again, turned to the students.

"Have you all rounded on your patients this afternoon?" The students all nodded their heads. "In that case, the next set of labs will probably not be resulted until after seven p.m. Make sure your pagers are on. I'm heading to the cafeteria to grab a bite to eat. Anyone else coming?" He raised a bleach-blond eyebrow at the group.

"Yeah, sure, I'll come," said Joe and then turned to his fellow students. "You guys coming?"

Neel's face brightened. "Sounds good man, I'm starving." Then he gave a little yelp as Neena's elbow dug into his side. She gave him a meaningful look and he quickly amended his statement. "Ow! I mean, um, no, actually, I just remembered I need to check on my patient."

Joe gave a little shrug. "Okay, suit yourself." He turned to join Duncan. Neena and Raj had each grabbed a random patient's chart and were busily flipping through the pages. Duncan's bright blue eyes squinted briefly at them before he too gave a careless shrug and sauntered away with his usual rolling gait.

Neel, rubbing his side, leaned toward Neena and lowered his voice. "Whatcha have to do that for?"

"Neel! We don't have time for you to stuff your face right now. Or have you forgotten the plan?" Neena demanded in an urgent whisper, attempting to scowl at him. She never could get her eyebrows to scrunch up for a truly impressive scowl.

"Okay, okay, keep your hair on! But, just to let you know, I do my best work on a full stomach. And you could use a little more meat on your bones too. That is one sharp elbow you've got there." But, Neena had already turned away from him, and was glancing anxiously at the nurses' station. Ron had seated himself at one of the computer consoles at a side station and appeared as if he'd taken root.

"What's he still doing here? I thought he'd go down to the cafeteria. Or down to the ER to troll for cases."

Raj glanced at his watch and then peered down the long empty hallway where the soft chime of the elevator was now clearly audible. He nudged Neena gently on the arm.

"Look. Right on time," he said, an appreciative gleam in his eyes. Neel's glum, and presumably hungry countenance, also lightened. They all watched as Cecilia hurried toward them, treading silently on her soft-soled sneakers. Her light blue scrubs were cinched tightly at her waist and even the boxy short white coat could not obscure her slim, graceful form.

"What's he still doing here?" she asked, arching a brow in Ron's direction. "To be perfectly honest, I was really hoping you wouldn't need me tonight."

"I know, Ceci, but we're so glad you're here," said Neena, giving her arm a gentle squeeze.

"Oh, of course, Neena. What am I saying? We girls need to stick together. I shudder to think what trouble these two could get into without us." She hooked a thumb toward Neel and Raj, a mischievous smile on her face.

"Ha ha ha," said Neel. "I think Raj and I are pretty capable, thank you very much." Raj nodded vigorously.

"Yes, yes you are," Neena said soothingly. "But I don't think either of you is as equipped for this stage of the battle as our friend Cecilia here." She turned to Cecilia.

"Okay, honey, ready? I think we will need at least fifteen minutes, right? But the longer the better."

"Okay, boss, you got it." Cecilia pulled out a slim tube of lipstick and quickly applied a light glossy pink color to her lips. She returned it to her pocket, gave her soft blond hair a final pat and straightened her short white coat.

"Wish me luck." She took a deep breath, exhaled slowly, and assumed her brightest smile.

"Do you think this will actually work?" asked Neel nervously. "I mean, it's Ron we're talking about."

Raj looked appraisingly at Cecilia's retreating form. Her hands were clasped behind her and it was clear that her fingers were crossed for good luck.

"If she can't distract Ron, no one can. If she fails, I'll shave off my mustache," he said with feeling.

"Really?" Neena asked, instantly distracted. "You'd actually shave off your mustache? I don't believe you. Anyway, we'd better pray she can keep him busy for long enough. Though, I'd love to see what you look like without that mustache."

Raj flashed a confident smile at her. "I think you will be out of luck then, Neena."

The three of them tried to watch unobtrusively as Cecilia glided up to the counter where Ron was seated. "Dr. Roberts? Can you help me with something?" said Cecilia in her clear, melodious voice. Ron grunted and then looked up from the computer screen, his bushy black eyebrows forming a thick ridge over his eyes.

"Yikes," whispered Neena, holding her breath. Cecilia then lowered her voice and launched into an animated speech. Her slim hands gestured eloquently, while her long lashes fluttered as if in a breeze. Her tinkling laugh punctuated the conversation and for a few minutes Ron appeared speechless. Then he harrumphed again and gestured brusquely for Cecilia to join him at the computer. She glided around the corner, leaned against the desk near Ron's chair, and looked interestedly at the computer screen. She had draped herself such that Ron could not easily see the other three students or the hallway leading to the resident's lounge. Cecilia lifted a slim hand to tuck a few strands of her fine hair behind her ear and then her co-conspirators saw her fingers wiggling furiously at them in a shooing motion.

Neena, Neel, and Raj, who had been watching with bated breath, now sprang into action.

"Right, let's go!" said Neena in a soft voice. "Neel, stay at this end of the counter and pretend to look busy." During their planning session on Saturday, she and Cecilia had decided that Cecilia would assume primary distraction duty while Neel and Raj functioned as lookouts and then would be responsible for secondary distraction or misdirection if needed.

"Come on, Raj, you can position yourself further down the hallway near the vending machine. If anyone comes in your direction pretend to be buying a snack." Neena and Raj quickly but quietly returned the charts they were looking at to their respective slots lest they attract the unwanted attention of Nurse Marge.

Neel reached out a hand to stop Neena. "Wait! How do I warn you if Ron leaves the nursing station? We didn't come up with a signal."

"Shoot! Yes, we need a signal." She looked at Neel and Raj, but both of them turned to her with blank stares.

"Okay, I've got it! Page us. Use 411 to let us know that he's finished with Cecilia. And if you think he's heading directly for the lounge then use 911."

"Good idea, Neena," said Raj with an approving nod. "Maybe we should put our pagers on vibrate?"

"Yes, good thinking," she said and the three of them pushed the little button to silence their pagers.

Neena shot a quick glance toward Cecilia and Ron. Her silvery blond head was bent close to Ron's black thatch and they seemed to be deep in discussion. Raj and Neena quietly left the nurses' station and hurried down the corridor. Raj didn't stop at the vending machine as planned but continued to walk beside Neena.

"Raj, I thought we agreed you'd be a lookout in this hallway?" Neena asked.

"Yes, yes, I will do that but I wanted to get my scrubs. I don't know when you found the time to change but I thought it was best to do so now before it gets busy."

"Yes, right. But can you be quick about it? I'm nervous about Ron coming back here too soon."

"Don't worry, Neena, I won't be but two minutes," he said and smiled down at her.

They walked swiftly to the resident's lounge. Once inside, they left the main lights off since the room was bathed in the glow of the afternoon sun which poured through the pair of windows along the back wall. Raj opened his locker and began to change his shirt. Neena joined Raj at the row of lockers and wondered where she should look first. She doubted she would find anything of value as there were no locks on them and people used the spaces simply to store their street clothing or lab coats. Anyway, she thought it was worth a try. Neena was not exactly sure which locker was Ron's so she started opening one door at a time. She opened the first door and sneezed as her nostrils were assailed by the overpowering scent of perfume. Seeing a pair of name-brand women's sneakers on the floor of the locker she surmised this one belonged to Victoria. Raj, now shirtless, was in the process of pulling a blue scrub top over his head. Neena, staring at his admirable musculature, was struck with a feeling of déjà vu. Raj's head emerged from the opening of his shirt in time to catch Neena gaping at him. He raised an inquiring eyebrow at her and unselfconsciously pulled his shirt into place. He smiled at Neena's flushed countenance.

"Don't worry," he reassured her in a teasing tone. "I seem to have forgotten my scrub bottoms so I will not be taking my pants off just now."

"Oh, ah, haha, um, okay, good," stammered Neena and turned her attention to the next locker. Raj pulled his white coat on again and strode toward the door.

"I will keep watch near the vending machine and distract Ron if I see him headed this way."

"Okay, great," Neena mumbled, still feeling embarrassed and slightly confused. She had seen other shirtless men before and even a few weeks ago she had seen Raj and many of her male teammates on the "skins" team during the soccer game in the park. So why did she feel so uncomfortable? She was going to be a doctor, after all. She felt silly and childish. *Get a grip*, she told herself sternly, and turned back to the lockers.

Neena recognized most of the belongings contained in the lockers and was thus able to identify the owners. As she opened the second to last locker she was met with another overpowering smell. This time it was the unmistakable odor of sweaty sneakers and unwashed clothing. Wrinkling her nose, Neena decided that this was likely Ron's locker. Reluctantly she put her hands into the pockets of the old gray sweatpants and sweatshirt hanging on the hooks. She fished out some coins, a few paper clips and a chewed-up pen cap. "Yuck!" she shuddered, shoving the items back inside and automatically wiping her hand on the front of her coat. She dragged a metal chair over to peer into the dark recess of the top shelf. There was a sheaf of papers which she quickly rifled through, but they were only old sign-out sheets with the initials RR scribbled on the top left corner, confirming that this was, indeed, Ron's locker. Stepping down from the chair she pushed the clothing aside to look at the floor of the locker. The only item there was a pair of scuffed, smelly shoes. Neena was about to close the door when a final thought occurred to her. She pulled on a pair of latex gloves from the stash she kept in her coat pocket and squatted down. Holding her breath she pulled the dirty gray socks out of the sneakers, turned them over and shook vigorously. She was rewarded with a clink of metal and a wink of light. Neena gasped. There, on the floor of the locker, was a gold chain with a small diamond pendant attached! *I can't believe I found it.* Feeling excited and nervous she scooped it up and dropped it carefully into the breast pocket of her scrub top. The handle of the door rattled and a little squeak of alarm escaped from her lips. Neena shut the locker door with a bang and swung around. To her relief it was only Neel.

"Neel!" she whispered. "You scared me half to death! Why did you do that? Why are you here? Why didn't you page me?" She peeled off her gloves and tossed them into the small waste bin in the corner.

"Calm down, Neena. I just wanted to give you some advance notice before barging in on you. I didn't page you since Cecilia is still keeping Ron occupied. I thought you might need some help. Well, did you find anything?"

Her eyes sparkled as she patted her breast pocket. "You bet I did! I found the necklace!"

"You did! Wow, where was it?" But Neena didn't answer since she was now trying the drawers of the metal desk. The tray in front of the desk opened easily and revealed only the usual clutter of pens, paper clips, and rubber bands. The large drawer on the right, however, was locked.

"Now, why do you think this is locked?" she asked Neel.

"I don't know. I've only ever seen Ron use this desk. But, I never noticed him locking it." He peered down at the small key hole. "Where do you suppose the key is?"

"Well, it's not in his locker, that's for sure," asserted Neena. She opened the small tray and fished about for anything they could use to pick the lock. She found some paperclips and a letter opener. She held them up. "Do you know how to pick a lock?" she asked Neel.

"No, how would I know that? Do you?" he countered.

She shook her head sadly. "No. Darn, what do we do now? We must be running out of time." They both jumped as their pagers vibrated.

Neena clicked the tiny button on the top of her pager to reveal the message.

"411, from Raj."

"Okay, let's just go then," Neel said. "You have the necklace, right? And, that's what we came for, isn't it?"

"I know but it makes no sense for this desk to be locked. Why lock a desk in a common space? Please, buy me a little more time." She pushed him toward the door.

"I don't know, Neena. Ron is going to be really PO'd if he finds you trying to break into the desk."

"And that's exactly why I need you to go distract him. Go on, hurry, there may be other evidence in here that we can use, and you wouldn't want Ron to destroy anything would you?" She turned away from him and bent over the lock again.

Neel opened his mouth to protest, then promptly closed it. He gave an exasperated sigh and quickly walked to the door. Neena turned her attention back to the lock, inserted two paper clips and tried to jiggle them around just like the heroines in her mystery stories did. The light in the room had been slowly fading as the sky darkened outside and a sudden streak of lightning flashed outside the window. Neena pulled out her penlight and held it between her teeth as she continued to struggle with the lock. She jumped as lightning flashed and the door opened again. This time it was Raj. He quickly slipped through and walked to her side.

"Neena, what are you doing? Neel said you were still in here. What are you looking for?"

"I really don't know but I have a hunch there may be something important locked in here. I don't know why he left the necklace in his locker rather than locking it up here, though he did hide it in an ingenious spot."

"Where?" Raj began, but Neena interrupted him.

"Never mind that now. I'll tell you later. Do you know anything about locks?" Raj joined her behind the desk and leaned down to examine the lock.

"As a matter of fact, I do," he said, and flashed her a smile. He pulled out his keychain on which hung a small Swiss army knife and squatted down on the floor. Selecting one of the notches along the side he extracted a thin metal tool. Then Raj picked up the letter opener from the desk and inserted both into the lock. His dark eyebrows were furrowed in concentration as he gently manipulated the tools. Neena held her breath, each passing second feeling like an eternity. Just as she was about to suggest they give it up, there was a slight click. Raj sat back on his haunches with a satisfied look on his face.

"There you are, madam," he said, and with a flourish gestured to the now-open filing drawer.

"What? Wow, Raj! How? Why? Okay, never mind that now. Great job. Come on, let's take a look."

The drawer was crammed full of green hanging file folders and each one was filled with manila folders. She and Raj each selected one at random, and flipped through the pages. Rain pattered loudly against the windows from the unexpected storm. Raj took out his own penlight and directed the little circle of light onto the papers on the floor.

"These look like medical bills and statements," he said. "All the patients in this folder have last names starting with the letter 'M.'" He looked at the front of the green folder which was marked with a large black 'M.'

Neena looked up briefly. "Mine has patients with last names starting with 'C,'" she said. "Yes, these are all medical bills as well." She returned her folder back to the drawer, carefully placing it in alphabetical order. She quickly flipped through the other green folders and found that each one represented another letter of the alphabet.

"Why are these here?" she asked. "This makes no sense."

Raj, who was closely examining the sheet in front of him said, "Maybe these are not medical bills, but payments?" He pointed to the fine print at the bottom of several pages which stated "amount paid" followed by a monetary value. The darkness of the room was making it increasingly difficult to see and Neena squinted at the numbers. An idea occurred to her and she returned to the drawer, pulling the file folders toward the front and reached to the rear of the drawer. However, her probing fingers only felt the metal back. She was about to close the drawer when she lifted the first few rows of folders out of their hanging slots. Feeling along the bottom of the cabinet, her fingers touched a large envelope.

"Aha," she said, as she carefully unwound the white string that was looped around the fasteners on the back of the envelope.

"Neena," said Raj urgently. "We've been here quite a long time. I think we need to get going." He was looking at his illuminated watch face and tapped on it with a long forefinger.

"Raj, look!" she said as she extracted a thick stack of checks. She fanned them out for him to see. Neena turned them over, trying to aim her penlight at the writing on the back. Just then, a helpful flash of light revealed the writing on the back. Imprinted by a neat black stamp was the name, "D.R. Healthcare."

Chapter 24

Neena and Raj looked at each other in astonishment. Then, Neena's big brown eyes widened in fear with the delayed realization that a corresponding crack of thunder had not followed what she had presumed to be lightning, and the sudden illumination in the room came from the overhead lights turning on. Unfortunately, the noise of the rain outside had drowned out the sound of the door opening. Suddenly, a pair of worn brown loafers were visible near the front of the desk.

"And what might you two be doing together on this dark and steamy afternoon?" said a familiar drawl. Duncan's face appeared over the top of the desk and his bright blue eyes looked at them.

Neena instantly sprang to her feet. "Hey, Dunk!" she said in an overly bright and cheery voice. "We were just, um, studying." She had quickly hidden the stack of checks behind her back and waggled them at Raj who was still squatting on the floor beside her. She felt him take them from her and wondered what he was going to do with them.

"Hello there, student-doctor Raj," said Duncan in a mocking tone.

Duncan's eyes moved to the drawer which was pulled wide open.

Raj, who was pretending to tie his shoelace, suddenly looked up and banged his forehead hard against the metal tray.

Neena whirled around. "Oh, no! Raj, are you okay?" A large goose egg was forming on the left side of his forehead, now giving him a matching set. Raj held his hand up to his head and nodded slowly.

"Yes, I'm fine," he said, and staggered back into the desk chair that had been pushed back against the wall. Neena noticed his eyes were slightly crossed. Duncan hurried around the desk to check Raj and placed a steadying hand on his shoulder as he swayed slightly.

"Okay, buddy. Just keep your eyes closed for a few minutes," he advised. Duncan then turned around and gave Neena his full attention.

"Now, why don't you tell me what's really going on here. Why is Ron's desk open and what are all these papers?"

"I, we," stammered Neena, her childhood stutter emerging in times of stress. Then she came to a decision. "Okay, Dunk, actually it's good you're here. I think, as our senior resident, we could use your help." She took a deep breath and plunged ahead. "We—Raj and I—think we know who killed that girl Linda and why."

Duncan lifted both of his bleach-blond eyebrows. "Really? Well, that's amazing." He sat on the corner of the desk, crossed one elegantly-trousered leg over the other and clasped his long fingers loosely over his raised knee. "Do tell," he said. His face was alight with curiosity but there was a gleam of amusement in his eyes as he leaned forward slightly.

"Look here. All these folders. They are all insurance statements. And, we found a huge stash of canceled checks. And you won't believe who cashed them."

"I'm sure I couldn't even begin to guess," he drawled. He flicked a finger toward Raj, who was still slumped in the chair, gently massaging the lump on his forehead. "What about you, Raj? What do you think about all this?"

"We think it's Dr. Roberts, Duncan." Raj tugged the stack from his coat pocket and held it out for Duncan to see. "Neena heard him arguing with that girl Linda a few days ago, down in the billing department. She works in an office near the radiology reading room." Duncan extended one long arm and took the stack from Raj.

"Hmm," he said, turning the stack over and looking at the imprinted name. "Very interesting. Okay, so what do you think happened?"

Neena answered as Raj now had his eyes closed. "I—we—think that Ron has been working with Linda from billing and stealing insurance checks from the hospital. I overheard an argument they were having last week. He was furious and kept asking where the rest of it was. I guess he thought that there ought to be more checks. Then on the day of her murder I saw him enter the ground floor lobby as I was getting a cup of coffee. I thought he would have been at the nurses' station before me, but he wasn't there when I got there. Remember, I bumped into you with the tape box? Ron only arrived after we did!"

"So, you think he was busy strangling Linda at that time?"

"Yes!" Neena nodded vigorously, her black curls bouncing and her dark eyes bright.

"And, look at the name on the back of these checks," she said and flipped the top one over so Dunk could see. "It matches the writing we found near Linda's body! 'D.R. Enterprises.' D.R.? Doctor Roberts?"

"Mmm, yes," said Raj, now holding his head with both hands. Neena turned to look at him.

"Are you okay? What's happening?"

"Just feeling a little dizzy and nauseous," he said slowly. "I will be alright in a few minutes."

"What was that about some writing near Linda's body?" prompted Duncan. "This is turning into quite the mystery story."

Neena resumed her tale. "After I finished doing chest compressions on Linda, I realized that, next to her right hand, written in red lipstick, were the letters D.R.!"

Duncan's eyes widened in surprise. "Wow! Now that is quite amazing! It seems Linda was quite a clever girl," he mused.

Neena looked searchingly at him. "I'm surprised you didn't already know that about her. After all, you and she were rather close, weren't you?"

"Now, what makes you say that?" he asked in mild surprise.

"Well, I noticed you both having lunch in the cafeteria last week and then we, Raj and I, came upon you and her kissing," she said, a faint blush diffusing her cheeks at the account of their voyeuristic encounter.

"Ah, that. I didn't realize we had been providing you both with free entertainment." Duncan gave her an appraising look and continued. "It was still early days in our relationship and we were keeping it to ourselves for now. It's quite sad that she's gone." Neena was slightly surprised by his bland tone regarding Linda's violent demise.

Duncan, who had been leafing through the checks Raj had given him, now re-stacked them neatly and placed them inside the pocket of his long white coat. He patted his pocket.

"I think it'd be safer for you two if I hold on to these, don't you? After all, this is certainly hard evidence of some serious insurance fraud and a motive to kill Linda if she was threatening to go to the authorities over it."

Neena gave a little sigh and nodded with relief. She definitely did not want to be found holding those incriminating checks.

"But this still does not prove he murdered her, does it?" Dunk asked.

"No, it doesn't, I guess. But I think the police may find his fingerprints on the murder weapon."

"What murder weapon?" Duncan asked sharply.

"The necklace! I noticed that she was wearing a necklace with a diamond pendant on it. It was there at the beginning of the code but by the end of the code it was gone!" Neena went on with mounting excitement. "And, I think I saw Ron take it. Why would he do that if not to avoid incriminating himself? That was actually the real reason we came in here today. To look for the necklace."

Duncan leaned closer to her. "And, did you find it?"

Before Neena could answer, she was distracted by the urgent vibration of her pager. Looking down she gasped as she read the brief, ominous message from Neel, "911."

Chapter 25

Neena hastily gathered up the folders on the floor and stuffed them back into the drawer. She slammed the drawers shut and heard the lock on the filing drawer click back into place.

"Raj! Come on, get up," she said, and tugged on his arms. He stood up a little shakily and allowed Neena to guide him to the worn sofa. Then, she ran to the bookshelf crammed with surgical reference books. Grabbing a few she dropped them onto the small coffee table in front of the sofa and opened them to random pages.

"Neel just paged 911," she whispered, leaning close to Raj's ear. "Ron is on his way! Look busy." Duncan unfolded himself from the desktop and followed Neena and Raj. He now raised a mocking eyebrow at her as he sank into the lumpy armchair near the sofa.

"Ron is on his way!" she told him in a low urgent tone. "You won't say anything about what we found, will you?"

Duncan pretended to lock his lips and toss away the key. "Your secret is safe with me, Miss Sherlock," he said with a sardonic smile, just as the door to the residents' lounge swung open and banged against the rubber door stopper. Ron came barging through the doorway, stopping suddenly as he saw Duncan.

"Oh, uh, hey Dunk."

"Ron." Duncan gave a slight incline of his head, the bright light from the overhead fluorescent bulbs caused his pale golden hair to shine like a nimbus.

Neena, who had been hunched over the textbook in her lap, hastily flipped it right side up and raised her head a fraction. Ron stomped over to the metal desk and slammed down the stack of scuffed, dark blue patient binders he was carrying. He dropped heavily into the chair and pulled the top one toward him.

"What are you looking at?" he asked in a low growl.

"Nothing, nothing," said Neena, turning back to her "studying." Raj uttered a soft groan and gently rubbed the newly injured side of his head.

"What's wrong with him?" Ron asked.

Duncan answered, "Oh nothing. He was tying his shoelace and when he stood up he banged his head on the side of the desk." He gave Neena a wink, looking pleased with himself for coming up with a truthful answer to Ron's question.

Ron snorted in disgust. "Like I said, this is the sorriest bunch of students to come through here. Hey, you know you're still on call tonight, don't ya?" he said, now training his glare at the back of Raj's head.

"Yes, yes, I'm fine Dr. Roberts," said Raj.

"You better be."

Duncan, who had been whistling a classical tune, got up and moved toward Raj.

"Don't worry, Dr. Roberts. I am going to take student-doctor Raj here to the treatment room and give him the once over. He'll be right as rain once I'm done with him."

"Come on," he said, reaching for Raj's arm. "Let's get you an ice pack and some Tylenol." Duncan and Raj had only taken a few steps when the door burst open once again.

Duncan held up his hand and stopped Neel's headlong rush into the room.

"Whoa, hey there cowboy, slow down! Your buddy here doesn't need any more head injuries tonight."

Neel skidded to a halt in front of Duncan and Raj. "What? What's happened? You're hurt, Raj?" he asked anxiously and then scanned the room. His gaze alighted on Neena and he mouthed, "You okay?" to which she gave a quick nod of her head.

Neena answered for Raj. "He's okay, Neel. He just banged his head on the desk."

"Oh, uh, okay then," said Neel, still sounding slightly skeptical. Neena continued to reassure him.

"He'll be okay. He's in good hands now." She then called out to Raj, "How about Neel and I meet you at the nurses' station in about ten minutes?" She glanced at her watch. It was only five-thirty? It seemed like an age since sign-outs. "We can still grab something to eat if we get to the cafeteria by five forty-five. Is that okay, Dunk? Dr. Roberts?" she asked, looking at each of the senior residents in turn.

"Fine by me," Duncan said, as he opened the door and led Raj out into the hallway.

She took Ron's grunt to be in the affirmative. Neena's mind was racing. What should they do next? They really ought to contact the detective and tell him about their findings today. And, to fill in the gaps about the writing she and Raj had noted at the crime scene. During what must have been the last few minutes of her life Linda had desperately tried to identify her killer. Now there was a clear link between what the dying girl had written on the floor and the initials Neena and Raj had found on the checks. Neena was sure that Ron had created a bogus healthcare company so that he could cash the insurance checks. No wonder he could afford a fancy watch and gold chain. *Too bad he hadn't seen fit to invest in some clean clothes and deodorant*, she thought dryly. Neena was picking up the textbooks that she and Raj had been pretending to study when a sudden, unusually loud crack of thunder caused her to jump and drop the books on the table. Ron, who was hunched over the desk and had been scribbling furiously in one of the charts, looked up to glare at her. Neena shrugged apologetically and returned the books to the shelf. She and Neel quietly let themselves out of the room.

Cecilia, who had clearly been pacing the hallway in anticipation, now came hurrying toward them.

"Did you find the necklace?"

"Yes, I found it, Ceci!" said Neena triumphantly. "He had hidden it inside one of his shoes, under his smelly sock."

"Ew!" said Cecilia, wrinkling her fine nose in distaste and then smiling brightly in admiration. "Now that's what I call dedication." She gave Neena a high five. "Where is it?"

Neena patted her breast pocket. "It's here. I was wearing gloves when I found it, so I think I'd better leave it there for now until we find a safe place to put it."

"Where's Raj?" Neena asked, looking around. "Dunk took him to the treatment room for some first aid."

"I thought he was with you," said Cecilia. "Wait a minute! Is he injured again?"

Neel grinned. "Yeah, seems he gave himself another goose egg when he and Neena were crawling around under the desk. Now he has a matching set."

"Why was he crawling around under the desk?"

"We'll tell you all about it once we find Raj." Neena shook her head at Neel. "Really, Neel, that's not funny. Poor Raj. He just seemed a little dizzy, Ceci, so Dunk said he was going to patch him up. You didn't see them go past here?"

"No, I was waiting for you at the nurses' station until I couldn't sit still any longer. Then, I just started walking around. I guess I missed them. Where's the treatment room?"

"It's over there," Neena said, pointing down the corridor to their right.

"That's so strange. You should have seen them if you were at the nurses' station." A small, puzzled frown creased her forehead.

"Come on, let's go find him then."

Neena had already turned on her heel and was heading down the corridor. She pushed open the door to the treatment room with Neel and Cecilia hard on her heels and they all came to an abrupt halt.

"I thought you said it was just a bump on the head," said Cecilia, looking around the small room in some confusion. It only took a glance to see that the room was completely unoccupied and was devoid even of the stretcher that usually stood in the middle of the space. The attention to detail at LCH was such that the nursing staff called housekeeping immediately after a patient left the room in order to clean up any debris that may have been generated during small procedures such as blood draws and IV placement. Occasionally, other procedures such as suturing or the placement of NG (nasogastric) tubes also took place here. Now the room, judging by the disarray and litter on the floor, appeared as if a major event had taken place. Packages of gauze and IV tubing were scattered on the floor and the door to one of the metal supply cabinets was hanging open. Items had tumbled from the shelves and bottles of alcohol, peroxide, and Betadine had rolled here and there. One of the bottles of Betadine had leaked and there were large dark brown streaks on the bright white tiles.

"What on earth?" said Neena, her eyes wide with astonishment.

"Did you have a code in here earlier?" asked Cecilia.

Neena's black curls shook vigorously. "No, not at all! We would have known since this is our floor."

Neel had advanced into the room. "Maybe another team performed a procedure here on someone our team is not following? There are other surgical specialty teams that admit to this floor. So maybe it was one of them and housekeeping hasn't been called yet?" He crouched down in the middle of the floor and pointed.

"This looks like blood, doesn't it?"

"Yes, it does. Maybe they did a more invasive procedure like a central line or a cut-down?" Neena suggested. She, too, had advanced into the room and was looking around intently. "Okay, then maybe they went to another treatment room or even the on-call room since this room was such a mess?"

"Yes, that has to be it," agreed Cecilia. "C'mon, let's go take a look." As Neena whirled back toward the door, she spotted something colorful on the floor. Stooping over she found a small bright yellow Lego piece. *Had it fallen out of her pocket?* She couldn't quite recall when she had last been in this room.

Cecilia, one hand on the door, turned back. "Neena, you coming?"

Neena picked up the Lego piece and added it back to the miscellany in her overstuffed pockets.

"Yes, yes!" she said, and hurried to join the other two.

They walked quickly back the way they had come.

"Did either of you try paging Raj?" asked Cecilia. Neena and Neel shook their heads.

"Okay, why don't I do that? I can wait here for a few minutes for an answer."

"Good idea!" said Neel. "Then, how about we split up?" he suggested. "Neena, why don't you check the on-call room, and Cecilia, if Raj doesn't answer can you run down to the cafeteria? Maybe he got confused and thinks we planned on meeting him there? And, I will check the treatment rooms on the other surgical floors. Okay?"

Both Neena and Cecilia nodded in agreement.

"Right, good thinking," said Cecilia.

"Okay, let's use the paging codes we came up with," said Neena. She turned to Cecilia. "Cecilia, we decided to use 411 for non-urgent info-related messages and 911 for emergencies."

"Oh, that's cute. Okay, sure."

The three friends each went in separate directions to accomplish their assigned tasks.

Chapter 26

Neena pushed open the door to the stairwell and ran the two flights up to the on-call rooms. She knocked on the door of the men's on-call room and, receiving no answer, opened the door, reaching for the light switch as she did so. The bright fluorescent lighting revealed two sets of bunk beds with fresh white sheets and pillows. There was no sign that Raj and Duncan, or anyone else for that matter, had recently been here. She went to the telephone and dialed the Four East nurses' station.

"Hello?" said a gruff voice.

"Hi. This is Neena, one of the med students. If any of the students or residents are there may I please speak to one of them?" she asked.

"No," said the voice, and hung up the phone with a bang. Neena instinctively pulled the handset away from her ear and looked at it in surprise. *No, they weren't there or, no, she couldn't speak to them?* Neena wondered irritably. Of course it would be Marge who answered the phone. She turned off the lights, shut the door and walked briskly down the hallway, considering her next move. Presumably, Cecilia and Neel were still checking their assigned locations. Should she try paging one of them to let them know that the call rooms were empty? She decided she was too impatient since she would have to wait by the phone until one of them called. Could Raj have been more injured than she had initially assumed and Dunk decided to take him to the ER instead? Her newly minted third-year medical brain automatically started catastrophizing. What if the second lump on Raj's forehead was not just superficial but actually extended into his brain? He could have brain swelling! He could be herniating! Neena was now running down the corridor. As she rounded the corner she ran headlong into someone and glanced up into a pair of startled dark brown eyes.

"Slow down there, little lady! I mean, Doctor," said Mr. Robinson. He had caught her by the shoulders to prevent her from careening into him. His tidy cart was parked next to him as he waited for the elevator.

"Mr. Robinson! So sorry, I didn't see you there," Neena gasped as she skidded to a stop. She held a hand to her right side where a stitch had developed.

"Is everything okay?" he asked.

"Yes, I mean no—that is, I don't know."

Mr. Robinson looked at her with kindly concern. "Can I help?"

"I'm looking for Dr. Goodwin. Do you know who he is?" Mr. Robinson's usually affable countenance assumed a slightly more guarded look. "Yes," he said, pursing his lips slightly. "I know who he is."

Neena, picking up on the change in the older man's expression, asked, "You don't like him? Why not?" She was surprised to find someone who had a negative opinion of Dunk. It had seemed to her that Duncan was well-liked by his fellow residents, the students, and the hospital staff. His easy smile and laid-back style put people at ease. Duncan never seemed to have any difficulty in getting people to do what he wanted them to do. *How strange and intoxicating such power must be*, Neena mused. Did Duncan always get what he wanted?

"That young man is trouble, Doc, if you ask me. I'd stay clear of him."

"Trouble? Duncan?" Neena asked in surprise. "He's a rich playboy, I know, but he hasn't approached me in that way, if that's what you mean."

"It's really not my place to say, Doc," said Mr. Robinson. As curious as Neena was to hear about Mr. Robinson's opinion of Duncan Goodwin, she knew she didn't have time for this now.

"I'm also looking for my friend, one of the medical students. His name is Raj. Tall Indian guy with a mustache. Do you know him? Have you seen him?" Neena asked urgently.

"Dr. Raj? Yes, I know him. What a nice young fella he is. Isn't he on one of the surgical floors, or maybe he went to the call room?"

"No," Neena shook her head. "He's not in the call room. He had a minor accident and Dr. Goodwin was going to take him to the treatment room but they weren't there."

Now Mr. Robinson's face looked slightly worried. "He's injured? But, it's minor you say? Did you check the men's room?"

"Ah! No, I didn't even think of that."

"Hang on, let me check the one right here." He went around the corner but reappeared in less than a minute, shaking his head. "Did you check the cafeteria? Maybe he went to get a bite to eat? They're serving grilled salmon tonight, I heard. You should get down there yourself. You look like you could use a meal," he said.

"No, no, I don't have time for dinner right now, but thank you for your concern. I really need to find Dr. Goodwin and Raj. My other friends, Neel and Cecilia, are also looking for him."

Mr. Robinson's forehead was wrinkled in thought, then he appeared to come to a decision. "There's a phone call I gotta make, Doc, I'll be right back. You just wait here a sec, okay?"

"Um, what? Why?" Neena asked but received no reply as Mr. Robinson had already turned away and was walking toward the telephone that was mounted in the hallway. She watched his retreating form, and wondered whom he suddenly decided he needed to call. She liked Mr. Robinson. He always had a kind word or a smile and even Raj had said how helpful Mr. Robinson had been to him as he was getting acclimated to the hospital. It was sweet of him to urge her to eat dinner, she thought. Although dinner sounded like an excellent idea she couldn't eat until she found her friends. And, they had to contact the detective to hand over all of the incredible evidence they uncovered this evening. Neena pressed the down-button for the elevator as she pondered her next move, being no closer to a plan than she had been a few minutes ago, before she had run into Mr. Robinson.

Neena's stomach gave a little grumble, as if to remind her that a salmon dinner would be just the ticket right now. Salmon. Salmon? *Stop thinking about your stomach*, she told herself sternly. The elevator door opened with a soft chime but Neena was suddenly transfixed. Salmon! It reminded her of something important. She was feeling anxious wondering about how Raj was doing. And where was he? She willed herself to breathe slowly and deeply, and allowed her mind to wander freely. Salmon was tasty, but also slightly smelly. Ron was smelly. This was about Ron then? Yes, and no. What else could it be? Salmon was pink. No, it was more peachy than pink. Neena immediately went to her mental filing cabinet, but her fingers hesitated before opening one of the drawers. What should she look under? What was the common thread? Neena loved color and she used color-coding to organize her closet, her notes, her bookshelves. *Okay, let's start there*, she thought and mentally rifled through items that were peach-colored. Peaches, cantaloupes, papayas, mangoes. Neena's stomach gave a gurgle of protest as she thought of all these delectable fruits. Mangoes were peachy-orange and were drawn like tear drops on textiles, and then called paisley. She loved the traditional Indian paisley prints that had been featured on many of her mother's sarees. She paused mentally at the image of a peachy-pink paisley print.

The elevator door closed again but Neena hadn't noticed. She stood still, deep in thought. Her brain was racing. Images clicked before her mind's eye, like slides in a View Master. Paisley prints, a little boy with golden hair shining like a nimbus, and the sudden startling similarity between two seemingly random men. She imagined their faces on a sliding scale, one of them becoming older as the other became younger, and as the faces overlapped, barring a few minor details, it was as if they were one.

Chapter 27

The elevator chimed again and the doors slid smoothly open. Neel and Cecilia burst through the doors before they had even fully opened and stopped short upon seeing Neena.

"Neena!" exclaimed Cecilia. "We can't find Raj or Duncan anywhere! He was not in the cafeteria and I even swung by the ER in case he was more seriously injured than you had believed him to be."

Neel shrugged his shoulders. "Where could they have gone? While I was waiting for Cecilia I tried to page him to the Four East nurses' station, but no answer."

Neena, whose mouth had formed a perfect "O," was staring straight ahead, her eyes unseeing. Cecilia and Neel looked at her and then back at each other in puzzlement. Cecilia took Neena by the shoulders and gave her a little shake. "Neena, are you okay? Why are you just standing here? Did you find Raj or Dunk?" Neena did not answer or even bat an eyelash.

"Neena!" shouted Neel.

Neena's eyes finally focused on him. "What? Why are you shouting at me, Neel?"

He gave an exasperated sigh. "Really? We've been trying to tell you that we still haven't found Raj or Dunk and you're just ignoring us."

"No, Neel," said Cecilia, as enlightenment dawned. "I think she's thought of something. Haven't you?" she asked excitedly. "What is it? Do you know where they are?"

Neena shook her head slowly. "No, I don't know where they are but a crazy idea just popped into my head and if I'm right then I think I know why all these accidents have happened to Raj and Neel. And, also why I was attacked. And, more importantly, I think I know who is behind all this. Come on, we've gotta find Raj! I'm really worried about him."

"Where are we going?" asked Neel, running to catch up with Neena, who, eschewing the elevator, walked quickly toward the stairwell. As they ran down the stairs, Neena called over her shoulder.

"I want to check the treatment room again for any clues. I found something on the floor that I think Raj may have dropped." She went on to tell them about the small yellow Lego piece. "Little Danny has been hiding Lego pieces in my lab coat pocket when he visits. He's not really allowed to have the little ones but he loves them and so he hides them in my pockets. But do you remember that day we all had lunch together in the cafeteria? I think I may have left some of my change on the table and maybe some Lego pieces as well. Did either of you see Raj pick them up?"

Cecilia nodded. "Yes he did! You raced off in a hurry so Raj pocketed some coins and a few Legos you had left on the table."

"He must have forgotten he had them," said Neena breathlessly. She tugged open the door to the fourth floor and the three of them ran down the hall, back to the treatment room.

"Look around for anything else that would suggest Raj was actually here," she said and started walking around the perimeter of the room. Neel and Cecilia examined the debris on the floor more closely.

"I think there is some blood mixed in with this betadine," said Neel, squatting next to some of the dark brown streaks.

"Was Raj bleeding from his head injury?" asked Cecilia, who was now also squatting on the white tile floor next to Neel.

Neena shook her head. "No, it was just a bump."

Cecilia turned worried blue eyes up to Neena. "My god, what do you think happened here?"

"I don't know. Looks like there may have been a struggle," Neena said.

"Who with?" asked Neel, standing up and dusting off the knees of his scrub pants. "Are you saying that someone attacked Raj and Duncan in this room?"

"No," said Neena slowly. "I think Duncan is the one who has been trying to hurt Raj. And, I think you, Neel, were the accidental beneficiary of the loosened door closer. I also believe that Duncan was worried that I had already figured things out and that's why he attacked me."

Cecilia and Neel looked shocked. Neena, who had been roaming around the room, stopped and bent over to pick up some papers that were partially visible under one of the rolling wire racks.

"Look! These are Raj's sign-out notes." She shook them under Neel and Cecilia's noses. She indicated the initials, M.R.M., printed neatly on the top corner of each page. Raj was very meticulous in his charting and his handwriting had not yet developed into the hasty scrawl she had seen the senior residents and Attendings use. She hadn't realized it was an acquired attribute, but it was one she hoped she could avoid since she liked her neat, cursive handwriting.

Cecilia reached out and put a hand on Neena's shoulder. "Neena, are you serious about Duncan? Why on earth would you think that? What possible reason could he have to hurt Raj?"

"One word," said Neena. "Money." She quickly explained her extraordinary theory to Cecilia and Neel. Now they both looked gobsmacked. Cecilia held her hands up to her mouth, her eyes wide with sudden understanding. Neel opened and closed his mouth but no sounds issued forth. After a few seconds he closed his mouth with a snap and looked quickly around the room.

"Okay, then we have to find him. I don't see anything else here of use. Do you?" Neel looked from Neena to Cecilia. "Come on, let's go!" He strode quickly out of the room, with Neena and Cecilia close on his heels. Neena occasionally broke into a little hop to keep up with his long, loping stride.

Neel headed directly to the nurses' station, thrust his head and shoulders over the counter, and did the unthinkable. "Excuse me, Nurse Marge?" he said in a rush. "We are looking for two of our team members. Have you seen Dr. Goodwin or student-doctor Raj?" Marge, who seemed to have fallen into a waking doze, gave a startled snort and shook her large grizzled head back and forth. Then her beady eyes came into focus and she fixed them on Neel like a predator sizing up its prey. Apparently, Neel's concern for Raj had superseded his common sense, but now he took a cautious step backward as Marge slowly lumbered to her feet. From her full height she scowled down at Neel. *She must be at least six-foot-three*, thought Neena in amazement.

"He went to the ER," she said gruffly.

"Oh, they were called to see a patient in the ER?" asked Neel.

"Dr. Goodwin went to the ER."

"What about our friend, Raj? Was he with Dr. Goodwin?" Neel pressed her.

Marge's lip curled in a sneer. "How am I supposed to know?"

"How long ago was that?" Neena asked Marge, throwing caution to the wind.

Marge bared her coffee-stained teeth at them. "You just missed him," she said, cocking a bushy eyebrow in the direction of the rear stairwell.

"But where do you think Raj is then?" asked Cecilia anxiously.

"I don't know," said Neena. Her small hands were balled into fists by her side and her face was grim. "But if we can find Dunk then we can make him tell us where he took Raj."

With a chorus of mumbled thanks Neena and her friends ran toward the rear stairwell. A bank of service elevators was also located there so that orderlies could take patients up and down to the ER and to the radiology suites. Neel ran to the stairwell and yanked the door open.

"Neel, wait!" called Neena. Bending down she picked up a small object and held it in her palm for her friends to see. It was a little red Lego piece.

"Where did you find that?" asked Neel.

Neena pointed to the floor near the service elevators. "I think it must have fallen out of his pocket."

"He took the elevator? Why? When it's so much quicker to run down the stairs."

Neena looked around frantically. Where could Raj be? And, how had Duncan managed to abduct a large able-bodied man like Raj? Well maybe he wasn't quite so able-bodied after his head injury, but he should still have been able to put up some sort of resistance. Oh god! Maybe Raj was already dead? No, he couldn't be. She would not even allow the horrid thought to linger in her mind. Glancing down at the usually immaculate, gleaming white tile floor she noted a set of black linear scuff marks.

"The stretcher!" cried Neena, pointing to the floor.

"Yes, the stretcher!" agreed Cecilia. Neena turned and jabbed at the down-button for the elevator.

"What stretcher?" asked Neel, confused.

"The stretcher that should have been in the treatment room!" said Neena.

Cecilia continued, "If Raj is hurt then Duncan would need to find a way to transport him, right? What better way in a hospital than to put him on a stretcher? Pull a sheet over him and then Dunk could then hide Raj in plain sight!"

"Right, good thinking!" Neel agreed. The elevator gave a ping and the large double doors slid open. The service elevator, though not as elegant as the ones in the front of the hospital, was still clean and well-maintained. Wide gray rubber rail guards ran around the perimeter to prevent the walls from getting scuffed by the sides of stretchers, carts, or laundry bins. They hurried into the elevator and Neel, with unexpected anger, banged on the button to close the doors with the base of his fist. "Come on, come on!" he yelled at the doors which paid no heed to his urgency but closed at their usual inch-by-slow-inch pace.

Neena was about to press the button for the ground floor when Cecilia stopped her.

"Neena, look!" said Cecilia, pointing to the row of buttons. Across the top-most button, labeled 'roof,' was a bloody fingerprint.

Chapter 28

Neena, trying not to get blood on her fingers, used the knuckle of her index finger to press the same button. Why was Duncan taking Raj to the roof? Was he planning on throwing him off the rooftop? Neena could imagine Duncan tipping the unconscious Raj from the stretcher over the edge of the building. Then he could leave the stretcher in an empty hallway and saunter back into the hospital, his blue eyes clear and a lazy smile on his face. If he proclaimed that Raj was hale and hearty after he had patched him up, who would ever doubt him? Then, with a casual shrug of his elegant shoulders he would simply deny any knowledge of Raj's current whereabouts. They had to catch him in the act!

This section of the hospital was eight stories high and in recent years a helipad had been installed so that trauma patients could be quickly transported. Neena and her team had thus far only gone to the helipad once to receive a patient who was being flown in from the site of a serious motor vehicle accident. Most of the team had raced up the stairwell leaving two of the residents to bring the stretcher in the elevator. Neena remembered squinting into the bright sunlight and holding her hands over her ears. The roar of the helicopter blades and the rush of the wind had created a thrilling experience. She and the other students had been bystanders while the trauma Attending and the senior residents performed their assessments at lightning speed and then whisked the patient into the elevator.

The elevator finally reached the roof and opened into a small glass-enclosed vestibule. Neena slammed her fist on the metal button on the wall. Even before the doors had fully parted, she and her friends were being spattered with sharp sprays of rain. What Neena had assumed was a brief summer storm seemed to have devolved into a minor hurricane over the last hour. Dark, menacing clouds were depositing torrents as if from a broken dam. And the fierce, whipping wind was directing the water in fantastical horizontal sheets. There was a sudden exponential increase in the noise and ferocity of the storm assaulting them. The effects of Mother Nature were now being augmented by the whipping blades of a helicopter!

They were all instantly drenched. The onslaught of wind and water, coupled with a sudden burst of lightning, gave them a moment of pause. There, illuminated like a portrait in a gallery, was a black-and-white rendering of a scene that Neena was sure would be permanently etched onto her brain. Crouched in the open doorway of the helicopter, his hair plastered to his elegantly shaped head like a golden sculpted helmet, was Duncan. In his arms was the dark shape of a man's torso. The man's legs appeared to be entangled in the blankets on the stretcher, which was now tipped precariously on its side as Duncan tried to wrench the man free. For an instant, Neena, Cecilia, and Neel simply stared in disbelief. The flash of light which had brightened Duncan's face had also served to illuminate the three of them. Duncan looked up, and his blue eyes pierced through the darkness, catching Neena's horrified gaze. One eyebrow and the corner of his lip quirked upward in a mocking challenge.

"That's Raj!" shouted Neena. The wind whipped her words away but her announcement was unnecessary as Raj's dark curly hair and mustache were easy to discern against the paleness of Duncan's shirt. Neel sprang forward and sprinted toward the stretcher, with Neena and Cecilia close behind him. He lunged with both arms, grabbing hold of Raj's legs, which were now encased in heavy, sodden bedclothes.

Duncan, his face now grim, turned toward the interior of the helicopter. "Go, go, go!" he shouted. Immediately, the helicopter rose a few feet off the ground. Neena could see the pale, startled face of the pilot as he turned to look at Duncan. The sudden movement of the helicopter dislodged Raj from the stretcher and Neel staggered backward, his arms filled with flapping blankets. He fell back into Neena, sending them both sprawling to the ground. Neena scrambled up, pushing hard against Neel's back to free herself. She saw Cecilia, who had swerved to avoid her two colliding friends, reach the helicopter and grab hold of one of Raj's legs with both of her hands. Neena raced forward to grab the other leg. Raj's leg was heavy from inertia and his water-logged pants. Neena struggled to find a purchase on the fabric which was now taut against his leg.

Duncan gave a roar of frustration as Raj's body started to slip downward fractionally due to Neena and Cecilia's determined and energetic efforts.

"Let go, you stupid bitches!" he screamed, his face distorted with rage. Duncan's lips were pulled back in a snarl. His eyes were narrow blue slits. "I am Uncle Mark's rightful heir! Not this monkey in a white coat!" Saliva frothed at the sides of his mouth and he spit on Raj's head. Gone was all resemblance to the affable, handsome persona he had presented to the world.

Neena gasped as she felt a sharp pull on her legs and her hands slipped a little farther along Raj's leg. Daring a quick glance backward, she saw that Neel had wrapped one long arm around each of the girls' waists and was pulling down hard.

"Hold on!" he shouted. Neena redoubled her efforts and took a firmer grip on the sodden fabric. Wrapping her arms tightly around Raj's leg she hugged it against her small frame and prayed for a miracle. Suddenly she felt Raj's leg stiffen. Looking up she saw his eyes flicker open and then widen. He met her frightened gaze and saw her eyes flick behind him. Neena could not even begin to imagine what Raj was feeling as he woke up to find himself in this bizarre life-threatening scenario. However, with an incredible presence of mind, Raj brought his head forward and then snapped it back hard against Duncan's chin, catching his captor by surprise. Raj grabbed onto Duncan's arms, pulled them away from his chest and twisted, desperately trying to free himself.

The helicopter had now risen a few more feet, and to her horror, Neena could no longer feel her feet touch the ground. Cecilia had emulated Neena and, wrapping her arms around Raj's right leg, had hugged it to her chest. The two girls now turned to look at one another. Water was streaming down their faces. Neena's bangs were hanging over her forehead, obscuring part of her vision.

"I can't feel the ground anymore!" called Cecilia, her eyes wide with panic.

Another quick glance downward revealed that now Neel was standing on tiptoe!

"Hold on, Ceci! Neel won't let go of us!" shouted Neena, with a confidence she did not quite feel.

As the helicopter exerted its upward pull, Duncan, whose position had been precarious to begin with, now slipped forward. His lower extremities found a frantic purchase on the helicopter's skid and he wrapped his legs around it. With grim determination he tightened his hold on Raj and pulled hard.

"Aarrgh!" yelled Neel from below. Neena looked down into his shocked face and realized that now he, too, was no longer touching the ground. Both she and Cecilia were inching slowly down Raj's legs, their cold, stiff fingers struggling to maintain a grip on the wet cloth. *I do hope he's wearing a belt*, thought Neena, suddenly imagining that she and Cecilia were holding Raj's empty trouser legs and he was dangling above them in his underwear. *Boxers or briefs*, she wondered. Looking up, she saw a slow, satisfied smile curve Duncan's lips as he came to the realization that Neena and her friends were now airborne.

For what seemed an eternity, Duncan, Raj, Cecilia, Neena, and Neel hung from the helicopter in a state of suspended animation. At the same time, Neena felt a new force being violently exerted on her lower limbs. Since she was still desperately clinging onto one of Raj's legs she felt as if her arms and legs would suddenly pop out of their sockets and she would be left dismembered like the Barbie dolls she had seen in her friends' toy chests. Neena shook her head in an attempt to move the wet hair off her face and risked a quick glance downward.

"Let go!" thundered a familiar voice. Even the noise of the storm could not drown out Ron's bellow. Ron? What was he doing here? Now they were trapped with Dunk on one end and Ron on the other. Ron was holding both of Neel's legs and gave a tremendous tug, almost causing Neena to lose her grip on Raj.

Raj, who had been pulling at the fingers that were entwined in his shirt collar, finally managed to loosen one of Duncan's hands. The pilot appeared to be struggling to keep the helicopter steady, and Duncan, who was now holding onto Raj with only one hand, clawed through the air with his free hand. One of Duncan's legs, which he had wrapped around the skid, slipped free. A sudden gust of wind buffeted the machine and then his second leg also lost its grip. The smirk that had been on his face an instant prior was now replaced by a look of disbelief. The helicopter, like a great tethered beast which now found itself free, took off into the air with a roar. Duncan hung in the air for a millisecond, anchored only by his grip on Raj's shirt.

Raj reached up and clasped Duncan's arm with both hands as the human ladder came crashing down. Their screams and thuds were muffled by the sound of the storm and the departing helicopter. Neena's fall was slightly cushioned by Neel, whom she and Cecilia fell on top of. However, the impact rattled her teeth and knocked the breath out of her. She and Cecilia were still holding onto Raj, who in turn, was holding onto Duncan. While Neel, Neena, Cecilia, and Raj had landed on the cement roof top, the only visible portion of Duncan was a white forearm clasped tightly by Raj's long arm. The rest of Duncan was presumably dangling over the edge of the building, almost a hundred feet in the air.

"Hold on!" Raj yelled at Duncan. He then shouted over his shoulder to his friends. "Help me pull him back!" Instinctively they all pulled on the person in front of them. Neena fervently hoped that Ron was helping to anchor Neel.

"Here! Take my other hand!" cried Raj. Neena and Cecilia, who were lying on top of Raj's legs, looked up. The muscles in Raj's arm were taut as he struggled to maintain his existing grip on Duncan's wet skin. Inch by inch, Duncan's face, scraped and bleeding, finally appeared over the ledge. Raj extended his other arm in an attempt to reach for Duncan's free hand. A flash of lightning revealed a familiar gleam in Dunk's eyes. With a sardonic twist of his lips he violently pulled himself free of Raj's grip and plummeted to the ground.

The fierce, erratic wind caught Duncan's final scream, whether it was one of rage or fear would never be known, and funneled it directly into Neena's auditory canals. Neena clapped her hands over her ears, rolled off of Raj's leg, and lay still, her eyes tightly closed. Rainwater and tears flowed freely over her face. Her eyes flew open as she felt a large pair of hands roughly patting down her lower extremities. The sight before her, as well as a sharp searing pain in her foot, made her recoil violently. Dark shaggy locks fell over a broad forehead, coalescing with a row of thick black eyebrows. Was this all simply a nightmare? Neena tried to push herself into a sitting position but now the hands were on her shoulder and pushed her back down.

"Don't move!" it yelled. Neena rubbed her eyes and pushed her damp locks off of her face. A demon from hell could not have been more frightening than the sight of Dr. Ron Roberts hovering above her. Was he here to finish where Dunk had left off? Would she and her friends find themselves being thrown off of the roof? She frantically tried to push his hands away.

"Be still!" he commanded. "I'm just making sure you haven't broken your back or your femur, or anything else. Can you move your legs?" Neena gave an experimental wiggle of her toes and felt a throbbing pain in the region of her left ankle. She nodded at Ron.

"Okay, good! Let me help you up." And suiting his actions to his words he put an arm under her shoulders and propped her into a sitting position.

"Wanna try standing up?" Seeing her nod, he gripped her under her arms and hoisted her into a standing position. As she put her left foot down she cried out in pain and hopped onto her right leg. Ron looked around, trying to judge if any of the other victims on the roof could be of any use. He spied Neel who was now upright and hobbling quickly toward them. Without warning, Ron gave Neena a great shove, propelling her forward. Her breath came out in whoosh as Neel clasped her tightly to him in a bruising embrace. She felt the side of his face rest fleetingly on top of her head. She suddenly felt exhausted. Just as she was about to relax into his comforting embrace, he roughly pushed her away. As she tottered on one leg Neel gripped both her shoulders in a vice-like grip and held her at arm's length.

"This is what you call being careful?!?" Neel yelled, his voice shaking. Neena was startled by the ferocity of his question. His face was suffused with emotion and his green eyes were blazing. His light brown hair, which had been darkened by the pouring rain, was plastered to his head and fell over his forehead.

"I, um, I . . ." stammered Neena. Neel looked more than a little frightening. Neena tried to pull away but Neel held on.

"Oh, no you don't!" And he half-dragged, half-carried her toward the door.

Raj, motionless at the edge of the roof, did not seem to have heard Ron. Cecilia was squatting near him, her arm around his shoulders. Raj stared blankly at his empty hands until Cecilia gently tugged on his shoulders, encouraging him to stand up. He got to his feet gingerly and slowly straightened. He and Cecilia, supporting each other like participants in a three-legged race, limped toward the elevator. Soon all four students were huddled in the vestibule.

Ron ran to the ledge and peered over. Then he turned around and shook his head. His grim face, illuminated by another streak of lightning, was then transformed into a look of utter astonishment. For a millisecond, all of his hair stood on end and a tremor passed through his body before he fell, like a log, to the ground. Neena, Cecilia, Raj, and Neel looked at each other and then back at Ron in horrified fascination. *Oh my god!* thought Neena. *Ron was just struck by lightning!*

Saturday July 18, 1992

Chapter 29

As Raj stood at the open French doors the light evening breeze ruffled his thick dark hair. He looked out at the wide expanse of emerald green lawn with a sense of wonder and gratitude. Wonder at the strange and beautiful turn his life had taken literally overnight, and gratitude for the loyalty and affection of the small group of friends who, even now, were waiting for him to join them.

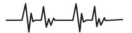

Neena gave a murmur of thanks as she accepted a cold glass of lemonade from Patrick. She, Neel, and Cecilia were sitting under a large canopy of trees in Mr. MacMillan's expansive backyard. She took a sip and relaxed back in her chair. A soft breeze blew her curls off of her face and the blue cloudless sky gave no indication of the violent storm that had occurred just a few days ago. Neena found it just as astonishing that after last week's chaos and tragedy she was now sitting in this lush, tranquil garden, calmly sipping a cold drink. *What a difference a few days makes*, she thought.

The days after Monday evening's tragic event had passed in a blur. They had all been subjected to thorough examinations in the emergency room and the Attendings had insisted they remain overnight for observation. Neena's ankle had been badly sprained but not broken. And after a few days of rest, ice, and elevation, she was able to walk almost normally on it. Ron, successfully resuscitated by her and her friends, would live to tell the tale and face the consequences of his actions. Not only was he guilty of fraud but also of obstructing justice by covering up for Duncan.

Miraculously, no one, other than Duncan, had sustained anything more severe than abrasions and contusions. Although emergency personnel, summoned by Neena, had raced outside in the storm to rescue Duncan, he had been proclaimed dead at the scene. Despite all that Duncan had done to them they had tried their best to save him. However, there was no doubt in Neena's mind that Duncan was beyond saving, in every sense of the word. Though the details of that bizarre night were seared into her brain Neena still found them to be unbelievable. Had she really been dangling from a helicopter? It was a miracle she and her friends had survived that night.

Then there had been the interminable meetings with the police and Detective Flannigan, during which Neena, Raj, and Neel told of all they had learned regarding the mysterious attacks on them and Linda's death. In addition to being a murderer, Duncan had made a successful career of forging checks. He had studied art and printing at his fancy liberal arts college and had put those skills to good use. He had come up with a scheme to subvert insurance payments into a bank account of the bogus company he created, thereby keeping him in expensive clothing, watches, and Mont Blanc pens. Ron, who had accidentally come across the insurance payments, confessed that he had put two and two together and the price of his silence was a share of the money. He had removed the necklace from Linda's dead body so that it could not be traced back to Duncan. Dr. Roberts had been loath to give up a lucrative revenue stream and without Duncan's talents, the insurance scheme would have fallen through. Neena did not doubt that eventually Dr. Roberts would have moved to the top of Duncan's hit list. Perhaps Linda, too, had been threatening exposure or blackmail. Maybe she had grown discontented with little baubles and had demanded even more, leading Duncan to silence her once and for all.

Neena turned back toward her friends who were having a lively conversation.

Neel, leaning casually in his chair with his long legs stretched out in front of him, looked as amiable as ever. She had exchanged brief phone calls with Cecilia over the past few days but she had not spoken with Neel or Raj since that fateful night.

"How are you doing?" Neena asked, looking hesitantly at Neel. The breeze ruffled his hair and his eyes were once again bright green and sparkling.

"I'm as good as new. How are you?"

"I think the shock has finally worn off. My ankle is mostly healed but I'm still black-and-blue everywhere."

"Glad to hear it," he said. Then with a slightly sheepish, apologetic smile, he added, "I'm sorry, by the way, for yelling at you on the roof."

Neena shook her head. "It's okay, Neel. I know you were just worried. We were all worried and scared. I mean, what a nightmare! We couldn't have made all this up if we tried."

"You got that right!" said Neel with a laugh. "Can you believe Ron was actually struck by lightning?" His face lit up in amusement. "That was so cool!"

"Neelesh Shah! That's not nice. Poor guy, he could have died!" scolded Neena, easily reverting back to her natural bossiness now that the air had been cleared between them.

"Well, he didn't die, did he? Thanks to my timely and vigorous chest compressions!"

"Yes, I think you saved his life," said Cecilia. "Thank god you were there.

He's such a big guy I don't know if Neena and I would have been as effective with CPR." A shudder ran through her slim frame. "What a night! I never want to go through anything like that again!"

Neena patted her friend's hand, "Don't worry, Ceci! I'm sure the rest of our rotation will be smooth sailing after all of this drama and chaos."

Cecilia's face brightened. "Fingers crossed," she said fervently. Then glancing at the elegant watch face on her wrist she added, "I wonder what's taking them so long?"

Neena looked toward the open French doors of the house. "Look, there's someone coming right now." They all watched as a man walked out of the house. Since the sun was in their eyes they could not clearly identify him until he came under the leafy canopy of the trees.

"Mr. Robinson!" cried Neena. "What are you doing here?"

Mr. Robinson smiled brightly at them, his white teeth gleaming in his dark brown face. "Why hello there, Docs! How are y'all doing on this fine evening?" he said with an affable nod. He shook each of their hands and, pulling out one of the heavy wrought iron chairs, he sat down. "Well, Mac invited me o'course."

"How do you know Mr. MacMillan, Mr. Robinson?" asked Neel.

"Aw, call me Ed, why don't you? Mr. Robinson reminds me of my old preacher father," he said with a chuckle. "Oh, Mac and I go way back. I used to work in his grandfather's clock factory. I worked there until it closed about ten years ago. I still come by from time to time to make sure that old clock in the hallway is still ticking along."

"So, last night, that phone call you left to make, was it to Mr. MacMillan?" asked Neena.

"That's right, Doc. Mac asked me to keep an eye on you young folk in that there hospital. Hospitals can be deadly places, you know." He pursed his lips and shook his head. "And that good-for-nothing nephew of his. I could tell from the first time I clapped eyes on him that he was bad news."

"You mean Duncan, right? Dunk is Mr. MacMillan's nephew?" asked

Cecilia, then nodded proudly at Neena. "Yes, that's what Neena guessed, but we still couldn't believe it. She had seen a picture of a young boy who resembled Dunk with a young woman on Mr. MacMillan's desk and wondered if they were Mr. MacMillan's wife and son."

"No, that was his lovely sister Annabelle with her only son, Duncan. Why she went and married that good-for-nothing man—Duncan's father—I'll never understand. Well, he was handsome and charming, I suppose. He had her fooled real good into thinking he also came from money. But he didn't have two nickels to rub together. Mac was so worried about his little sister."

"Where are Duncan's parents now, Mr. Rob—I mean, Ed?" asked Neel.

Ed shook his head sadly. "That beautiful girl was taken from this earth too soon. Breast cancer, it was. And that man is behind bars, which is where he belongs. He had been stealing from her and Mac for years, but nothing was ever enough. He then got into armed robbery and during his last heist he killed the old woman whose house he was trying to rob."

"Oh my!" gasped Neena. "That's horrible. Poor Duncan, to lose both his parents like that."

"Don't you go wastin' any of your precious sympathy on that blackguard, Doc. He tried to kill you, didn't he?" Ed said with a cluck of his tongue.

"Yes, of course. And, he almost accidentally killed Neel here too," said Neena.

"Yeah, but he wasn't accounting for my thick skull, was he?" said Neel with a laugh.

"That he didn't," said Cecilia smiling, and reached over to pat his arm. "And," she added, "he hadn't counted on Raj." As if on cue, they heard Raj's voice mingling with another's, from the open French doors. Two figures walked toward them. The sun was behind them, bathing them in its fiery glow. They matched each other in height and in stride. Gradually, the outlines of the two men were visible and when they moved from the sunlight into the shade Neena let out a gasp. The faces she had seen merging in her mind's eye just a few days ago were now right in front of her.

But the only thing Neena could think to say was, "Raj, you shaved off your mustache!" He flashed her a bright, sheepish grin.

"Hi, Neena! Yes, that I did! Even though I didn't lose our bet." He addressed Cecilia and Neel, "I don't believe you two have met Mr. MacMillan yet." And turning toward that gentleman he said with another bright smile, "Neel, Cecilia, I would like to introduce you to my father."

Chapter 30

Although Neena had already prepared them for this momentous news, the announcement was met with a moment of stunned silence. The resemblance between Mr. MacMillan and Raj was so obvious now that they were standing next to each other and since Raj was also clean shaven. Neel and Cecilia pushed back their chairs and hurried around the table. Ed simply beamed at father and son.

"Oh my god, Raj!" exclaimed Cecilia as she threw her arms around his neck and hugged him tightly. "I couldn't believe it when I heard!" It was a few seconds before Raj, startled by this display of affection, put his arms lightly around her and returned her embrace. However, he quickly but gently disengaged himself and turned toward Mac. "Father, this is Neel and Cecilia. Classmates and good friends."

Neel grasped Mac's hand and wrung it enthusiastically, all the while saying, "Wow, wow, wow!"

Mac, his hand finally released by Neel, extended it toward Cecilia. But she ignored this and hugged him as fiercely as she had his son.

Raj turned to Neena. "Of course, Neena you already know." Neena had also stood up from her seat and came around to shake Mac's hand.

"Mr. Mac—I mean Mac, I don't know what to say." Tears welled up in her eyes.

He took both of Neena's small hands in his large ones and clasped them warmly. "There is nothing you need to say, my dear, it is I who have to say 'thank you' to you. Thank you to all of you. You all saved my son's life, with great risk to yourselves, as I'm sure I don't need to remind you."

Ed, still beaming, said, "Yes siree, you could have blown me over with a feather when Mac here told me his long-lost son was coming to work at the hospital! He told me to keep an eye on you, young man." He leaned across the table to give Raj a pat on the shoulder.

"Thank you, Ed," said Mac. "But if Ed was Raj's guardian angel, who do you think was Neena's?" he asked, his eyes twinkling.

"Me?" squeaked Neena. "I don't have a guardian angel!"

Mac laughed. "Well, he is rather stocky to be an angel but he's light on his feet and looked out for you as best as he could." Then he sobered. "Thank god he was there the night Duncan tried to strangle you."

"The night Duncan . . ." Neena's voice trailed off. "You don't mean Mr. Patel, do you?" she asked incredulously.

"Of course that's who I mean! Remember I told you about Dash, he once worked as a security guard in my building?"

"Oh! Dash is short for Darshan?" she asked, as enlightenment dawned. "And you mentioned that he always shared his chai and samosas with you."

"Yes, what a happy and amazing coincidence that you found housing next to his store. Now, everyone, please sit. I think I have a lot of explaining to do."

Once they had all been seated, Neena poured tall glasses of ice-cold lemonade for Mac and Raj. Mac took a few long sips and put his glass down. He looked around the circle of bright, inquisitive faces and launched into his tale.

"As a young businessman I traveled to India numerous times. No, no, let me go further back than that. My grandfather, Roderick Duncan MacMillan, was a skilled maker of fine watches and timepieces in Scotland, and had even supplied the royal family on several occasions. However, at the beginning of the twentieth century there was mass unemployment in Scotland and not much use for fancy timepieces, so he emigrated to America, as so many Scots were doing at that time. He had already married so he and my grandmother, Anna, decided to carve out a new life for themselves here. I was named after him and my sister was named after our grandmother. My grandfather had an innate talent for the mechanical as well as for the artistic, so he continued to make quality clocks, timepieces, and eventually wristwatches as well. He became wildly successful and sold expensive pieces to masters of American industry like wealthy oil and steel barons. Basically, the new American Royalty." Mac paused to take another sip of his lemonade.

"My grandfather, who was not an educated man, greatly desired that his sons be educated. My father, Marcus MacMillan, was the first in our family to graduate from college. Being mechanically inclined, like his father before him, he went to RPI and became a mechanical engineer. He continued to work in my grandfather's shop but expanded into small machines and appliances such as typewriters and self-playing musical instruments like pianos and music boxes. As soon as I was knee-high, my father would bring me to his workshop and let me tinker with gears and other mechanisms, thus sparking my own interest. I studied computer science, but was always fascinated by the hardware that went into computers. As you may know, in my early twenties I developed a small piece of hardware that is now found in almost every computer, which is when my business exploded.

"As there was a dearth of engineers in America, I started going overseas to recruit new talent. Which is how I found myself in India all those years ago. However, during one of my visits I had a minor accident. As I was crossing a busy road in Madras, I jumped aside to avoid a two-wheeler, tripped over some stones on the road and hit my head."

"Oh no!" cried Neena.

Mac smiled at her. "Luckily, it was not a serious injury, just a gash on my head, which bled profusely, as you know head wounds can. A helpful passerby put me in an auto and directed the driver to drop me off at GH, the government hospital. And that"—he said, glancing briefly at Raj—"is where I met your mother, who was a doctor-in-training." A deep sigh escaped his lips. "As you know, your grandfather was ahead of his time in many ways, otherwise he would not have allowed his daughter to study medicine. No doubt he had already lined up a suitable groom who was also a doctor so she could be married soon." With a rueful smile he added, "Unfortunately, he didn't count on me. From the first moment I set eyes on Leela, I was enchanted." Neena saw Mac's eyes glisten with unshed tears.

Raj, his voice gruff with emotion, said, "My mother always had a great love for all things American. Now I know why."

"Leela and I had a prolonged but intermittent courtship since I lived in the States. But, I returned to India every chance I could. Then, we married secretly during the December holidays of her final year at school. We spent several idyllic weeks in one of the hill stations near Madras."

"How on earth did she get away from her family?" asked Neena in astonishment.

Mac laughed. "That turned out to be surprisingly easy, actually. She and several of her college friends had already planned on vacationing together, so that was the cover story. Your mother had several dear friends who were reliable accomplices."

Now it was Raj's turn to look surprised. "You don't mean Lakshmi Aunty, Neelam Aunty, and Kamala Aunty?"

"The very same! They called themselves the four musketeers."

"Yes, I know! I had three surrogate mothers growing up. What I did not have was a father."

Mac turned worried hazel eyes toward Raj. "I know, dear boy. And how I wish I could have been a part of your life before now. When Leela and I came back to the city we went first to your grandparent's home. I am sure that no Bollywood screenwriter could have scripted a more devastating scene than the one that ensued that night." He gave another long, sad sigh. "Your grandfather was apoplectic with rage and banished me from the house. Your mother, as his only child, was the apple of his eye, so I hope he was kinder to her afterward than he was with me."

"Until the day he died, my grandfather would look at my mother with only sadness in his eyes. Theirs was a very strained relationship," said Raj. "He eventually warmed toward me as his only grandson. I think he had finally even convinced himself of the story he wove to explain my presence. I had grown up being told that my parents met somewhere in the north of India where my mother had gone for a school conference and that she had entered into a hasty love marriage. My father, supposedly an engineer, went to the Gulf to work and died there in a workplace accident, before I was born."

Raj turned to Mac. "My mother told me that my father's name was Markendaya, which is why I have the letter 'M' as the initial before my name."

"Your mother always called me by my middle name, Mark, short for Marcus. She thought it suited me better than my given name of Roderick."

"But, Mac, why didn't you contact Raj's mother before this?" asked Neena. Her heart ached for Raj.

"But I did!" cried Mac, clearly anguished by the long separation with his family.

"I called, wrote, sent telegrams. I even tried to come to the house but Raj's grandfather, who was a well-known judge in the district, had many resources, and had posted guards outside the gate forbidding me to enter. After several terrible weeks I had to return to the US. There, I received two telegrams. One supposedly from Leela which said she no longer wanted to be my wife and then three months later, another, even more devastating telegram, telling me she had died in a scooter accident. There was even a clipping from a newspaper of her obituary." He turned back to Raj. "Your grandfather was a wily one. How he managed that article, I will never know. I never even knew Leela had been pregnant with my child." A single tear escaped and slowly ran down Mac's cheek. Raj reached into his pocket and pulled out a small white linen handkerchief. He handed it to Mac who looked at the initials embroidered on it in astonishment.

"These are your initials, M.R.M?" he asked.

"Yes, for Markendaya Rajendran Muthuswamy. Muthuswamy after my grandfather." Raj explained to his friends.

Neena and Cecilia, who by this time also had tears flowing unchecked down their own faces, were fumbling in their handbags for tissues. Neena pulled out Raj's handkerchief which she had laundered and meant to return to him.

"This belongs to you, Raj," she said, and handed it to him. Raj looked at the small row of letters embroidered in the bottom right corner and gave a little laugh.

"I always thought my mother had a moment of dyslexia when she embroidered this since my initials are all jumbled up." He held up the square of linen for them to see.

"R.M.M," read Neel, who was sniffling a little himself.

"Those are my initials," said Mac with a watery smile. "Roderick Marcus MacMillan. I have one of the handkerchiefs your mother embroidered for me and it is the only thing of hers that I own. She must have kept the others and given one to you by mistake, Raj."

"Yes," said Raj, shaking his head slowly in wonder.

"So, Mac, how did you learn about Raj then?" asked Neena, having wiped her tears.

"It was thanks to Raj's grandmother. I don't know how she found me but she wrote me a letter, an aerogram, as you may know." Neel and Neena nodded their heads in understanding as they had both received and written such letters when they corresponded with their grandparents in India. "She finally decided to break her silence after your grandfather died. While he lived, she didn't feel that she could betray him but it seems she never agreed with him about keeping your mother and you from me."

"Amazing," said Raj. "I never would have thought my Ammamma had such gumption."

"You can imagine how I felt when I found out, six months ago, that not only was Leela alive and well, but that we had a son together. I have wondered recently if it wasn't the stress, grief, and surprise of it all that caused me to have a coronary."

"I imagine it felt much like learning after twenty-three years that my father was alive and well. Luckily, I did not have a coronary," Raj teased gently.

Raj turned to Neena. "Neena, how did you figure out that Mac was my father? Did you see the resemblance when we first came to the house to help him change his bandages?"

"No, that was not it at all," she said. Sitting across from them now, Neena marveled at the likeness between father and son. She wondered why she had not seen it before. "I never would have thought to connect a middle-aged American man with a young brown kid from India."

Cecilia smiled and nudged Neena's shoulder. "Go on, tell them how you knew. Tell them about the salmon."

Mac laughed. "Salmon? What can salmon possibly have to do with Raj and me?"

"The dining room was serving salmon on Monday night and that reminded me of peachy-colored foods like cantaloupes, peaches, and mangoes. And mangoes reminded me of paisley and paisley reminded me of your birthmarks." A dull flush started to creep up her neck. "Um, well, I think I am the only one here who has seen you both with your shirts off."

"Oh, ho! Really?" asked Neel with a grin.

"Shut up, Neel!" said Neena irritably, as a bright pink bloom now spread to both of her cheeks. Neel continued to grin unrepentantly at her so she ostentatiously turned her head away from him.

"As you well know, I was the one who was sent to take Mac's staples out and that's when I saw the paisley-shaped birthmark on his chest. And Raj, on Monday night in the residents' lounge you were changing into a scrub top when I caught a glimpse of a similar mark on your chest.

"Mac, didn't you tell me that this particular birthmark has been found in many of the male descendants on your father's side?" Neena asked. "Duncan probably knew about this hereditary feature and he must have seen Raj's during that soccer game in the park. Remember, Ceci? Raj was one of the 'skins.'"

Cecilia nodded vigorously. "Yes! And it was just after the match that the first attempt on your life happened, Raj. It must have been Duncan who followed you home and then pushed you into the road!"

"My god," said Raj and gently touched his forehead where now a fresh, neat line of sutures were superimposed on the first, now fading, bruise. "I didn't even think of that, Cecilia."

"Yes, he failed to eliminate you that day, so he had to think of something else. I think he purposely loosened the door closer on the call room door and then tried to send you to the call room ahead of all of us. Unfortunately for Neel, he finished up first and was the recipient of that attack." Neena turned to Mr. Robinson.

"Ed, did you by chance notice Duncan that evening?"

Ed nodded slowly. "Yes, Doc, I did. He was up on a chair fiddling with the closer. He said it looked loose and he was tightening the screw. I should have checked it myself later on. I knew that man was trouble. Trouble with a capital 'T.' I could just feel it in my bones. But that night I was covering for one of my buddies who was out sick and had to see to several other floors in addition to my usual ones." He looked at Neel with sad brown eyes. "I'm so sorry you got hurt, Doc."

Neel patted Ed's arm and said, "Forget about it, Ed, and call me Neel. I think we've already established the thickness of my skull." He gave Neena a cheeky smile.

Neena pursed her lips. "Well, at least that is something we can agree on. Yeah, don't worry about Neel, Ed."

"Neena," said Raj. "I've just thought of something. Do you think that the 'D' and 'R' that that poor girl Linda scrawled on the floor could have stood for Duncan and Ron?"

"It certainly could have!" agreed Neena, her black curls bouncing. She told Mac and Ed about the macabre message written in red lipstick near the dead girl's body. "We thought it stood for the bogus healthcare company Duncan created so he could steal insurance payments. And since Linda was his billing contact we assumed she was trying to point a finger in that direction. But maybe in her last moments she was only trying to identify her killer and his accomplice. I guess now we'll never know for sure."

"Oh my," said Ed, his brown complexion taking on a decidedly gray hue. A somber silence fell over the group.

Then Mac looked up. "Raj, Neel, Neena, Cecilia . . . I owe you all an apology," he said. "I could have prevented all of this, if only I had let Duncan know that he was not my sole beneficiary. He never was, he simply assumed. Duncan, handsome and suave on the outside, was dark and manipulative on the inside, just like his father. My poor sister fell for Sebastian Goodwin's handsome face. Goodwin!" He shook his head in disgust. "A misnomer if ever there was one! But my father was quite astute and though he didn't prevent her from marrying Sebastian, he made sure that that scoundrel would not inherit a penny of his money. My father put in ironclad stipulations that my sister would receive her share of the family assets and then it would go directly to her children."

Mac paused to take another sip of lemonade. "Duncan inherited quite a bit from his mother. No doubt he has made great inroads on that money considering his extravagant lifestyle. I never intended to leave the family business or the majority of my wealth to him. Yes, certainly I had bequeathed him a generous amount but most of my fortune would have gone to charity and then equal shares to all the stockholders of the company."

"Mac, there's no way you could have known what he'd do," said Neena soothingly. "It's unbelievable that he even connected all the dots and figured out who Raj could be. But he couldn't have known for sure, could he?"

"Duncan was always incredibly intelligent. He was an expert at reading people and situations. But, it's possible that he ran across letters in which Raj was mentioned. He would have had ample opportunity to snoop in my study since he was a frequent visitor here."

"I almost feel sorry for him," said Raj, at which he received outraged stares from his friends. "No, really, can you imagine how he must have felt the first time we met? I think Duncan noticed the family resemblance as soon as he met me. Several times that first day I caught him looking intently at me. I just assumed he was unhappy that an international student suddenly joined the team."

But he now turned back to his father. "Speaking of which, did I really win a scholarship to this medical school?" His dark eyebrows were knitted together, whether in mild distress or indignation, Neena couldn't tell.

Mac looked sheepish and held up his hands in a placating gesture. "There had been an opening in this medical school class and I appealed to the board of directors to start a scholarship program, on the condition that this year it was awarded to you. Raj, they reviewed all of your transcripts from India, which your grandmother so obligingly sent me, and agreed you were a worthy candidate. And each subsequent year the scholarship will pay for the last two years of medical school for a similarly worthy recipient."

"I don't know. That sounds more like a bribe to me. This is what happens in India, but I didn't think this would happen in America."

Mac placed a hand gently over Raj's hand which had clenched into a fist. "Son," he said, and then stopped, as if savoring that word. "Son," he repeated. "Do you not believe you are a worthy candidate for this scholarship? It was clear from your transcripts and recommendations that you were a top student in your medical college. Is that not true?"

Raj, instead of answering Mac's question, posed another one. "So, my grandmother knows about this but my mother does not?"

"Raj, I am so sorry that I deceived you. But, I wanted so badly to see you and to finally be able to help you. I did not have the courage to contact your mother."

"Are you and my mother still married then?" Raj asked slowly. "You never remarried?"

Mac shook his head. "There has never been anyone else for me."

Mac's hazel brown eyes pleaded with Raj's light brown ones. Please don't be angry, they said. Raj, holding his father's gaze, seemed to be searching Mac's face for the truth. After a long moment, he gave a small nod. "I understand, Father. I am grateful that my grandmother wrote to you." His hand unclenched and he gave Mac's a slight squeeze. "She always told me that there is a right time and place for everything. This must now be our time."

Neena, who was wiping fresh tears from her face, said, "I am so happy for both of you." She paused to blow her nose noisily. "What a story! This could definitely be a Bollywood movie."

"Not without a dance sequence in the Alps, it couldn't!" countered Raj with a laugh.

"Haha, true!" agreed Neena.

Mac stood up and raised his glass of lemonade. "I would like to propose a toast! To my son." Everyone raised their own glasses and Raj, before clinking glasses with Mac, said, "To my father."

There was a chorus of, "To Mac and Raj!" and much tinkling of glass against glass. After they had each drunk another glass of lemonade and polished off all of the shortbread cookies that Patrick had left on a large plate, Neena pushed her chair back and stood up.

"Raj, do you need a ride back to your apartment?" she asked.

He shook his head. "Thank you, but no. I have been staying here the last few days as Father and I have much to discuss."

"That sounds like a great idea," she said, beaming at Raj and Mac. She turned to Cecilia who was still sitting in her chair.

"Ceci? Ready to—" and she stopped abruptly mid-sentence.

"Neena, what's wrong?" asked Ceci, her delicately arched eyebrows knitted together.

"I'm fine," Neena said slowly. "But do you realize The Curse of the Surgical Rotation has occurred?"

Mac looked confused. Ed turned to Neena. "Come on, Doc. You're pulling my leg, right? What in tarnation is The Curse of the Surgical Rotation?"

Cecilia explained and Neena, using her fingers, proceeded to tick off the various incidents. "One, Raj was almost run over by a car. Two, Neel suffered a head injury. Three, Duncan fell off of the roof." She grimaced slightly at this, then finished, "And four, Ron was struck by lightning!" Neena looked at her three friends, her brown eyes twinkling with humor. Suddenly, a beautiful medley of laughter rang through the garden and was carried away by the warm summer breeze.

Epilogue

The early morning sun, filtering through the trees near the wrought iron gate, created a dappled pattern over the freshly scrubbed stones in the courtyard. The distant toot of auto rickshaws combined quite harmoniously with birdsong. A light breeze, carrying the delicate scent of jasmine, made his breath catch in his throat. He looked down at the small hands that rested lightly within his much larger ones. Once again, after twenty-four years, his hazel eyes were transfixed by her dark brown ones.

"Leela," he breathed.

"Mark," she whispered.

THE END

About the Author

Niru Mohandas, a practicing pediatrician, combines her passions for medicine and mysteries in her debut novel, *A Pre-Med(itated) Murder*. She lives in Montgomery, New Jersey, with her husband, Govindh, and her dog, Ruby.